M000164716

# PRAISE FOR WILLIAM BERNHARDT AND THE DANIEL PIKE LEGAL THRILLERS

"William Bernhardt is a born stylist, and his writing through the years has aged like a fine wine…."

— STEVE BERRY, *NEW YORK TIMES*-BESTSELLING AUTHOR OF *THE KAISER'S WEB*

"William Bernhardt knows when to soar and when to dive, when to make you sweat and when to let you breathe, when to throw this flying machine into a barrel roll that will absolutely shock you and when to bring you home safe and satisfied."

— WILLIAM MARTIN, *NEW YORK TIMES*-BESTSELLING AUTHOR OF *THE LINCOLN LETTER*

"Thrillingly interwoven plots are Bernhardt's forte, a talent he once again demonstrates full-blown in his latest superb thriller…"

— *BOOKLIST* (FOR *DARK JUSTICE*)

"Bernhardt keeps his readers coming back for more."

— *LIBRARY JOURNAL*

"Once started, it is hard to let [*The Last Chance Lawyer*] go, since the characters are inviting, engaging, and complicated….You will enjoy it."

— *CHICAGO DAILY LAW BULLETIN*

"[*Court of Killers*] is a wonderful second book in the Daniel Pike series...[A] top-notch, suspenseful crime thriller with excellent character development..."

— TIMOTHY HOOVER, FICTION AND NONFICTION
AUTHOR

"I could not put *Trial by Blood* down. The plot is riveting—with a surprise after the ending, when I thought it was all over....This book is special."

— NIKKI HANNA, AUTHOR OF *CAPTURE LIFE*

"*Judge and Jury is* a fast-paced, well-crafted story that challenges each major character to adapt to escalating attacks that threaten the very existence of their unique law firm."

— RJ JOHNSON, AUTHOR OF *DREAMSLINGER*

"*Final Verdict* is a must read with a brilliant main character and surprises and twists that keep you turning pages. One of the best novels I've read in a while."

— ALICIA DEAN, AWARD-WINNING AUTHOR OF
*THE NORTHLAND CRIME CHRONICLES*

"*Exposed* has everything I love in a thriller: intricate plot twists, an ensemble of brilliant heroines, and jaw-dropping drama both in and out of the courtroom. William Bernhardt knows how to make the law come alive."

— TESS GERRITSEN, *NEW YORK TIMES*-
BESTSELLING AUTHOR OF THE RIZZOLI & ISLES
THRILLERS

"William Bernhardt returns with a stunning piece of fiction....In a story that mixes fiction with the deadliest realities, Bernhardt provides readers with a novel unlike any I have read in a long while. With graphic depictions told in a highly realistic fashion, William Bernhardt proves why he is at the top of his game and eager to share his skills with readers!"

— *BOOK REVIEWS TO PONDER* (FOR
*PLOT/COUNTERPLOT*)

"*Splitsville* is a winner—well-written, with fully developed characters and a narrative thrust that keeps you turning the pages."

— GARY BRAVER, BESTSELLING AUTHOR OF
*TUNNEL VISION*

# PARTNERS IN CRIME

# PARTNERS IN CRIME

## DANIEL PIKE LEGAL THRILLER SERIES
### BOOK 7

## WILLIAM BERNHARDT

BABYLON BOOKS

Copyright © 2023 by William Bernhardt

All rights reserved.

No part of this book may be reproduced in any form or by any electronic or mechanical means, including information storage and retrieval systems, without written permission from the author, except for the use of brief quotations in a book review.

*For my family*
*Nothing matters more*

Alone we can do so little; together we can do so much.

— HELEN KELLER

## Part One

# WHEN DEATH ITSELF COMES CALLING

# CHAPTER ONE

I'VE ALWAYS WONDERED WHAT HAPPENS WHEN YOU DIE.

But that doesn't mean I was in a big hurry to find out. And when the answers finally arrived, I wasn't ready for them.

I don't know how I got into this mess. I don't know why I'm being hunted. All I know is that I shouldn't have stayed late at work tonight. But when you're a social worker, there's never enough time. I spend most of my day in an Indianapolis social services office convincing people who get SNAP—what we used to call food stamps, sort of—to buy nutritious foods rather than grabbing garbage at the nearest 7-11. I'm always behind on the paperwork, my illness caused me to be absent several days, and since I had no other plans, I thought this would be a good night to catch up.

One of my clients, Chantelle, is a single mother with two small children. I've been trying for months to instill concepts apparently not introduced in her own childhood—like balanced meals and discipline.

"Honey." She always calls me "honey" for some reason. "You can get those big boxes of beef jerky at Dollar General for nearly nothin'."

"Chantelle, processed meats are not the best meal for your girls. They need more variety. Three colors on the dinner plate."

"They like that beef jerky. And I can make lunch cheap by getting chips and pouring that Cheez Whiz on it. Instant nachos!"

"Instant junk food. You need to use your EBY card wisely. Don't fill your pantry with pseudo-food. Get fresh produce. Go to the farmers market."

"Sorry, Mrs. Zimmerman, but my girls won't eat fruit."

"They will if there are no other choices."

"Mia throws tantrums if she doesn't get what she wants."

I clenched my teeth. Not my job to teach someone how to parent. "She'll get hungry, assuming there are no readily available snacks. She needs fruit and vegetables and fiber and—"

"Is there fiber in Cap'n Crunch?"

"Maybe try shredded wheat. Or oatmeal."

And the next thing I knew I was writing a detailed shopping list and meal plan. And about an hour behind schedule.

Just as I was thinking about getting out of there, the phone call came. On the land line. I picked it up.

No one answered. But the line wasn't dead. Someone was there, just not talking. So what was the point?

Knowing where I was, obviously.

I hung up and ran for the elevators.

I didn't see him. Her. It. Anyone. But as soon as I punched the down button in the office lobby, something hard clubbed me over the head. I tumbled to the floor. Managed to protect my teeth, but my forehead hit the ground hard enough to make me dizzy.

I tried to crawl back to my feet, but something grabbed me. I twisted away. My clothes tore. The buttons on my blouse popped, gaping open, with one sleeve dangling around my wrist. I tried to get up again, but my head was still clouded. Someone pushed me down. I tried again.

Someone slapped me across the face.

"Stop!" I screamed. "Why are you doing this? If you need money—"

I heard a laugh that creeped the hell out of me. Wasn't sure if it was a man or a woman or a supernatural beast. Which made it all the more unsettling.

"Why are you doing this?"

I felt as if the entire lobby went into suspended animation. No one spoke. Nothing moved. Until at last, the laughter gave way to a few words.

"You're number four." The voice sounded distorted, unnatural.

A vicious blow hit the right side of my face, swinging my neck around so hard I feared it might snap. I didn't understand any of this. I didn't know what to do. I felt paralyzed.

My attacker straightened, rearing back for the fatal blow. Something glistened in the refracted overhead light.

That dark figure held a knife. A very big knife at the end of a long handle.

The elevator made its familiar dinging sound. The doors opened.

For the first time, I got a good look at my attacker. Dressed in black. Wearing a long robe. And a mask that looked like it was Halloween. A white skeletal face.

Was he dressed like Death itself? The Grim Reaper?

Something hit me over the head. The knife? A scythe? Didn't matter. I staggered across the tile floor, realizing that if I didn't do something fast, the Reaper would be dispatching another soul to the afterlife. In horror movies, this would be when a fire axe or knitting needle or letter opener would suddenly appear conveniently within my grasp. Where were they now?

I'd been in this lobby a thousand times and I'd seen a fire extinguisher. Didn't really focus on it, but I knew it was there. I staggered in the general direction. Found the handle to the glass case. Opened it...

I could feel the Reaper moving, rustling....

I summoned all the strength I could muster, raised the extinguisher over my head, then slammed it down on top of my attacker.

There was no noise. No cry of pain. But the Reaper crumbled.

I ran for the elevator and slipped between the doors just in time. They closed behind me. Thank God! I descended to the ground floor. Nothing was going to stop me.

But that didn't mean I'd escaped.

As soon as the elevator doors opened, I raced out, torn clothes dangling from my upper body. My skirt was torn, too. I was a mess. Didn't let that stop me. I pushed through the outer doors onto the street and plunged into a downpour. I screamed for help. I knew I must look like a crazy person, but I didn't care what people thought. I just wanted to be safe.

No one came. No one helped.

Behind me, I saw a black robe emerge from the building.

Tearing down the streets. Splashing through the rain. Giving myself a running bath. I made noise and waved my arms. I thought if I acted whacked enough, a cop might pull over to check me out. No such luck.

In ten minutes, I could be back in my apartment. But I didn't have that long. The Reaper was behind me somewhere. I could feel it. It was the chill in the marrow of my bones. The shiver in every step.

I ran to Maryland, one of the main downtown arteries. Raced past Buca di Beppo and the Sugar Factory. Convention Center. Lucas Oil Stadium. Where were all the people? How late had I been working?

Glanced at my watch. Broken. Searched for my phone. I put that in my clutch...which I must've lost during the struggle.

I was on my own.

I looked behind me. Was it my imagination, or had the black shape returned? Hard to see anything clearly in this deluge, plus my head still throbbed. Was the Reaper behind me, closing in? What did he want?

I raced across the street—too fast, as it turned out. The sidewalk was slick and I fell. I hit something hard. It hurt. Not so much in my legs as my lower back. I managed to push myself to my feet, but it felt like a surgeon had cut me open with a scalpel. Searing pain. Almost unbearable.

I ignored the stabbing torment and started moving again. It was more like a hobble than a run. But I inched forward.

I could see where the alley emptied out onto the street. The downtown canals were easy to navigate if you understood how they worked...and difficult to navigate if you didn't. One wrong turn and suddenly there was a wide waterway between you and your prey.

I could only hope.

Fifty more feet and my apartment would be within sight. If I got there, what could happen to me? I'd be able to rest and relax and figure out how my already difficult life suddenly become so much worse. I could see the light at the end of the tunnel—

Something grabbed me by the throat and yanked me to the concrete. My head hit hard and the world started spinning. After that, I wasn't thinking too clearly.

I felt a hand clutch my throat. A slender bony hand. Exactly what you would expect from the Grim Reaper.

And just as the barely visible light began to dim, I returned to my initial question. The one I'd had to confront, not just now, but every day for the last three years.

What happens when you die?

I stopped struggling. I wasn't accomplishing anything. It was as if my entire body had accepted the inevitable. Which, I suppose, I had.

In my dying moments, the Reaper, still choking the life out of me, spoke.

"You should have withdrawn," the voice rasped. "You aren't the first. You won't be the last."

And in that moment, the light dimmed. My life did not flash before my eyes. I did not see angels. It was more like when you wake just a few minutes before your alarm sounds. You could get up. But you don't. You nestle in for a few more moments of, maybe not asleep, but peace.

I've spent most of my adult life helping others. But when I needed it most, I couldn't help myself. And no one swooped in to save the day.

The light did come. So bright I had to close my eyes.

Was it really there, or did I just want it to be there? And what did it mean?

My eyelids fluttered shut for a final time.

I've always wondered what happens when you die.

Looks like I'm about to find out.

# CHAPTER TWO

DAN WATCHED MARIA GATHER HER NOTES FOR CROSS-EXAMINATION. IN the past, she preferred to work behind the lines, out of the courtroom limelight. But since he agreed to help run the Last Chance Lawyers network, she'd been forced to take lead chair on many occasions. He was glad to see her gaining confidence. She sounded just as smart as she looked—today sporting a Sergio Hudson tailored tuxedo-style midnight-blue blazer.

But watching her tackle a hostile witness made him a bit wistful. Did he miss practicing law? Of course not. What a hassle. One irritation after another. Dealing with judges, juries, opposing counsel, and worst of all…clients. How did he ever stand it? He was able to accomplish so much more on a larger scale since Ben Kincaid handed over the reins. He was content.

And yet, here he was, Monday morning, on a beautiful Floridian St. Petersburg day, inside the courthouse, sitting beside Maria's client. Spectating.

"Agent Clarkson." Maria cleared her throat. "May I call you that?"

"You're the lawyer, so I suppose you can do anything you like," he groused. "But I retired from the FBI over ten years ago."

"But you were in the FBI."

"As I told your client. First time we communicated."

"Did you tell her why you were dismissed?"

"Objection." Clarkson's lawyer, a young kid named Barclay, rose to his feet. "Relevance."

Dan instinctively pressed down on the toes of his Air Jordans—then froze. Stay in your seat, he told himself. You are just watching. Not your problem.

"It is relevant," Maria insisted. "Goes to the fraudulent portrait he painted of himself."

"She asked about something he didn't say," Barclay replied, "not something he did."

"Omissions can be just as misleading as false statements."

Judge Littlefeather tossed her head from side-to-side, mentally deliberating. "I'll allow it."

The witness, Emil Clarkson, looked as if he would rather be anywhere else in the world. But that wasn't unusual. Being on the witness stand was uncomfortable for everyone, even those with nothing to hide. Clarkson was a large man with a scarred face. Dan would not want to meet him in a dark passageway.

"When did you first meet my client, Darleen Fielding?" Maria asked. Darleen sat at the plaintiff's table with Dan, barely concealing a sneer. She was just over forty, brunette, plump, and still kicking herself for giving this man money.

"About three years ago. Assuming you were asking when I met her online."

"Right. You swiped right on Tinder."

"Correct."

"And then you engaged in an extended dialogue."

"We talked for weeks. Eventually switched to email. Then telephone. And finally I met her in public."

"Because you wanted money."

"I felt we had something."

"But you did take her money."

"I knew about an investment opportunity and mentioned it to her. I didn't make her do anything she didn't want to do."

"And then you spent all the money?"

"I didn't spend it. I invested it."

"And now you say the investment is kaput."

"Investments don't always pay off. There's always risk."

"You risked my client's money."

"With her full knowledge and consent. She understood the risks. We gambled. We lost."

And that had been the sticking point. Darleen was suing Clarkson for fraud, hoping to recover some or all of the money she gave him. But if she gave the money voluntarily, their chances of success were slim. He claimed he invested it at her direction, and thus far, despite extensive discovery, they had been unable to find any evidence of him converting her money to his personal benefit.

Still, Dan had to admire how well Maria controlled and contained the witness. This was a tough case to win but she was going after him full throttle.

Since they bought a house and moved in together, Dan and Maria solidified their relationship in a way that rarely gave him anything but pleasure. They had always spent so much time working together that this current life didn't seem all that different. But it definitely had side benefits. Having been a lone wolf his entire life, he was genuinely surprised by how much he enjoyed living with her. And she had never once suggested that he "put a ring on it." Her clock was ticking like everyone else's, but still no stress. She didn't appear to care about conformity or normality or obtaining the approval of Middle America.

This was the best relationship of his life, though that perhaps was saying too little since he was approaching forty and had never been in a relationship that lasted long. The most serious relationship of his previous life had been with the city's mayor, and…well, that hadn't worked out so well. Maria strove to please him and to coordinate their busy lives. As far as he could tell, she was ecstatic.

Until lately. Maybe. Was he imagining it? He thought maybe he detected a trace of…something. He couldn't even tell what. The way she looked at him these past few mornings over coffee. The way she hugged him longer than before. Especially at night.

"Agent Clarkson, was this a romantic relationship?" Maria asked.

"We did have a personal relationship. For a time."

"There was also a professional aspect, correct?"

Clarkson exhaled heavily. "Yes. Darleen was charged with possession. Years ago. Before medical marijuana was legalized in Florida. I tried to help."

"Didn't you tell her she was on some kind of secret probation?"

"Absolutely not. I don't even know what that would be."

Dan had no idea what that would be either, other than a really good way for a former Feeb to get money from a wealthy widow. She said he claimed he could get a judge to terminate her probation, but all his travel and related expenses ending up nickel-and-diming her into the five-digit numbers. He claimed he took what he didn't need for the judge and invested in a venture-capital fund that lost everything on a bankrupt phone app. He claimed his financial records had been stolen and, unfortunately, Darleen never asked for any copies or receipts.

"Isn't it true that you told my client you'd been assigned to mentor her so she could avoid prison time?"

"Not true."

"Did you ask her to report her activities to you on a daily basis?"

He shrugged. "Sometimes I asked how her day went."

"And you told her not to tell anyone about this."

"Why would she want to?"

Maria took a step closer. "You told her that if she told anyone about the 'secret probation,' she could be thrown into jail. She'd lose her job. Might even lose custody of her children."

"I don't know anything about this secret probation. But since she'd been arrested on drug charges, obviously, she might lose child custody."

"But there were no pending drug charges, right? She reached a plea agreement and paid a fine."

"As it turned out. You can never be too careful."

"So you extorted money from her by threatening that if she didn't comply she would lose her children and her freedom."

He straightened, looking indignantly at the jury. "I did no such thing. I've worked in law enforcement my entire adult life. That is not something I would ever do."

"And someone left recorded messages on her phone, claiming to be from the Intelligence Center of the DEA. Of course, no such thing exists. You know that. Darleen didn't."

"I know nothing about any such calls."

"The calls didn't begin until after my client gave you her phone number."

"Coincidence."

Maria paused a moment. Dan knew what was going through her head. It was make-or-break time. The jury might be suspicious, but Clarkson was absolutely resolute in his denials, and they had the burden of proof. She had to somehow convince the jury that Darleen was more trustworthy than this ex-FBI tool or she was going down in flames.

"Sir, all totaled, my client gave you over two-hundred-fifty-thousand dollars. Most of it in cash."

"Barely one hundred thousand. Which she gave me because she saw an investment opportunity."

"You created a fake narrative. You gaslighted her."

"Not true."

"I can give you the bank records. They show how much she withdrew. In cash."

"But you can't show a matching deposit into any of my accounts, right?"

"Because she paid you in cash."

"Because the money she gave me wasn't for me."

Baloney. He either hid it or spent it. Somewhere.

"You talked about marrying Darleen and buying a house together, correct?"

"We did. I still would."

Not mutual. "And you bought a house recently. But for yourself."

"Unfortunately, the lawsuit has soured the relationship."

"You know what I think? I think you used my client's money to buy that house."

"Not true."

Maria returned to counsel table and opened her briefcase. He himself had switched to a backpack long ago—much more comfortable, roomy, aerodynamic, and better for the back. But Maria was a traditionalist.

She removed a folder. "Since you have a house now, the next likely move would be to buy a car."

"Not with her money. I've got a 2007 Honda Accord that still does fine."

"Is that your only car?"

He hesitated a moment. "What difference does it make?"

"I don't doubt that you may have an old Honda tucked away somewhere, but I don't think it's your only ride. May I approach?" Judge Littlefeather nodded. Maria handed the witness a photo. "Recognize this?"

Lines crossed Clarkson's forehead. "I'm...not sure..."

"It's a Mercedes. Specifically, it's the Mercedes you drove to the courthouse this morning." She handed him another photograph that showed him standing outside the car with keys in his hand. "To be specific, it's a Mercedes AMG E 63 sedan, which currently runs for about $113,000."

"I...uh...rented—"

"It's not a rental tag."

"I have a friend—"

"We already checked. The car is a recent purchase and it is registered to you."

Clarkson coughed into his hand. "Well, I didn't want you to confuse everyone by asserting stuff that isn't true. I bought that car with my own money. I had some savings."

"I think you bought it with my client's savings."

"You can believe anything you want. You can't prove it."

"You must believe that. Driving it to the courthouse was a bold move. But you probably didn't expect me to have an investigator in the parking lot watching for you." She winked at Dan. "Our friend Garrett is relentless."

Clarkson's throat tightened. "I'm an American citizen and I can buy a car anytime I like."

"With your own money, sure."

"I already told you—"

"A complete lie." Maria withdrew another document. "Garrett is one of the best researchers in the world. He took your license number and went online." Using databases he should not be able to access, but she wouldn't dwell on that. "Turns out you bought that vehicle from Carvana a mere four days ago. And you know what the most remarkable part is?"

"I—I don't—"

"You paid cash. Which definitely made an impression on the dealer, who would be happy to testify. Where'd you get all that cash, sir?"

Clarkson looked thunderstruck. He stuttered a few times but never managed to actually pronounce a word. "I-I-I...This is all...so confusing..."

Maria pivoted and faced Clarkson's lawyer. "Your honor, could we have a ten-minute recess? I think it's just possible we might be able to settle this case out of court."

———————

HALF AN HOUR LATER, DAN AND MARIA STOOD IN THE COURTHOUSE corridor with their client.

"I can't believe he's going to make restitution," Darlene said. "You're amazing."

Maria shrugged. "There were a lot of loose ends in his story."

"No," Dan said, "Darlene is right. You're amazing, Maria."

She fanned her face. "Well, gosh. If you both insist."

"I was such a fool," Darleen said. "I thought I'd never get that money back. Thank you for saving me from my own stupidity."

Maria shrugged. "We've all made mistakes. They should be teaching moments. Not dead ends."

"I'm going to tell all my girlfriends they should hire you to be their lawyer, Maria."

"Or better yet," Maria replied, "tell them not to give money to some guy they met on the internet."

"Or even better," Dan added, "tell them not to give money to some guy *ever*."

Darleen signed the letter agreement and left, a huge smile on her face.

Dan laid his hands on Maria's shoulders. "Good work, superstar."

"Stop. I know I don't have your courtroom flair. But I'm getting more comfortable with it."

"You're my superstar." He kissed her lightly on the lips. "And you always will be. I have to run a few errands. Wanna meet later at my office? Maybe we could get lunch."

"I'll go there now. I need to answer some email."

"Another big case?"

"Someone calling and messaging me from Australia. I don't know what it's about yet."

"You cannot try a case in Australia!"

She stepped in closer, almost nose-to-nose. "Oh yeah? Are you my boss now?"

"No." His voice dropped several notches. "But I'd miss you."

She grinned. "If I were going to try a case in Australia, I'd want you to come with me."

He brightened. "You would?"

"Of course. Someone has to second-chair."

He watched, smiling, as she disappeared.

*Second*-chair?

# CHAPTER THREE

MARIA APPROACHED THE FRONT DOOR OF DAN'S UPSCALE OFFICE SPACE in downtown St. Petersburg. She thought she had a little time to get comfortable before he arrived. Which was good. She had a surprise for him.

Okay, she'd been shopping. That wasn't the surprise. That was her passion. The new Sundial St. Pete Mall was her new best jam. She realized getting such a charge out of retail therapy was possibly not healthy. But she had other hobbies. Kitesurfing. Scuba diving. Paragliding...

Okay, those were Dan's hobbies. But she'd done them so many times they were starting to feel like hers.

Dan accepted Ben Kincaid's offer to help manage the Last Chance Lawyer offices nationwide, but he didn't want to move, so he needed this additional space downtown. He could still get to the beach in fifteen minutes, which allowed him to start his day with extreme watersports, risk his life a few times, and still put in a full day at the office.

She'd rather shop. Nothing wrong with that. Good genes and frequent trips to the gym had given her an excellent figure, and she knew Dan appreciated it, so why not show it to its best advantage?

That didn't make her any less feminist or lawyerly. It didn't mean she was superficial or some '50s hausfrau stereotype. It was simply a matter of...leading with her strong suit.

The salespeople knew her well enough to offer the best deals on sight. Some people shopped online, but she thought that was so much less fun, surfing Poshmark or The RealReal. She wasn't a snob but she worked hard to get where she was and if that allowed her to dress well, what was wrong with that? She didn't want to be upstaged by someone who scored a pair for less by obsessive clicking.

She switched into some midleg straight Gucci jeans she'd left in her car. They looked awesome on her. Skinny jeans were so yesterday and she for one was glad. She had an actual figure. She watched what she ate but didn't starve herself. And they were Gucci, for heaven's sake, *Gucci*, and she got a great deal on them at Ellenton Premium Outlets.

One thing was certain. Dan would notice she had new jeans. He always did. He would say she looked great in them. He always did. And if they got a little privacy, he might show her how much he liked them. They'd been together for several years now, but he didn't seem to have lost his enthusiasm. Maybe it was because they hadn't married, hadn't had children. They still had room for one another, but...

She stepped inside Dan's office and closed the door.

The lights were off in the lobby. Not surprising. He didn't have a full-time receptionist or assistant.

She took two steps forward, then stopped.

Her foot hit something.

She couldn't make out what it was in the dim light, so she pulled her phone from a tight jeans pocket and turned on the flashlight.

Books, files, papers, and folders littered the floor. An entire file cabinet had been overturned. Broken glass littered the carpet.

Someone had ransacked the office and made a mess in the process.

Did she hear something? The tiniest sound of weight shifting...

She felt a chill trickle through her body.

Was else someone here? She started to call out, then stopped.

She turned off the flashlight, then pressed herself against the wall and held her breath. Dan's private office was just around the corner. The only other room was a kitchenette.

She was certain Dan had not beaten her here. She came as quickly as she could and she would've noticed his Ferrari in the parking lot.

Maybe it would be smarter to call someone. She was getting seriously concerned and she didn't need any trouble. Maybe she should just tiptoe out...

The hood appeared before her with such suddenness it seemed supernatural, as if it had materialized out of the ether. And then the skeletal face emerged.

She jumped. She hated being startled, but who could blame her? It looked weird, gaunt, twisted...

And a hand was traveling toward her throat.

She ducked. She would've preferred to have a calm conversation and determine what the hell was happening, but that didn't seem to be an option at the moment. She swiveled around, dodging a blow, then raced toward the front door.

It wouldn't budge.

Damn. She'd locked it behind herself on her way in, hadn't she? She twisted the deadbolt—

Too late. She felt a hand on her shoulder and a second later, a hard shove. She smashed into the glass door, making a titanic noise and briefly losing her footing. Her assailant grabbed her neck. Her head whipped back so fast it cracked the glass. She felt glass tumbling around her head, but at the moment, that was the least of her concerns.

Her phone was still in her hand. She beamed the flashlight toward her assailant.

And gasped.

The Grim Reaper had come calling. And now had her by the throat, so there was little question about who Death wanted to be the next passenger to the netherworld.

The dark figure knocked her phone out of her hand. It skidded across the floor.

"What—What do you want?" Maria gasped.

No reply. Seemed Death was not much for small talk.

But the grip around her throat tightened.

She had to do something and she had to do it fast. She pounded the arm pinning her down, but it didn't make any difference. She aimed a blow at the elbow, where everyone's arm was most vulnerable.

Death didn't budge. That skinny arm did not buckle in the slightest.

She guessed she probably could survive another thirty seconds of this choking before she lost consciousness. And then finishing her off would be easy.

"Why—are you doing this?" she managed to croak.

No answer.

She kicked the cloaked figure hard in the leg.

Death responded by clubbing the side of her head.

Ohmigod. The pain was so intense she forgot how to breathe. She felt the little air left in her lungs spill out. Her legs weakened. She would've fallen to her knees, except Death's steady grip held her upright.

"Are you…going to kill me?" she choked. She didn't expect a reply.

But she got one. The voice was weird and distorted. "You're not on the list. You're just in the way."

Was that good? Bad? She wasn't sure. "Is that why you're trying to kill me?"

"You aren't the first. You won't be the last."

That sounded ominous, even if she didn't have a clue what the Reaper was talking about. "Are you looking for Dan? I expect him here any moment. And believe me, he is going to kick your ass so hard it'll probably end up in the Pacific Ocean."

No response. Other than an increased tightening, crushing her trachea.

Kicking Death's leg didn't accomplish anything, so she switched to a swift kick between the legs. Male or female, didn't matter. That didn't feel good to anyone.

Right after she landed the blow, she felt the choking grip relax slightly. This was her opportunity. She screamed, loud and defiant, then pushed back as hard as she could. The Reaper stumbled, then tripped and fell.

She knew she had seconds at best. She unlocked the damaged door, started through—

Death grabbed her foot. Technically, grabbed the bottom of her straight-leg Gucci jeans. She fell forward, scraping her hands on the pavement.

The sudden burst of pain helped clear the fog in her head. She kicked backward, trying to force him to let go.

He did not.

She rolled over. By God, she'd worked hard to establish her rep as a lawyer, and she'd worked even harder to get Dan to pull his head out of his butt and notice that she adored him. She was not going to let this bastard take it all away from her.

She waited until Death's head was close. Then she swung around with both fists and pounded the sides of the hood.

Death winced. She knew that hurt. She'd used the same move on creeps at frat parties and law school keggers. It still worked.

But the grip on her neck did not relax. She couldn't see a face, but she felt the rage.

An angry psycho dressed like the Grim Reaper held her captive. Not a promising scenario.

She was pinned down on the concrete. She tried screaming again.

Death slapped her hard across the face.

Then the fog set in, much too quickly. It was already so dark. Was this the final darkness?

What had she interrupted? What was Death after?

She didn't want to die, but in the end, she had to admit she'd lived a dynamite life. She couldn't complain.

Except she really did want Dan to see her in these jeans. And to tell him about her surprise...

Too late.

# CHAPTER FOUR

Mitch Theroux did not relish being summoned to his faculty advisor's office. Not because he had any academic problems. He had an excellent grade point average, played piano for the student orchestra, and was on track to graduate in May.

But he suspected this summoning had nothing to do with any of that.

More than a year had passed, but the entire university music department was still haunted by the brutal murder of Claudia Wells. Clubbed over the head while she was alone in her dorm room. Her violin stolen. And from the start, one of the chief suspects was Professor Herwig, even after someone else was arrested. Understandable. Mitch had seen the way Herwig looked at Claudia. And he'd seen the way he looked at her violin, too. He wanted both.

The door was open, so he entered Herwig's tiny office. Herwig might be a department head, but apparently that didn't translate into better digs. The professor faced the bookshelf opposite the door.

Herwig glanced over his shoulder. "That you, Mitch?"

He nodded. "I got your email."

Herwig brushed off his hands and stepped back. "Books get

misplaced. You know how it is. At least once a week I have put every-thing back in order."

Mitch peered at the shelf. "Are your books...alphabetized? By author?"

"Of course. How else would I find anything?" Herwig smiled. "Okay, I'm a bit OCD. But I don't see anything wrong with keeping your dwelling space in apple-pie order. Do you?"

Mitch didn't answer. Herwig pointed toward the only chair oppo-site his desk. "Take a seat."

Mitch complied.

"Let me apologize in advance. Call it a trigger warning, if you will. I didn't call you in to talk about graduation or your grades. Truth is, I didn't call you in to talk about you at all. I was hoping to talk about Claudia."

Thought so. Just couldn't let it go, could he?

"You know David Donovan, right?"

"Of course. We stayed in the same dorm. Most of the music students do. And of course, I frequently saw him at Claudia's."

"That must've been an irritant."

Meaning what? When the police questioned Mitch, they initially had pursued some idea that he committed the murder out of jealousy. He had to gently inform them, not that it was any of their business, that he was gay. He loved Claudia, but not the way they meant, and even if he had, he could never bring himself to harm her, much less over a violin. I mean, he had another friend with a fabulous Steinway, but it didn't make him want to commit homicide.

"I thought he was not the best choice for her," Mitch said, choosing his words carefully. "But Claudia was a big girl and she could handle herself. Or so I thought."

"So we all thought. Pity. So talented. Best work-study I ever had."

So he was going with that? Regret that he lost his favorite inden-tured servant?

"You've probably heard that David is coming back to court again. Seems a jury verdict wasn't enough to put him away."

"Another trial?"

"Hearing. He's trying to get the case reopened."

First he'd heard of this. "Is that likely?"

"I have no idea. Seemed cut and dried to me. Jury convicted unanimously in the blink of an eye, right? But you never know."

Mitch waited patiently. This was interesting, but he still had no idea why he'd been summoned.

"This is what I wanted to ask you, Mitch." Herwig leaned forward and spread his arms across his desk. "Do you know anything about Claudia's doctor?"

"Sorry...no."

"Her name is..." He glanced down at his desk. "Southern. Marilyn Southern. Female doc. Ring a bell?"

Indeed it did. But she wasn't Claudia's doctor. Her patient was David. The man convicted of her murder.

He considered correcting Herwig, then decided against it. Why should he? He didn't even know why this guy was asking. Claudia was gone, but he still thought the less this man had to do with her, the better.

"Too bad. Friend at the police department told me Southern had some connection to the case. He thought Claudia gave her some money."

"David is very ill, of course. But as far I know, Claudia was perfectly healthy when she...you know."

"Right. Heard the doctor might be having financial problems. And the one thing we know for sure is that Claudia was not hurting for money."

Most of his fellow college students were neck-deep in debt and could barely afford cafeteria food. But Claudia always had more than enough. "I'm sorry. I really haven't followed any late developments. I've kind of put the whole thing behind me." Pause. "Or tried."

"Completely understandable. I'm just thinking of the department. We went through hell when she died. I don't want to see it happen all over again."

"I'm sure it won't. Most of the people Claudia knew are about to graduate. Like me."

"Right, right. I'm probably too cautious. I just...thought you might know something. Thanks for coming by."

As he rose and left, Mitch couldn't help but think that was the weirdest faculty meeting of his entire life. And he'd had some weird ones.

He didn't believe for a minute that this was about the department. Herwig only thought about Herwig. What was he worried about?

Ten minutes ago, he believed this case was behind him. Now his interest had been rekindled.

He didn't know Dr. Southern. He'd never had any reason to meet her.

But he knew where she worked. And he was curious why Claudia would give her money.

Not that he was nosy. He wasn't. But he did not want Claudia's memory tarnished.

And if Herwig was coming after him, he might need to defend himself.

He'd escaped police attention once. He was not about to let them target him now. He'd come too far. And he had too much to lose.

# CHAPTER FIVE

DAN DROVE TO HIS OFFICE WITH A SMILE ON HIS FACE. HE USUALLY DID, but that was typically because he'd spent a pleasant hour in the ocean, kitesurfing or snorkeling. Back when he worked as a lawyer, his colleagues called him Aquaman, because nothing made him happier than getting wet and licking salt water off his lips. He felt sorry for tourists and locals who stayed on the beach. They were missing out on the best part.

This was Monday, however, and on Mondays he visited his mother at the assisted living facility where she stayed. She suffered from dementia and he was never quite sure whether she knew who he was, but she appeared content and at this point in her life that might be the best he could hope for. The smile on her face as he left each week was almost enough to erase his memories of the many years when her life had been anything but happy, when she worked her butt off to support him after her husband was locked away. When his father was an active-duty police officer, she worried night and day that he might be hurt. When he was behind bars, a cop incarcerated with the worst criminals in the state, some of whom he'd caught himself, she had even more reason to worry. And eventually, all that worry caught up with her.

As he pulled into the parking lot, he spotted Maria's car. He walked to the front door—and immediately realized something was wrong. He had what Maria called "a knack for noticing," a gift for observing and eventually connecting the dots to grasp the larger significance.

What was wrong with this picture?

He didn't need superpowers to answer that question. The front door glass was cracked. Burglars?

He stepped inside and flipped on the overhead light. The office had been ransacked. Trash everywhere.

Plus definite signs of a struggle.

He walked cautiously to his inner office. The door was closed, just as he'd left it. No sign of forced entry. Not here or in the kitchenette.

And no sign of Maria.

He pulled out his phone and speed-dialed her.

He'd been with Maria for several years and he knew she always had her phone with her. Usually in her hand.

The call went straight to voicemail.

She wouldn't blow off a call from him unless she had a good reason.

Or was physically unable to answer.

His inner office was as bad as the lobby. Maybe worse. Crumpled papers were strewn across the floor. Two of the file cabinets were knocked over, two drawers still out. His desk was a mess. The CPU for his desktop computer was missing. A mirror was smashed.

Someone was looking for something. Did they find it?

He knelt by one of the overturned file cabinets. Difficult to reach any conclusions, given the mess. Most of his files had spilled onto the floor.

He gritted his teeth and pulled the file cabinet upright, no small feat since the drawers still held a lot of paper. But he managed it. Even lawyers needed muscles on occasion.

Just as he thought. Nothing had spilled out of the middle drawer because nothing was in it.

A large file was missing.

He knew what that file was, too.

But if the intruder had any brains, he should've been able to find the file immediately. Why ransack the office?

Only one likely answer. Because he didn't get everything he wanted. Which meant he would have to go somewhere else.

He paced around, pondering, trying to push the mounting panic from his mind. Hard to solve a mystery when Maria was missing and not answering her phone...

He noticed something near the front door.

A stain. More evident once he cleared away some of the paper.

There was blood on the carpet.

"*Maria!*"

Of course there was no answer, but while he was down low, he noticed something else.

A cellphone rested under the nearby reception station. Probably slid there...

During a fight. Or someone threw it there so she couldn't call for help.

He clenched his eyes shut and took a deep breath. Don't let your imagination run away with you. There are a million possible explanations for this. Don't jump to any conclusions...

He gingerly picked up the phone, careful not to obliterate any fingerprints that might be there. Pink floral seashell case. Definitely Maria's.

He touched the screen. It asked for a six-digit code. He knew her code.

It wasn't her birthdate. It was his.

Once inside, he scrolled for anything that might explain the event so catastrophic as to separate his girl from her beloved phone. Email looked normal. No threatening texts. No apps were open. He almost let the screen go dark before he noticed something else.

The WhatsApp icon. It had a little red 2 in the upper right-hand corner.

He tapped the icon. Maria had received two phone calls through WhatsApp. Why not just call the normal way?

Because the call came from a foreign country. Australia.

She mentioned that, back at the courthouse. Why would anyone from Australia be contacting her? He tapped Recent Calls, but there was no profile or ID. He tried making a return call, but no one answered.

Panic seeped into his heart. This was not a simple misunderstanding. She was not going to magically come through the door and explain the confusion.

She had been taken.

He felt a sudden tightness in his throat. His heart raced.

He loved Maria. Told her so almost every day. Hoped to spend the rest of his life with her. But he may not have realized how important she was to him until this moment.

He stood in the middle of the room, trying to think what to do next, when suddenly his legs flew out from under him.

"*Wha—*" He tumbled to the floor, landing hard on his side. For a moment, he feared he'd popped his arm out of its socket. Hurt like hell, but it wasn't quite that bad.

What hit him?

He searched the room for answers as he scrambled to his feet…and took another hard blow to the neck. He tumbled sideways, breathless —and he still hadn't managed to lay eyes on his attacker.

Until he did. And gasped.

The figure before him was dressed in a dark hooded robe.

Dan raised his hands to block the next blow, deflecting it to the left.

Good thing, too—because his attacker's hands held a large blade.

*A scythe?*

The deflected blade missed his face but sliced his right forearm. He cried out in pain, but before he fully understood what was happening, he saw the blade headed his way again. He rolled, favoring his wounded arm, avoiding the next blow.

The Reaper pounced on him, gripping his wrist. They wrestled back and forth, each trying to gain control, neither quite making it. Dan gritted his teeth and brought all his strength to bear, but the assailant had a big advantage, being on top, armed, strong—and vicious.

He felt the enormous power his attacker mustered. He knew he couldn't prevent that blade from descending for long.

"What...did you do to Maria?" he managed to ask.

No reply.

They were practically nose-to-skeletal-nose. He could feel sweat dripping from the Reaper's eye sockets.

"Why...are you...trying to kill me?"

This time, Death spoke, with a harsh electronic voice. "You are not on the list. But you must be eliminated."

Dan managed to throw the Reaper off and scramble back to his feet. His eyes darted around the office, looking for anything that could be made into a weapon. A lamp? A letter opener?

"At least tell me why you're killing me."

No verbal response, but the Reaper inched toward him...

Dan was never so happy to hear a siren in his entire life. The Reaper heard it too. It was getting louder.

"Your death has been postponed. Not cancelled," the metallic voice said.

The Reaper fled through the front door. Dan followed, but by the time he reached the parking lot, there was no trace of anyone. The Reaper had disappeared.

Just like Maria.

---

Fifteen minutes later Dan spoke over the phone to his friend Jake Kakazu, Chief Detective with the SPPD.

"Someone reported that they heard loud violent noises coming from your office. I recognized the address and sent over a patrol car."

"Glad you did. That lunatic was going to kill me. And I have no idea what happened to Maria." He paused. "I'm worried."

"On it," Jake said. "Issuing an APB right now. I'll have two detectives at your office in ten minutes, plus a forensic team."

"Very much appreciated."

"Do you know of anyone who might want to harm Maria?"

"No. Everyone adores her." He swallowed, trying to keep the panic out of his voice. "But she is a lawyer."

"Any idea what happened to your office?"

"No. But someone seems very interested in the LCL cases."

"Don't touch anything else. My team will want the scene as pristine as possible."

"Understood. Jake—there's no telling where Maria is or...what might be happening to her. Please hurry."

"You don't have to ask. This is Priority One, starting now."

———

DAN PACED OUTSIDE THE OFFICE SO MUCH HE WORRIED HE WOULD DIG A hole in the ground, like the circular moat in Uncle Scrooge's worry room. While Jake and his forensic team did their work, he called all Maria's friends. No one had seen her. He called every hospital in St. Petersburg and Tampa. He even called some of her favorite apparel stores.

No trace of Maria.

The empty feeling in the pit of his stomach intensified. He could barely think straight. He wanted to run into the street and cry out her name. He kept that buried inside. He had to remain professional. Crumbling like a cookie would not help Maria.

But he had an aching in his chest that felt like someone had rammed a knife into it.

Even before he spoke, Dan could see Jake had nothing positive to impart. "The good news, Dan, is that I don't think there's any chance she was...seriously wounded here." Dan could see he almost said "killed," but modified the sentence to make it less painful. "There are only a few drops of blood. The forensic team is finding some trace evidence, but so far it appears to have all come from you or Maria."

"Could she have been knocked out? Taken somewhere?"

"That's certainly possible."

"Then she's been abducted."

"Perhaps." Jake wasn't going to say it out loud. But they both knew there was a worse alternative.

"Why?"

"I was planning to ask you that question. There must be someone who has a grudge. Disgruntled client. Angry opposing counsel. Offended judge."

"Maria would never offend a judge."

"Guess she doesn't take after you. What about all these Last Chance Lawyer cases lying all over the floor? Any of them controversial? Didn't you say a file was missing?"

"True. But it wasn't anything Maria has worked on. Hell, it wasn't anything I've worked on. I only had it because I'm supposed to be supervising."

"Maybe she was just in the wrong place at the wrong time."

"But if so—why abduct her?"

"I can't imagine. I'm going to have every available man walk the streets this afternoon. I'll get the governor to call out the National Guard if necessary. I'd release the bloodhounds and drag the ocean if I thought it would help. We're going to find her. If it's...possible."

"I appreciate that." But at the same time, he had a strong feeling that none of Jake's usual moves were going to help. He tried to maintain an outward calm, but inside, he was falling apart.

And there was another problem. He was good at reading faces. And right now, there was something major going on in Jake's head. Something he wasn't saying out loud.

"Of course, Dan..." Jake cleared his throat. "I know you and trust you, but in most cases involving disappearing spouses or paramours..."

"The cops assume the significant other did it."

"Because in most cases, they did."

"What are you saying? Am I a suspect?"

Jake shrugged. "Everyone's a suspect until we find the evidence to eliminate them. We have to consider—"

"Maria has been taken. Or worse. My office has been robbed.

Someone in a Halloween costume tried to kill me. And if that weren't quite enough, the police are now accusing me of murder."

"There's no evidence anyone else was here!" Jake sighed heavily. "What more can you tell me about this missing file?"

"Not much. It's a West Coast case."

"C'mon, Dan. Put me in the loop. I can't do my job if I don't know—"

Dan grabbed his backpack. "I think maybe I should keep my thoughts to myself for now. Since I'm a suspect."

"Suit yourself. I don't need to tell you that you should obtain legal counsel. The lawyer who represents himself has a fool for a client. And...you know the drill. Don't leave town."

"I have to find Maria."

"All the more reason to stay here."

"Am I accomplishing anything here?" All he could do here was stand around and stew. Until the police decided it was time to make an arrest. "You have no reason to suspect me, Jake. You're taking the easy way out. Arresting the guy who's here instead of finding the guy who's missing."

Jake pursed his lips. "I haven't told you the weirdest part yet."

"What could possibly make this weirder?"

"Your doorbell cam."

He installed that. An Amazon gizmo that let you look at your phone and see who's at the front door. It recorded the footage and stored it on a cloud. "Have you reviewed the footage?"

"I asked a plainclothes officer to review the entire tape on high speed."

"Who's passed through the front door today?"

"Just Maria and you."

"And before or after? Or in between?"

"Not a soul. If someone attacked Maria, they're completely invisible. Or a vampire." He paused. "But this intensifies the appearance that...the only person other than Maria who's been here today...is you." Jake looked at him levelly. "Let me say it again, Dan, and I hope you understand that I'm serious. Don't leave town."

# CHAPTER SIX

"FATHER FORGIVE ME FOR I HAVE SINNED."

The Reaper wondered if this was the first time the priest, Father Lamont, ever had Death personified in his confessional. Probably, but given how little light seeped from one part of the confessional to the other, he might not have noticed.

"It's been two weeks since my last confession." A long time, but these were busy days. And most of the recent activities would not be endorsed by the Catholic Church. "Father, I have taken a life. And more deaths are in my future."

Father Lamont began talking, but the Reaper didn't hear most of it, too torn up inside to listen. The Church would not approve of murder or other criminal deeds. But the priest would eventually offer a home-work assignment—some Hail Marys and a rosary, whatever—and then forgive all the sins. Which was the only reason to make this stop.

"I am glad you seek forgiveness," Father Lamont said. "But I cannot grant absolution while you hold evil in your heart. Are you planning to kill again?"

Tough question. Especially after that run-in with Pike. The Reaper spent the rest of the day observing Pike's office from a discreet distance, watched the police investigate and organize. They lined up single file, ready to scour the beach, the park, every street and alleyway in the area. Someone was pulling out all the stops—

The Reaper took a cleansing breath, then released it.

What difference would it make? Once the streets of St. Petersburg calmed a bit, he was heading west.

There was more work to be done.

Props to SPPD for trying. The target in Indianapolis had been dead for days, and as far as anyone could tell, no one had even noticed. That job had been a piece of cake. But the lawyer woman in the tight jeans knew how to fight. Not that it helped her much, ultimately.

There was much to be done and no time for this indulgent church visit. But the Reaper felt torn apart from the inside. Didn't everyone hate what was happening to this country? Shouldn't everyone be trying to do something about it? Didn't everyone seek peace?

And that could only come from one source.

"Father, I know I have committed evil deeds. But I did so for a reason."

"The ends cannot justify the means. That is not how God works."

"God doesn't have family. He doesn't have to deal with mortgages and health insurance and—"

"We all have secular commitments and temporal lives. They cannot override the will of God."

"But Father—look what's happening to this world."

The Reaper blamed the media. They always favored liberal causes. If a white guy had been murdered and chopped into pieces, it probably wouldn't get a footnote on page fourteen. But if something happened to a wealthy female Hispanic lawyer with connections to city government—that was a completely different story. Every day, this nation seemed less and less like America. They had to do something to take this nation back before it was too late.

And it had to start somewhere, right? Granted, this costume wasn't red, white, and blue, but it was appropriate for the task at hand.

Maybe life hadn't been all it could be. Whose fault was that? Every upward path was blocked by rules and regulations, artificial qualifications, quotas, tests and trials and prohibitions. It was not a level playing field. Why was there no affirmative action for real Americans? There'd been too much emphasis on outsiders, foreign nations, global problems. It was time America started taking care of its own.

"Let God worry about the world," Father Lamont advised. "You must save your soul. Make no mistake—God still has plans for you."

"People always say that, but I never received my marching orders. Or any help paying the bills."

"God helps those who help themselves."

"That's what I'm doing."

"If you're sinning, that is not what you're doing. You're indulging your basest instincts and rationalizing evil deeds."

"Father, I'm just trying to survive."

"I know the road before us often seems insurmountable. But God takes care of his own."

Sounded good in theory. Where was the evidence? And since there was no evidence, why come? It seemed that no matter what, the Reaper still wanted to believe it was possible to be right with God, the Twitch Upon the Thread that could never be completely severed.

The media reports were all the same. Blood found in the office. No trace of the woman. Strong hints that Pike was Suspect No. 1. APBs issued. Televised pleas for assistance. Every available officer on the case.

Even the mayor appeared, making a personal plea for help. Apparently she and Maria Morales knew each other. Nice that she would speak up for her friend. Women often were their own worst enemies, judging and criticizing and backstabbing.

The DA also made a pitch, and of course, that was another woman, also claiming to be a personal friend. Did Morales know everyone in town? The DA said she was working closely with the police and they would do everything imaginable to learn what happened.

The standard claptrap. I am woman, hear me roar.

But when asked if Pike was a suspect, she dodged the question.

"I'm going to be traveling soon, Father. May I have your blessing?"

"May God bless your travel and keep you safe." He paused. "But that blessing will not forgive intentional evil deeds. You know the law. Thou shalt not kill."

The priest's words like a knife to the heart. Why would anyone be willing to take...such extreme actions? This country had gone very wrong and someone had to take a stand before it was too late. God instructed the ancient Israelites to seize Canaan and kill the inhabitants after they lost their way. How was this any different?

The Reaper was God's Angel of Death. So he dressed accordingly.

Father Lamont mumbled a few more words. Took the blessing and the priest's instructions and rushed out the door. Much work to do.

All the key players had appeared in the media reports—except one. Pike himself. Of all the players in this scenario, he was best positioned to screw things up. And if that happened, immediate action would be required. There was too much at stake.

Jesus would just have to understand. The needs of the many...

And after so many deaths, what possible difference could a few more make?

# CHAPTER SEVEN

BEN KINCAID LEANED BACK IN HIS RECLINER, SUDDENLY REALIZING that, for once in his checkered life—he felt contented. And why not? He'd earned it.

That was what the Oklahoma Bar Association said in the letter informing him that he was about to get a special lifetime achievement award, something he never expected. Sure, he'd defended a lot of clients against false accusations. But that didn't always make you popular in a red state like Oklahoma. He'd also been arrested a few times, accused of numerous crimes, and trashed on social media. He constantly clashed with law enforcement (even though his best friend was now Chief of Police). And some people have long memories, especially for anything negative. He'd built the Last Chance Lawyer network, but he always kept that on a low profile. A national law firm for clients too controversial or too poor for other lawyers sounded wonderful to some and dangerously radical to others.

No, there was only one explanation for this award. He was getting old. Someone probably thought he looked fragile and worried that if they didn't give him an award soon they might lose the option…

He had agreed to appear and accept the award. Which meant he had to think of something to say.

"Just say thank you and sit down. Really, that's the safest course."

He swung his chair around and saw Christina, his wife, former law partner, and mother of their two daughters. Her eyebrows bounced. "Don't get me wrong. You did learn how to speak to a jury. Eventually. But a speech before a packed audience of peers? Just asking for trouble."

"I was thinking I might reflect on the evolution of the law during the decades I've been practicing. Perhaps contrast that with parallel evolutions in other fields, technology and literature and—"

She patted him on the shoulder. "Just say thank you and sit down."

She appeared to be wearing a hip-hugging black dress with fringe at the sleeves and the bottom. And looked darn good in it, too.

She followed his eyes. "Too eccentric?"

"Not if you're going to a Halloween party as Morticia Addams."

"*Tres amusing.*" She scowled, then glanced at the items on his desk. "Did you look at those links I sent you? The houses?"

Ben sighed. "Do we really have to move? Again?"

"That's what we agreed. A long time ago. When we came back to Tulsa."

"I know. But moving is so…exhausting."

"We don't need all this space. A big house is just a money pit. The girls are both in college. It's time to downsize."

"I know, I know. But my piano is perfect where it is. And heavy."

"We'll get movers."

"Movers are expensive."

"We can afford it."

"We're not rich, Christina."

"We're comfortable."

"If we're comfortable, we can pay for whatever expenses arise in our current money pit."

"Ben, you agreed to this. Why are you arguing?"

"I don't know. To stay in practice?" He swiveled around and stared at the wall. "I don't like spending my father's money. I mean, for a nonprofit, sure. But for myself, no."

Christina knelt beside him, brushing her long strawberry blonde hair behind her shoulders. As far as Ben was concerned, the traces of gray made her more appealing. "Heads up, hubby. It's not your father's money anymore. It's yours. And it came to you through your mother, who loved you dearly. Sock some of it away for the girls, sure. But that doesn't mean we can't have a little fun. And it certainly doesn't mean we can't move to a smaller house."

He clasped her hand. "This is why I let you make the important decisions. You have a much better grasp of the big picture."

Her lips trembled a bit. "You old romantic. I'm gonna get teary-eyed."

"Please don't."

"And while you're in a sappy mood, let me also say that it's time we traveled more."

"We already went to France."

"And it was wonderful, wasn't it?"

"Certainly interesting. Would be better if they put ice in the soft drinks."

"You could've ordered espresso."

"Coffee? Ick."

"Okay, chocolate milk. If you insist on eating like a seven-year-old."

"Look, you wanted to go to France and we did. Mission accomplished."

A sly smile crossed her face. "They speak French in Monaco, too. Also Belgium, Madagascar, Chad—"

"Monaco?"

"Casinos. Art museums. Four-star restaurants. The most beautiful beaches in the world."

"I never know what to do at beaches. I can't just lie around doing nothing."

"Bring some Trollope. You'll have skin lesions before you finish."

"Which raises another point. My dermatologist says I shouldn't go out in the sun."

"Wear a hat."

"Or just stay home, where I can read in comfort."

"Ben, in some ways you haven't changed since I first met you at Raven Tucker & Tubb thirty-plus years ago."

"Is that a problem?"

She ran her fingers through the thinning hair on the side of his head. "No. That's why I love you." She rose. "I'm going to the store. Big sale at Dillard's. And we need cat food."

"Home in time for dinner?"

"We have leftovers. But in the meantime." She ran to the kitchen and returned carrying a plate. "I made you a snack to tide you over."

"Grilled cheese?"

"Your doctor told you to lay off dairy after that last batch of kidney stones."

"He said reduce, not eliminate." He glanced at the plate. "What is it?"

"A very healthy, tasty spinach salad."

He sighed. "Yum."

"Be back soon." She waggled her fingers and headed for the garage.

He'd reached a point where he could actually digest a salad, but he was never going to like it, at least not without Ranch dressing, which according to Christina completely defeated the point of eating a salad. He appreciated the fact that she was watching his health. He just wished there was a way to do it other than by eliminating everything that makes food taste good...

He walked to his home office, a Marquis Captain's desk wedged into the side of their bedroom. Christina was a bundle of energy, but he felt older every day. And now the Bar was giving him a metaphorical gold watch, putting him out to pasture...

And he didn't blame them. He felt tired.

Captain Dunsel? Grandpa Useless?

He wasn't sure how much time passed before he heard urgent pounding on the front door, accompanied with shouting he could not understand.

His pal Mike Morelli had told him to prepare for emergency situations like this. Call 911. Get a dog. Get a gun. None of which he ever did.

"Who is it?"

More pounding.

Well, faint heart never won fair maiden…

He walked to the front door and peered through the glass.

*Dan?* Daniel Pike? Florida attorney and current Chief Administrator for the LCL network? What was he doing in Tulsa?

He opened the door. "Dan? What—"

"Come with me if you want to live."

Ben squinted. "Have you been waiting your whole life to say that?"

"I don't have time to explain. We need to go."

"Stop being so mysterious. I'm not going anywhere."

"You will. You must. Is Christina home?"

"No, she left to—"

"Good. Thought that was her. We can call her and tell her not to come home."

"What are you babbling about? How did you get here?"

"I flew."

"You could've called first."

"I didn't think that would be wise. Someone wants to kill me and quite possibly you too."

"Would you slow down already? Why don't you want Christina to come home?"

His voice erupted. "Because I don't want her to end up like Maria!"

Ben still didn't understand, except he grasped that Dan was seriously upset and trying to help him.

"I'll explain in the car, Ben. We need to leave."

"You just got here."

"No. I've been parked down the street for an hour. You're being watched."

"*What?*"

"The black van obviously watching your home just left. Possibly to follow Christina. So we need to get out while we can without being spotted. Tell Christina to call your daughters and go somewhere safe. You have police friends, right?"

"One very good one."

"Get Christina some protection. Or hire security." Dan checked his watch. "Are you coming voluntarily?"

"Absolutely not. You'll have to go without me."

"Can't. We're making an important stop and you can get me inside. Plus, you're the boss of the network and—"

"I thought you were the boss of the network."

"No. I'm the worker bee. You're the founder and CFO and everyone knows it." He looked as if he were about to rip out his hair. "Look, I can explain all this in more detail later. Will you just get in the car?"

"I will not."

"Have it your way." Dan reached into his backpack and withdrew what looked like a black hood. He draped it over Ben's head, then pulled a drawstring to tighten it around his neck.

Ben tried to yank off the hood, but Dan knocked his hands away. He shouted, but the hood muffled the sound. "What are you doing, you insane maniac?"

Dan grabbed his left wrist and pulled it behind his back.

"*Oww!*"

He snapped handcuffs around Ben's wrists.

"Are you completely delusional?"

"Not completely. But I don't have any more time to waste." He grabbed Ben and steered him toward the door.

"This is kidnapping!"

"Only in a...technical way."

"Could I at least pack a bag?"

"No. We'll buy anything you need."

"Have you forgotten I'm your employer?"

"I guess you can consider this my resignation."

"I do not accept your resignation!"

"Then we're both taking a leave of absence." He shoved Ben outside and slammed the door behind them.

# CHAPTER EIGHT

GARY QUINCE HATED LA TRAFFIC. HE'D LIVED HERE IN THE CITY OF Angels his entire life, so he should be used to it. But it seemed like traffic was always at its worst when he was short on time.

You loser. Stop making excuses. Shouldn't a grown man in his mid-forties be able to get out of bed on time? Especially when he had a court date?

His problem this morning wasn't insomnia. It was the cause of his insomnia. Namely, this case. David Donovan's case. He was sweating bullets over it. He appreciated the LCL assignment. But he was in over his head. And if he botched this, his client's life was at an end.

He parked his Mini Cooper and raced toward the back courthouse door. LA's downtown courthouse was one of the largest in the country and could be a giant rat maze if you didn't know your way around. Or if it was crowded. Or half the elevators were non-functional, which seemed to be true most of the time.

By the time he got to the courtroom, he was sweating profusely. The marshals had already brought in his client, who was still in shackles and coveralls since today he would only be seen by a judge, not a jury. The marshals stood at a discreet distance, though Gary knew they could pounce in a heartbeat.

He slid behind the table beside his client. "How are you feeling?"

Donovan's face was lined and drawn, as if he'd been up all night and hadn't eaten for a week. "Trying not to think about it."

Trying not to think about which? The fact that he had received a life sentence—tantamount to an execution order, for him—or that the flimsy motion Gary filed was the only thing that could prevent him from going back to prison. "I'm going to give it everything I've got."

"You know what I read online? These motions are successful less than one-tenth of one percent of the time. They say it's a pro forma motion lawyers file but never expect to succeed."

Damn Wikipedia anyway. He knew he couldn't dislodge people's faith in anything they read on their phones. Especially since, in this case, it was accurate. "I don't want to inflate expectations, but I think we've got a shot. The police did not investigate several possible suspects and the case against you was full of holes."

"But they still convicted me. Quickly."

Yes, there was that. "Juries are more easily manipulated than judges. There is definitely reasonable doubt here." He said that, careful to not actually ask his client if he committed the crime—a question defense attorneys rarely asked. He hadn't handled the trial, but he knew it was complex and left many questions unanswered. The college student David allegedly killed had a safe in her dorm room and many sketchy friends. A priceless violin. Stalkers. "That's why LCL sent me your case."

"The Last Chance Lawyers? That does not sound promising."

"You might be surprised by our success rate."

"Tell me that means we're going to win."

Gary took a deep breath. "It means you've got the best shot you could possibly have." Especially since he was broke and no one else would take his case. "But we've still got a tall mountain to climb."

A uniformed bailiff entered and half-heartedly announced the imminent arrival of the judge. They rose. So did his opposite number, a young woman from the DA's office. Seemed this hearing was so unthreatening they sent a baby to cover it.

Judge Durant was the worst possible choice, at least for them.

Durant had decades on the bench, a thick shock of white hair, a craggy face, and an expression that suggested he had been doing this job far too long. He had a rep for being a prosecutor's judge, not because he was a Republican appointee but because he seemed too far gone to volunteer for the considerable work required to overturn a verdict.

The judge stared at the papers on his bench as if he had no idea what they were doing, which seemed rather unlikely.

"Motion for New Trial," the judge mumbled, as if speaking to himself. "The defendant unsurprisingly wishes to set aside the jury verdict and start over, making various allegations of misconduct by law enforcement." He looked up. "Does that about cover it, counsel?"

Gary rose. "We also have newly discovered evidence that casts doubt on the fairness of the verdict, your honor."

The judge nodded. "I see that. You've summarized the evidence but not attached it."

"The evidence is in the form of testimony, your honor. We will need to call witnesses."

"Were these people born recently? Was their existence known at the time of trial?"

"Well, yes…"

"Then why didn't you call them then?"

Gary took a deep breath. "I didn't handle the trial below, your honor, but—"

"You stand in the shoes of whoever did."

"I know, your honor."

"Are you alleging incompetence of counsel?"

What a can of worms that would be. "Not at this time."

"Then the court does not grasp how these witnesses can be considered newly discovered."

His opponent, Assistant District Attorney Lynn Chee, rose. "On that point, we agree. This case has been fully and fairly litigated, your honor. The defendant lost. We don't want to start retrying cases every time the defendant doesn't like the verdict."

Judge Durant shuffled a few more papers. "The court is not seeing a compelling claim of newly discovered evidence. Therefore—"

Gary raised his hands, desperately trying to hold back a ruling. "Your honor, one of these witnesses only came forward a few weeks ago."

The judge shook his head. "The fact that trial counsel may not have adequately researched the case before it went to trial does not—"

"Your honor, there's no way any defense lawyer could have known. The prosecutor gave us no indication—"

Chee interrupted. "We are only required to produce evidence we intend to use or that might be exculpatory. Which we did."

"Then we must have differing definitions of 'exculpatory.' Because they buried at least one important witness. A credible witness. A medical doctor. And maybe more."

Judge Durant sighed. It wasn't hard to guess what was traveling through his brain. The last thing on earth he wanted to do was retry this case. But he also didn't want to leave himself open to attack by an appellate court that might think he should've at least heard the supposedly relevant evidence being proffered. "The court requires a very high level—"

"Your honor." Gary knew it was dangerous to interrupt a judge. But if he waited till the judge reached the end of his sentence, it might be too late. "Let me make an offer of proof. In writing. I can have it on your desk by the end of the day."

The judge bit down on his lower lip.

"There's no harm. I'll submit today." He could feel sweat seeping through his shirt. He'd left his jacket on, of course, so the pit stains didn't show. But sweat was also dripping down the sides of his face. "If the court thinks this bears merit, set it for full hearing."

"Your honor," Chee said. "The judicial system needs to have some sense of finality. Otherwise, no case will ever end."

Judge Durant peered down at his papers. "Yes, the case needs to end at some point. The question is when we've reached that point. And this is a murder case, so we must ensure that every relevant rock has been overturned." He looked up. "I'll expect your offer of proof to arrive before the close of business today, counsel. The State will have twenty-four hours to respond. I will instruct the court clerk to set this down for hearing at the first possible setting."

The clerk, a gray middle-aged woman who appeared almost as lifeless as the judge, replied. "Monday morning at ten."

"There you have it. If the court is not persuaded by your offer of proof, then the motion will be dismissed. If the court determines that the motion has some possible validity, however remote, we will have a hearing and call witnesses on Monday. And then this matter will be full and finally over. One way or the other. The court will not grant any more extensions, so don't bother asking."

He couldn't believe it. He thought they were dead in the water. Maybe he was a better lawyer than he thought...

Or maybe he'd just gotten lucky. Either way, he was going to take the opportunity and run with it.

"Thank you, your honor. I'll have the offer to you immediately."

The judge turned. "Does the State understand the ruling?"

Chee rose again. "Of course, your honor. We strongly disagree, but—"

"The court has ruled." Judge Durant banged his gavel. "Court dismissed."

Gary watched the judge leave the courtroom.

David clutched his coat sleeve. "That was good, right?"

"Very good." He saw marshals approaching. Bastards. Couldn't give them five minutes to talk? "Not a slam dunk. But at least we have a chance. I've already drafted the offer of proof. I'll polish it up and send it out. I think we'll get the hearing."

"And what happens there?"

"We put on our evidence. And hope the court will see that, in its rush to convict the obvious suspect, the police failed to investigate other suspects to such a degree as to call the whole process into question. If the judge grants our motion, we get a new trial."

David nodded. The marshals looked impatient. He knew they didn't have much more time. "Are you ready for this?"

Which was exactly the same question Gary had been asking

himself ever since LCL assigned him this case. It was nice having someone else find his clients, finance his cases, and pay him a generous salary that wasn't dependent on success rates. But this time, he might be in over his head. He'd never tried anything so serious in his entire life. Ever since the case began he'd been an anxiety-ridden mess.

David's eyes were pleading. "I won't be able to get the help I need if I'm behind bars. Don't let them put me away for a crime I did not commit. I'll be dead inside of a year."

There it was. Unbidden but still answered. He claimed he was an innocent man. And a lawyer's highest and best use was to prevent the innocent from being railroaded. But he felt desperately unsuited for the task. Like an imposter. And this man needed the real deal.

"I'll do everything I possibly can," he said, but even as he spoke the words, they felt weak and inadequate.

Out the corner of his eye, he spotted someone racing out of the courtroom. He wasn't aware they had spectators. Was someone monitoring the case?

All at once, a tremor rippled through his body with such intensity that he could barely remain standing.

What had he gotten himself into?

The marshals tugged David toward the door. "I'm counting on you, Gary. You're my only hope."

And then they were gone and Gary was left standing alone. Feeling terrified and nervous and on the verge of mental collapse.

David Donovan needed him. And he was very much afraid he was about to let him down. Fatally.

# CHAPTER NINE

BEN KNEW HE WAS IN A CAR. AND HE KNEW IT WAS MOVING. BUT THE black hood prevented him from drawing any conclusions about his current whereabouts. And since his wrists were cuffed to...something...he couldn't explore much.

"So now you're a kidnapper?" Ben asked, the edge in his voice not remotely concealed.

"In a friendly sort of way," Dan replied.

"There is no friendly way to hold someone against their will."

"I haven't demanded a ransom and you haven't been harmed."

"You forcibly took me from my home."

"Not an ideal scenario, I grant you, but—"

"It's a felony!" Ben's voice magnified. "I've made it possible for you to do exactly what you've always wanted to do professionally without worrying about money. And you repay me with an abduction."

"Let me explain."

"There is nothing you could say that would make this acceptable. Here in the civilized world, we talk first, kidnap later. Or perhaps—"

"Maria has been taken," Dan said, cutting him off.

"—you think that—*what?*"

"Maria. Morales. You know. Also your employee. Plus, we live together."

Ben's voice lowered. "What happened?"

"I don't know. But she's gone, there's blood on the carpet, someone tried to kill me, and the police haven't been able to find her."

"Maria disappeared in Florida—so you came to Oklahoma?"

"The police are doing everything they can back home, and my sister Dinah is coordinating with them—while staying out of sight." He omitted the part about him being the cops' top suspect.

"You think she's in danger too?"

"I don't know. I'm not taking any chances. I've told all my close friends and colleagues to get somewhere safe. And like I said before, you should do the same. This has something to do with you."

"I don't know anything about it."

"Someone ransacked my office in Florida but didn't get everything they wanted. So the next logical place to look—"

"Would be my office? Why didn't you just say so? You could've called…"

"I had no way of knowing who might be listening. Or watching. You have files in your downtown office, right? On Boston Avenue?"

"True."

"Look out the window." He yanked the hood off Ben's head.

Ben winced as the sudden infusion of daylight made his eyes water. "That's my office." He squinted, trying to shut out the offending light. "Why is the door open?"

"Exactly. Any chance Christina is in there?"

"None."

"Good." He parked the car and unbuckled his seat. "I'm going to check it out."

"Uncuff me. I'll go with you."

"I can't do that."

"Why the hell not?"

"Because you'll flee. And I need you."

"If you leave me here, I'll scream for help."

"No, you won't. And even if you did, no one would hear you."

"This is a completely unacceptable denial of my fundamental human rights. This is—"

"—only going to take a few minutes." Dan slid out of the car and slammed the door behind him.

---

As soon as he entered the office, Dan knew two things with certainty. First, someone had torn this place apart just as they'd done to his office. And second—that person had disappeared.

Five minutes later, Dan returned to the car. Ben was not screaming, but he didn't look happy, either. "Suspicions confirmed."

"You found something in my office. Which I myself was not allowed to see. But now that you've found my office felon-free, I assume you'll let me go."

"Not yet."

"Why the hell not?" Ben swiveled as far as the cuffs—hooked to the passenger seat door—allowed.

"I still need you."

"For what?"

"Figuring out what's going on."

"That doesn't require handcuffs."

Dan ignored him. "Tell me about *State of California vs. Donovan.*"

Ben tucked his chin. "The homicide case?"

"Yeah." Dan started the car and slid out of the parking space. "The guy who attacked me took what I had on the case. But I didn't have much. So your office was the logical next stop."

"I probably had a lot more than you, but the primary files on that case will be in the LA office. That's where the case is pending."

"I also found weird calls on Maria's phone. From Australia. She mentioned them to me last time I saw her. I tried calling back but the numbers were unidentified and no one picked up."

"Does Maria have something going on down under?"

"No."

"Maybe something came up she failed to mention?"

"Maria does not keep secrets. Like, ever."

Ben chuckled. "All women keep secrets. Also all men."

"Not Maria. She has no cause. We're completely upfront with one another."

Ben continued to smile. "Okay. Let's focus on her disappearance. Has anyone asked for ransom money?"

"No."

"Have they offered to return her in exchange for information?"

"No."

"But there's no...no..."

"No corpse. I'm confident she's still alive."

"Because...?"

"I have a feeling."

"Anything more?"

"No. But I...don't believe she's gone. I would know."

Ben fell silent for a long time. "I think I'm beginning to understand. Please uncuff me."

"If I uncuff you, will you try to escape?"

Ben paused a few moments before answering. "When the proper moment arises."

"At least you're not a liar. But I'm responsible for Maria. And I won't do one thing that might endanger her or prevent me from finding her. I—I just—I couldn't—" He turned his head away. Fighting back tears.

Ben's voice softened. "No worries. We'll find her."

"You don't know that."

"I know how important she is to you." He cleared his throat. "Okay, uncuff me. I won't try to run."

"Promise?"

"But you're going to have to tell me everything about this."

"Deal." Dan pulled up to a stop sign, then reached over and unlocked the cuffs.

Ben massaged his wrists. "Thank you so much."

"Better?"

"Not really. But at least I can feel my fingers again."

# CHAPTER TEN

BEN TALKED INTO HIS CELL PHONE, HOLDING IT SIDEWAYS PARALLEL TO his mouth, like his daughters did. He wasn't sure why it made a difference. But he didn't want to seem clueless. Ever since his last birthday, he'd been more sensitive about not looking like a befuddled old fogey.

"That's right, Chris. We're in a car. A..." He looked around him. "What is this, anyway?"

Dan had his eyes fixed on the road. "Mercedes convertible. C-class. Rented it at the airport."

Ben's eyes widened. "You rented a Mercedes?"

Dan shrugged. "I wanted a convertible. I prefer the Ferrari F8, but none of the rental dealers had one."

"Imagine that."

"I think better when I have the top down."

"Should I be concerned that, at the moment, the top is up?"

"I was afraid you'd scream for help."

"Sound thinking." Ben returned his attention to the phone. "Did you get that, Chris? I'm confined to a ridiculously overpriced German convertible. Apparently we're going to McAlester." Pause. "She wants to know why."

"Got an old friend I want to visit. Then back to the car. We could drive to the LA office in about twenty-eight hours. An all-nighter, basically."

"Wouldn't a plane be faster?"

"Maybe. But I prefer to travel without being observed, particularly by the people who took Maria and want me next."

Ben gave him a long look. "You're afraid if we go to an airport, I'll cause a scene or report you for kidnaping."

"The possibility did occur to me."

"I told you I wouldn't run. So I won't." Ben glanced at the road ahead. "You know McAlester is not on the way to California, right?"

"Think of it as a scenic side trip."

"I can tell you've never been there." He returned his attention to the phone. "Christina wants to know when you'll be returning her abducted husband."

"Tell her as soon as possible, because you're starting to get on my nerves."

He relayed the message. "She wants to know why she shouldn't call her close personal friend, the Tulsa Chief of Police Michelangelo Morelli, and get your sorry ass arrested." He coughed. "Sorry about the language. That was a direct quote."

"Ask her to give me a chance. Wouldn't she want you to move heaven and earth if she disappeared?"

They talked a few more moments, then Ben ended the phone call.

Dan looked sideways as he merged onto the highway. "That's it? She's not calling cop friends?"

"Not yet. She reserves the right. But she thinks you're probably not a coldblooded killer, and she's worried about Maria, so she's giving you a little rope."

"That all she said?"

"Not remotely."

"Can you bottom line it for me?"

"She expects me back by Friday or she'll come looking for you. And she will have someone arrest—"

"My sorry ass? I heard that part. Anything else?"

"She says if anything happens to me, she'll hunt you down and kill you like a dog."

"I admire a woman who doesn't mince words."

"Me too. For thirty-odd years now."

"How do I know she won't come looking for you? With friends?"

"Well…"

He snapped his fingers. "Do you have Location Services on your phone?"

Ben appeared confused. "Do I have…what?"

"Location Services. That's an iPhone, right?"

"I…think so."

Dan rolled his eyes. "Old people."

"Who's old? I'm barely…my current age."

"What about Find My Phone? Is that activated?"

"I'm…not sure."

Dan swore under his breath. "No wonder Christina's confident she can find you." He snatched the phone from Ben's hands, rolled down his car window, and tossed the phone outside.

"*Hey*!" Ben screamed. "What the hell do you think you're doing?"

"Keeping us safe."

"That phone cost me a thousand bucks!"

"You should get an Android. Apple products are ridiculously overpriced."

"This from the man who wanted to rent a Ferrari."

"Look, we're safer if you don't have a phone. Christina's not the only one who could use it to track us. So could the FBI. Or the NSA. Or a criminal with tech skills."

"Did you throw away *your* phone?"

"Of course not. We need some way to communicate with the outside world. But thanks to my colleague Garrett, my phone is equipped with every anti-surveillance device known to man."

"Smart precaution for a kidnapper."

"Look, when this is all over, I'll buy you a new phone."

"You damn sure will. But I still don't get why I had to lose my phone but you get to keep yours.

Dan's voice dropped several notches. "Maria might call."

If that remained possible.

# CHAPTER ELEVEN

Dan drove for over an hour without saying a word. Chatting with Ben seemed pointless. He was more than a bit on the cranky side, and honestly, who could blame him?

He slowed as he approached the Oklahoma State Penitentiary in McAlester, one of the most notorious in the system, home of one of the worst prison riots in history. Not a typical tourist destination. Unless, of course, you know someone who lives there.

Not a visit he looked forward to. But if there was any chance it might provide a clue about what happened to Maria, he would do it gladly. He would walk barefoot over hot coals every day for the rest of his life if it would help Maria.

Assuming she could still be helped. Which seemed more unlikely every moment.

He was relieved when Ben chose to speak. "I assume we're visiting someone incarcerated, not the warden."

"How'd you figure that out?"

"You're a defense attorney."

Flawlessly logical. "I know this guy. Knew him when he was on the outside and working for ICE. In fact, I was instrumental in putting him away."

"Well then, this is going to be a joyous reunion. What makes you think he'll agree to see you?"

"I brought him a present."

Ben nodded. "Probably doesn't get a lot of gifts in maximum security. Does he like you?"

"Last time I saw him, he tried to kill me. When I was briefly... sharing space with him."

Ben's eyebrow arched. "And when you say sharing space, you mean...incarcerated?"

"Briefly. It was a big misunderstanding."

"I'm sure. But if he's behind bars, he can't be the one who attacked Maria. Or ransacked our offices."

"True. But he still might know something. I told you I found Maria's phone. There was a call from this prison. A call placed after she disappeared."

"Why would this guy call Maria?"

"That's what I'm about to find out."

---

DAN ORIGINALLY PLANNED TO LEAVE BEN IN THE CAR. HE FOUND SOME offroad brush about a mile away where he could park and walk. But Ben wasn't keen on the idea—he kept talking about his allergies and tick phobia. Eventually Ben agreed to behave, but only if Dan let him come inside. He swore he wouldn't create a scene or inform the prison officers that he'd been kidnapped—and left phoneless—by his top employee.

"Very amenable of you," Dan said.

"I'm sick of being in the car. And I will admit to being curious."

"About the prison?"

"Nah. I've been here many times. I'm anxious to see you in action. I've read your case reports. But this time I've got a front-row seat."

Dan had called ahead, which streamlined the process of getting inside. There was a lot of paperwork, but Ben introduced himself and flashed his bar card and the guards waved them both inside.

"These guys seemed to know you," Dan noted, while they waited.

Ben shrugged. "I've had several clients lodging here at various times. Including a priest. Plus, I'm getting a big award from the bar association. Just announced."

"Congratulations. I'm jealous. I don't think the Florida Bar thinks much of me."

The corner of Ben's lips turned up. "I took a different approach."

"Meaning?"

"You're a showboat. Flashy, theatrical. I'm the opposite."

"Boring?"

"Low key. I suggest possibilities rather than ramming them down the jury's throat. I think most jurors appreciate that."

"You'd be more agressive if you'd been arrested on trumped-up charges."

Ben pressed his lips together but said nothing.

"So," Dan said, "I guess we use the good cop-bad cop approach?"

"That's original thinking. Am I the bad cop?"

Dan chuckled. "I don't think so."

"Meaning?"

"Nothing. It's just...you're...you know."

"Weak?"

"Mmm...unthreatening."

"You're planning to threaten this guy?"

"Possibly."

"Then you'll need backup."

"Sure. Just don't move too fast, Grandpa. Don't want you to fall and break a hip."

Ten minutes later, two guards brought Jack Crenshaw in to see them. When Dan first met him, several years before, he was dressed in cowboy garb, hat and boots and a bolo tie. But today it was orange coveralls with DOC emblazoned on the back.

Crenshaw looked like he'd aged two decades. His teeth seemed black and his face hollow, with dark circles around both eyes. He knew Crenshaw had problems getting along with fellow inmates back in Florida, which eventually led to him being relocated out-of-state.

Crenshaw sat opposite them, on the other side of a round metal table affixed to the floor. "Well, well, well now. I do declare. Daniel Pike. Never thought to see you again, pardner." His head twitched. "Who's the new guy?"

Dan was succinct. "My boss."

"Someone tells the Great and Powerful Daniel Pike what to do?"

"More of an overseer, really," Ben said.

"Do tell." Crenshaw grinned. "What brings you here today, Danny Boy?"

He saw no reason to mince words. "I want to know why you called Maria."

Crenshaw nodded. "Lovely woman. I heard you two hooked up. How is she these days?"

He didn't want to answer. Because he suspected Crenshaw already knew. "Why'd you call her?"

"To warn her."

"About what?"

Crenshaw leaned away from the table. "Hold on, sheriff. Why should I tell you anything? I wouldn't be in this hellhole if it weren't for you."

"I wasn't expecting you to help out of gratitude." Dan pursed his lips. "I brought you something."

Crenshaw clapped his hands together. "Goldarn you. Is it my birthday?"

Dan reached into his backpack and withdrew a large ornate kaleidoscope.

Crenshaw let out a soft sigh. "You remembered."

"That you love kaleidoscopes? Hard to forget." He signaled the nearest guard. The gift had been inspected and approved in advance. Once the guard nodded, he handed the kaleidoscope to Crenshaw.

Crenshaw pressed it to his left eye and turned the wheel. The delight on his face was unmistakable. He looked like a little kid who just found the best Christmas present he could imagine under the tree.

"This is...remarkable." Crenshaw continued gazing for several minutes. "You know you're experiencing a miracle when you can hold something to your eye and see the beauty in this joint. Kaleidoscopes are magical. They allow us to see the world as it should be."

"So you like it?"

Crenshaw seemed less threatening when he was holding a toy. "Sho'nuff."

"Tell me why you were calling Maria."

He lowered the kaleidoscope. "Word travels fast behind bars. I heard what happened to her."

"Then you understand why I want some answers."

"You may recall, Dan, that there's a certain El Salvadorean cartel that is not so happy with you."

"You mean an ex-cartel. The one I helped destroy."

"Funny thing about crime families. They're like that multi-headed hydra, you know what I mean?"

"I didn't just cut off the head. I smashed it to a pulp."

"But some people still carry a grudge. And some of them are in this very prison. Proximity to the border, I guess. I got information indicating that someone important—someone related to that little girl you got adopted—wants revenge against you. And everyone associated with you."

"Why didn't you call *me*?"

"Because I don't like you." He looked away. "But Maria never did anything to me."

"Isn't that taking a big risk? If someone finds out you tipped off their intended victim—"

"I'm in prison on a life sentence. How much worse can it get?"

"You could be dead."

"Would that be worse? The cartel wants to rub you off the face of the earth. But first they target your loved ones. Because they know that will cause you the greatest pain. They have hunters, snipers, assassins...bizarre, crazy Day-of-the-Dead guys who can find anyone. And seriously mess them up."

Several years back, Dan helped a young orphan girl who was about to be deported to her nearest relatives—a family connected with an El

Salvadorean cartel specializing in sex trafficking. It was obvious what would happen to Esperanza if she was delivered to them. Dan managed to keep her stateside and get her adopted by a dear friend, but only after causing serious problems for both Crenshaw and the cartel.

"If this cartel is active stateside, they must have some people over here. Someone I could question. Someone who knows who took Maria. Where can I find them?"

"Roswell."

Ben blinked. "As in Roswell, New Mexico?"

"Where else would you expect to find aliens?" All at once, Crenshaw burst out laughing, loud and hearty. Perhaps he was overcompensating, since no one else was amused.

If anything, Ben looked annoyed. "Where in Roswell?"

"He runs a museum."

"Is that a cover?"

"It's a job that doesn't take up much time. Being point man for a cartel is more time-consuming."

"Can you give us his name?"

"Eduardo Ramos. Tell him I said hi."

"Is he the one who attacked Maria?"

"Couldn't say. I've given you all I got."

Dan pushed against the table. "Sounds like this conversation is over."

Ben placed a hand on his wrist. "There's something more I'd like to ask you, Mr. Crenshaw."

"Don't beat around the bush, Pops. What is it?"

"Why are you being so helpful?"

"How can I refuse someone who brings me an expensive kaleidoscope?"

"I'm pretty sure you could. If you wanted to. But you don't. You're helping the man who got you locked away for a long time. And you don't seem all that surprised he came to visit you. Why?"

Crenshaw looked back at Ben, then his eyes drifted to the table. "I knew you'd see the phone record and come see me. And I am...let's say…aware that I've made some mistakes. I mean, I've always tried to do the right thing in a screwed-up world. But I may have…strayed from the path. Too focused on the ends, which sadly, do not always justify the means. I've been working on myself. Trying to become a better person. Trying to see if there isn't some way I can…redeem myself."

Dan stared at him. Could this possibly be genuine?

"I have a little girl. Caroline. Well, not so little now. She's twenty-seven. I never married her mother but that doesn't matter. She's mine, I love her, and I think it's time I started being a decent daddy. Better late than never, right?"

Dan thought it best he didn't comment.

"I've reached out to her and, to my surprise, she responded. Calls every week. Came to visit a few times, even though she lives in Texas. Not bad, huh?"

"You're very lucky," Ben said. "I have two daughters, and they totally transformed my life. Hold onto yours with both fists."

"I intend to. But that means I have to improve myself. Become a daddy she can be proud of. At least a little bit."

Good luck with that, Dan thought. Were they supposed to believe this soft-soap routine? Was he rehearsing for his next parole-board appearance?

"But Caroline has medical problems. Needs an operation she can't afford. You know what medical care is like in this country. Only the one percent can afford to be healthy. And she doesn't have insurance."

"You expect a quid pro quo."

"I expect nothing. I've already told you what I know. I hold no cards. But if you two rich bastards wanted to help out…"

"We'll cover her medical bills," Ben said without hesitation. "Every penny."

Crenshaw's head fell back. His body trembled. It was as if an enormous weight had been removed from his shoulders. "Thank you," he said breathlessly.

"Thank *you*." Ben started to rise. "Give me your daughter's contact info. I'll ask my wife to make the financial arrangements."

"I can't tell you…how much…this…"

"Whatever the mistakes of the past, you'll be her hero now."

Crenshaw clenched his eyes shut. The words appeared to be balm for an aching soul.

"Unless you screw it up," Ben added. "Or lie to us. Or hold something back. So don't."

"I won't. I promise."

"If you hear anything else that might help us, let us know immediately."

"I will. Should I call you or your compadre?"

"Call Dan," Ben said, rising to his feet. "I seem to have misplaced my phone."

"I will. Hey—be careful."

Dan slowly pivoted. "Is that a warning?"

"Of course not. I'm locked up. I can't hurt you. But these cartel people can and will. Maria is just the tip of the iceberg. I hear people have been murdered. More than one."

"And on that cheery note…"

Crenshaw suddenly leaned across the table and grabbed Dan's hand. "I'm serious. These rustlers are absolutely relentless. They will stop at nothing to get what they want. And the top item on their agenda is getting even with you."

# CHAPTER TWELVE

THE REAPER WAS GLAD TO DITCH THE BLACK CLOAK. NOT NEEDED AT this meeting. Spending time with right-thinking people was appealing, thought the constant frustration of inadequate funds was not. Soon there would be enough money to grease every wheel in the hierarchy. To paraphrase Benjamin Franklin, only two things are certain in life. Patriots would never stop fighting to reclaim this once-great nation. And they would always be fundraising. Because the fight for supremacy was expensive.

And the Reaper was no millionaire. Back in the '70s, Ben Klaasen famously funded the "Church of the Creator" using the millions he'd made in real estate, and that worked well—until he committed suicide. In the 2000s, Bill White self-funded "White Homes and Land" and acquired more than a million dollars' worth of rental property—until he took bankruptcy. Most of his friends' operations were funded by large outfits like the League of the South and the National Socialist Movement (which despite sounding liberal, was actually a band of patriots typically dismissed by the media as "Neo-Nazis"). They raked in millions selling memberships and merch, $50 swastika flags that cost thirty cents to make, that sort of thing. Their website did more traffic than Etsy. Some groups were even crowdfunding online and distributing funds in bitcoin so they would be near-impossible to trace. He had to pay $20 to get into this event, billed as a "super-concert" sponsored by the Charles Martel Society. The music sucked, but that wasn't the draw. That was the cover.

The Reaper guessed there were maybe a hundred people in this church basement. Someone was speaking up front, but it was all too familiar, even when the crowd hooted or hollered. It was much like a political rally, except smaller and with fewer codewords. They didn't call Hispanics "bad hombres." They didn't talk about "states' rights" or "law and order." They didn't pretend that building the wall was a security issue.

"Have you noticed how many times the loony liberals and fake-news media talk about diversity? Why do they assume that it's good to completely transform the nation that was once the greatest on the planet—because of white men? Why would bringing in people and colors and religions and deviants from less successful parts of the world make this nation better?" The crowd responded with cheers. They waved banners and pennants. "A unified nation will always be stronger than a divided one. And that is why all true Americans need to stand up and fight! Before it's too late."

Same old same old, although these meetings were good for the soul and motivation. But the Reaper had work to do and probably should never have made this stop.

The search of Kincaid's office had produced precious little. Most of the critical files apparently resided with the attorney now handling the case in LA, a Gary Quince.

And Pike's arrival in Tulsa was no great surprise. But kidnaping his boss? That was a bold move. If foolish. This was a skeet shoot, picking off helpless clueless birdies who had no idea what was really going on.

A paid associate followed them as they left the penitentiary. They were heading west, presumably to Los Angeles, but if so, they were not taking the quickest route. An interception might be necessary, before they got too far out of reach. Some bad weather was headed to that part of the world.

"You will not replace us!" the crowd shouted, raising the rafters in this relatively small basement. People slapped one another on the back, sharing their enthusiasm for the cause. But how many would actually do anything? How many were willing to perform the work necessary to make a positive difference? Most of these people were followers. Not leaders.

"You will not replace us!"

Time to leave. There was work to do. And the Reaper's work would enable these people to do so much more than they had done in the past.

Only took a minute to find the car and head down the road, buoyed by knowing the battle was for a just cause. The stakes were high, and a couple of liberal lawyers were not going to ruin what had been so carefully planned.

After all, they were only fighting for money. The Reaper was fighting for God and country.

# CHAPTER THIRTEEN

Dan noticed Ben remained silent as they drove down the highway. Fine by him. Visiting the prison was a sobering experience, and hanging around Crenshaw, asking that despicable man for favors, was probably deeply disturbing to the Oklahoma idealist.

"This should take us back to I-40," he said, as if Ben couldn't see the GPS screen for himself. "We'll take it most of the way through Amarillo, then dive southwest to hit Roswell."

Ben made a grunting noise. "You really think you're going to find a cartel kingpin in that dusty UFO tourist trap?"

"I don't know. But it would be a mistake to ignore a lead."

"You think Crenshaw is a reliable source?"

"It's worth checking out."

"I saw the look in his eyes. He hates you. Big time. He wouldn't tell you anything without a reason."

"Which he admitted. He wants to help his daughter."

"I don't trust him." Ben gazed out the window. "But there's no daddy on earth who wouldn't do anything to help his daughter."

"I talked to the guards. He hasn't been outside those prison walls for months. Verified."

"If nothing else, prison does give people a chance to reevaluate their lives," Ben said. "And when they realize they've screwed up, some people genuinely try to improve themselves."

"Probably thinks I might be grateful enough to put in a good word with the parole board." He glanced across the car. "You okay?"

"It's the prison. Hideous place. And it hasn't improved any over the years. I keep thinking someday we'll find a better way. We've been locking up criminals for centuries and it hasn't reduced crime in the slightest. Mostly it destroys lives and guarantees some people will never find a better path."

"We have to do something with dangerous people."

"True. But most of the people in prisons today aren't violent. More than half are drug and alcohol addicts. Some places it's close to eighty percent. They should be in rehab, not prison. And those who must be detained should be getting therapy, medication. Today we have the ability to deal with violent tendencies, mental illness. But that's not what's happening in prison, and worst of all, whenever someone suggests spending money to actually help inmates, they get backlash from those who just want to punish."

"This sounds pretty radical for an Oklahoma boy."

"I've also noticed that violent murderers do not typically come from wealthy or well-educated families. There's a reason for that." Ben held out his arms. "You forgot to cuff me."

"Are you planning to escape?"

"No."

"You'll come willingly?"

"I'll ride it out. For now. You might need some help."

Dan grinned. "You going to bail me out if it comes to fisticuffs?"

"I have taken some self-defense courses. Not by choice. My wife and friends keep insisting. I go to the gym twice a week."

"For what, yoga classes? I can't imagine—"

The back car window shattered with an ear-splitting explosion. The Mercedes swerved wildly. Ben ducked, covering his head with his hands. Dan fought to maintain control of the car. He veered right and came within a hair's breadth of hitting the guardrail.

"Are you okay, Ben?" he screamed.

"I'll live. What the hell happened?"

"Don't know. Can't see out the back."

Ben unbuckled his seat belt and crawled into the backseat. A second later, the unmistakable sound of a bullet whizzed past their heads.

Dan was impressed by how well Kincaid maneuvered in the car. He was pretty spry. "Stay down. That was gunfire."

"No kidding." Ben knocked some of the clinging safety glass away so Dan had a better view out the back.

"Don't panic," Dan shouted. "I know being shot at is probably terrifying."

Ben didn't blink. "Been there, done that."

"Look! There he is. In the van. Black, of course. Tinted windows. About five hundred feet behind us." Other than the two vehicles involved, they appeared to have this stretch of highway to themselves. Which was probably why the assailant picked this time to attack. Stay out of the line of fire."

"More invaluable advice," Ben muttered. "You have a weapon in here?"

"Of course not. You?"

"Sadly, I didn't know I was going to be abducted and—"

He saw the change in Ben's facial expression first. He glanced at the rear view just in time to see the van rocketing forward.

"Brace yourself!"

The van rammed them on the left side. Dan tried to maintain control while being flung forward so hard his chin banged against the steering wheel.

Ben curled up in the passenger seat, his back braced against the rear, his feet against the glove compartment.

"Are you okay?" Dan shouted.

"Just stay on the road."

"I'm trying but—"

The van slammed into them again, even harder than before. Their car swerved into the opposite lane. Dan spun the wheel around, trying to stay on the road.

"Can't take much more of this," he muttered, teeth clenched. He pushed down on the accelerator. "We're not going to—"

Three more shots rang out. One hit the frame of the car and ricocheted...somewhere. It didn't hit them, fortunately. One whizzed between them. Another hit the back of the car.

They weren't just trying to scare them. They were playing for keeps.

"Serpentine," Ben muttered.

"Huh?"

Ben drew a curved line with his finger. "Haven't you seen *The In-Laws*? Stop driving in a straight line. You're making this too easy for them."

Dan took his advice. He swerved into the other lane, then swerved back again. If he remained erratic and unpredictable, they might stay alive a little longer.

But what was the endgame? They couldn't drive forever. Eventually, the shooter would land one of those bullets. They needed to do something. But what?

Another trio of shots rang out. And with the third one, Dan cried out.

The car veered aimlessly to the left.

Dan looked down. His right arm was bleeding and he could barely move it.

The car was out of control. And he couldn't do a thing to stop it.

# CHAPTER FOURTEEN

W<small>ATER WELLED UP IN</small> D<small>AN'S EYES</small>. H<small>IS ARM HURT AND HE COULDN'T</small> steer the car, which was why they were currently careening across the lanes.

Ben grabbed the steering wheel, trying to correct their course. "Are you okay?"

"I'm hit."

"I can see that. Are you going to pass out?"

"I...don't think so. Hurts like hell though."

"Good."

"*Good?*"

"Pain will keep you alert."

Ben ripped open Dan's shirt sleeve. "Looks like the bullet went clean through, thank God. A little more than a graze but certainly not fatal."

"I...can't move that arm."

"That's a problem." Ben inched closer. "I'll be your right arm."

"You mean that figuratively?"

"Not today." Ben eased the car back onto the proper lane. "If we stop or slow down, we're toast."

"He's gaining on us," Dan muttered through clenched teeth.

"Anything you can do about?"

Dan nodded. "You're about to be grateful that I rented a luxury car." He floored it.

The car surged ahead with a burst of speed that took even Dan by surprise. He watched the speedometer. A few seconds later, they were flying faster than 100 mph.

"Is this safe?" Ben asked, wild-eyed.

"No. But it's better than being plugged by a maniac in a murder van. That low-rent bucket of bolts can't possibly move this fast."

"He's trying."

In the rear view, Dan could see the van closing the gap. "I've reached my upper limit. I can't drive any faster."

"Serpentine."

"At this speed?"

"You're not just dodging bullets. You're baiting him into driving too fast and swerving too much."

The light dawned. "Here we go." Dan started swerving, without decreasing his insanely excessive speed.

Behind him, their pursuer tried to match his moves. He could hear tires squealing.

"Just a little more, I think," Ben said. "But not too much."

"How much is too much?"

"If you smash into a tree, it's too much."

"Piece of cake." He increased his speed so he could surge ahead, then started swerving, even wider than before. The van tried to follow, but it probably didn't have the same degree of control. He pushed harder on the accelerator.

"You've got him sweating bullets. As well as firing them," Ben said.

"Wait till he sees what's coming next."

Dan kept his eyes on the rear view, and when he saw the van positioned directly behind him, he hit the brakes. The sudden deceleration sent the van into a frenzy. It slammed on its brakes, then swerved to avoid a collision. The van went one way, then the other, then jackknifed, doing a complete 180 and skidding off the side of the road. It plummeted across a ravine and straight into a cottonwood tree.

The van hit with such impact Dan thought he could feel it. Smoke rose from the hood.

"He won't be bothering us again," Dan said. "At least not for a while. Thanks to my expert driving."

"Expert? I was a second away from taking your place behind the wheel."

"Sure. Let's go back and see who it was."

"Are you joking? That driver is armed, remember? And possibly not alone."

"He's stunned. Or unconscious."

"You don't know that. If you go back, he might be waiting for you."

"But I want to know—"

Ben didn't release his grip on the wheel. "We got away, Dan. Don't screw it up. Besides, we need to deal with your wound."

"No doctors or ERs. I don't want anyone to know where we are."

"Just find a drugstore so I can sterilize and bandage the wound. Still hurt?"

"Like hell."

"Ibuprofen is the best we can do without a prescription."

"Fine. And then back on the road, right? Finding out who put a target on our backs?"

Ben nodded. "Or at the very least, spotting a UFO."

# CHAPTER FIFTEEN

HOURS LATER, DAN PEERED THROUGH THE WINDSHIELD, TRYING AS BEST he could to navigate in the darkness. And snowfall.

It was just past two in the morning. Ben was sound asleep, as evidenced by a heavy, brain-rattling snore that could not possibly be faked. Dan wasn't annoyed, except that the snoring reminded him that Ben was sleeping and he wasn't. The days when pulling an all-nighter seemed fun were far behind him.

He'd stopped in Amarillo to rent another car. Not that he turned in the previous one. He didn't have time to explain bullet holes and a shattered back window. He left it on the side of the road near the rental car station. Maybe Garrett could deal with that mess. He rented another car—a Ford Explorer this time, just to prevent Ben from criticizing—and continued the journey. All seemed well and he expected to hit Roswell by morning, maybe about the time that museum opened.

Except, snow.

Weren't they in a desert? How much snow could New Mexico get? And yet there it was, coming down faster by the second. He didn't know how much longer he could keep moving forward. He wasn't a big fan of driving at night, much less in hazardous weather. In a Ford.

Although in truth, he might be better off. Some foreign cars were less than ideal on slick roads. They were made to fly, not crawl. At least this Explorer had four-wheel drive. He wished he'd thought to get snow tires. But the sun was shining when he rented it and they were in the desert. Who knew?

Probably anyone listening to a weather report. But he'd been busy...

He gripped the steering wheel tighter, taking deep breaths to keep himself awake. The wipers were doing their best, but they couldn't cope with the increasing precipitation. He'd already slowed to half his normal speed. If the snowfall didn't let up, they would not make Roswell by dawn.

Ben stirred a bit. "Kinda cold in here," he mumbled.

"I've got the heater on, but it can only do so much."

Ben popped one eye open. "Is that snow?"

"Indeed."

"In New Mexico? In March?"

"So it seems."

"I hate climate change." Ben straightened. "How are the roads?"

"Getting worse by the second."

"Maybe we should pull over somewhere. Wait for the snow to stop. Or the sun to rise."

"I can do this."

Ben wiped sleep from his eyes. He laid a hand on Dan's shoulder. "Look, I know you're anxious about Maria. But getting to Roswell a little later is better than not getting there at all."

"I can do this." Almost the instant he said it, the back tires lost traction and began to slide. "Whoa!"

Dan corrected the steering and managed to get the car moving straight ahead again. But his grip on the road seemed even more tenuous than before.

"Tell me if I'm wrong," Ben said, "but I think I see black ice."

"You're not wrong. I'm trying to avoid the super-slick patches."

"Which is impossible. Sometimes you can't see them till you're on top of them. I really think we should pause a moment."

"Not an option."

Ben glanced out the passenger-side window. "How long has it been snowing? Looks like there's six inches on the ground."

"Probably more."

"Your arm must be killing you." While in Amarillo, they'd bought supplies and Ben bandaged his arm. "I really think—"

"We're not stopping!" Dan's eyebrows knitted together. There was an unaccustomed harshness to his voice. "We'll be fine. I'll take it easy and—"

As if on cue, the rear wheels swerved sideways.

Dan took his foot off the accelerator and tried to correct course, but he'd lost control. The back of the Explorer slammed into the center median with a resounding crash. He kept adjusting the wheel, making the car turn one direction, then the other.

"Stay out of the ditch," Ben said, a sharp edge in his voice. "Better to batter the median than—"

Too late. The car spun out of control. They crossed lanes, swerved around, and a few seconds later went spiraling into the incline off the side of the road.

Dan felt as if his teeth had slammed into his nose. The car tumbled sideways down the ledge like they were plummeting off a high cliff, even though he knew that they were tumbling six feet at best toward a barbed-wire fence. The car brought down the fence, but the fence stopped the car from sliding farther into the forest.

"Damn!" Dan pounded his left fist against the dash. "Damn, damn, damn!"

Ben leaned forward, arms locked. "Are you okay?"

"I'm fine. You?"

"I'll live. You're not going to get this car back on the road, though. Not even after the snowfall stops. We'll need a tow truck."

"We don't have time for that. And no one will come for us while the snow is falling."

"Probably right. Does your cell phone work? I lost mine recently."

"Can't get a signal. We're out in the boonies."

Ben looked livid but said nothing.

Dan admired him, if nothing else, for containing the "I-told-you-so" that must be on the tip of his tongue. "We'll walk."

"You can't be serious."

"We'll stay on the road."

"Where cars are careening out of control?"

"We'll walk to the next town. We just passed a sign. We're only three miles from…something."

"From what?"

"I don't exactly remember. It didn't seem important at the time."

Ben appeared incredulous. "You just want to start walking? And hope for the best? It's cold and snowy and only a complete idiot would go out there."

"You'll be fine. Don't you have a coat?"

"How would I have a coat? I didn't get to pack a bag, remember?"

"You can have mine."

"You'll freeze to death!"

"At least out there we can move. Get some blood going."

"This is the stupidest thing that has ever happened to me in my entire life." Ben paused. "And there's a lot of competition."

"Consider it an adventure."

"I consider it a blunder by a complete bumbler who—"

Ben stopped. All the air seemed to seep out of his chest.

Dan understood why. He'd remembered. About Maria.

"Fine. We'll walk. But I'm not happy about it."

"It would be a strange surprise if you were."

# CHAPTER SIXTEEN

DAN TRIED TO STOMP OUT A TRAIL IN THE SNOW FOR BEN TO FOLLOW, but it was hard work and they made slow progress. The snow on the ground was well past their ankles, so they walked on the road, which was easier but inherently dangerous. He'd given Ben his coat and a stocking cap, but neither were sufficient for this kind of weather.

And the snowfall was not abating.

"I think we could persuade someone to give us a lift," Dan said. "If we saw someone pass by."

"But we haven't. Because everyone else on earth had the sense to pull over or go home when the blizzard started."

"If we can just find a town, we'll get another car." Which would be his third rental car in twenty-four hours...

"You think there will be an agency in whatever Podunk town we hit next?"

"If not, we'll call someone. Get an Uber."

"Assuming we make it to the next Podunk town," Ben continued. "Assuming we don't die of hypothermia on our way over."

"We're not going to freeze to death."

"My hands and toes are icicles."

"You'll survive. I won't let you freeze to death."

"Are you planning to keep me warm with your body heat? Please don't."

Dan smirked. "Whatever it takes."

"This was supposed to be a simple road trip. I didn't expect it to go all Donner Party."

"This is not remotely—"

"I have to warn you, if I'm hungry, I won't hesitate."

Dan brushed the snow from his face. "Just keep walking. Three miles shouldn't take that long. Even in this weather."

———

AN HOUR LATER, DAN STARTED TO WORRY, NOT ABOUT HIS DESTINATION, but his companion. Ben was a trouper, not even complaining. Of course, that could be because his jaw was frozen shut. Or because frostbite was setting in. Or something worse. He'd taken an elderly lawyer and put him in extreme survival mode.

He didn't make a fuss about it, but he made sure Ben was in his line of sight at all times. If he slipped and fell, Dan wanted to be in a position to catch him.

He could see how cold Ben was. His entire body shook. His movements slowed. He suspected Ben was losing feeling in his feet. Which meant it was all the more likely he might fall. And be unable to catch himself.

He'd dragged Ben into this mess. He had to make sure he didn't die before the journey was complete. It would be pretty pathetic if they avoided the Grim Reaper only to be killed by Mother Nature.

"I think I see something up ahead." He shouted so Ben could hear him over the wailing wind.

"Frosty the Snowman?"

"No. A building." Dan squinted. "See it? Just off the side of the road."

Ben tried to follow his gaze. "Gas station?"

"Maybe. Lights aren't on, though."

"If it has a roof, it would be an improvement."

"True. And it might have a landline. We could get a call out."

"Let's go for it."

They trudged in the general direction. By now, the snow looked ten inches deep, possibly more. They followed the exit ramp, slipping and sliding with every step, and eventually made it to the building.

It was a gas station with an ample shopping area. Dan wondered if it had closed because of the weather…or had gone out of business permanently. The look of the place suggested the latter, although viewed in a snowstorm in the dead of night, appearances might be deceiving.

He tried the door. Locked. No surprise there.

"Can we get in?" Ben asked.

"We could try the windows, I suppose. One might be unlocked."

"Unlikely," Ben's voice trembled as he spoke. "There might be a back door."

"I could break a window."

"And then it would as cold inside as it is outside."

"I see your point. Stand back."

"Stand back? What does that mean? What are you—?"

Dan lifted a snow-encrusted boot and kicked the front glass doors as hard as he could. He kicked right between the two double doors, hoping to break the lock without smashing the glass.

"Didn't work," he muttered.

"You made progress." Ben pointed. "See where the door frame is dented. Try again."

"If the door breaks—"

"We can plug a small gap. But we have to be inside first."

Dan reared back and gave it another hard kick.

The lock snapped. The door swung open.

Dan beamed with pride. "Guess I'm stronger than I thought."

---

AFTER INSPECTING THE PREMISES, DAN DETERMINED THAT THE WARMEST spot in the empty unheated station was between the third and fourth aisles, far from the door which now did not completely close. He considered huddling in the bathrooms, which had no windows at all, but decided he wasn't that cold. Yet.

He heard a humming sound from time to time, but got no indication that the heat was running. He couldn't turn on the power, which meant he couldn't heat his hands over the hot dog warmer. He decided this joint was not only closed but had been closed for a long time. Maybe closed in a hurry, since a good deal of merchandise had been left behind.

The snow kept tumbling down, even harder than before.

They weren't going anywhere any time soon.

Best thing he could do, he decided, was to stay warm and get as comfortable as possible. Surely by the time the sun rose, the sky would clear, and even if it didn't, they'd spot snowplows driving by—especially if they spotted the vacated Ford Explorer on the side of the road a few miles back. He needed to be patient until help could arrive.

Could be a long night. Long and cold.

Ben scrounged together some seat cushions and a neck pillow he found on the shelves, then made a small pallet on the floor. He even scored a blanket, still in its plastic wrapper, advertising some sports team.

"Hey! Look what else I found!" Ben said grinning.

In his hands, he held a long thin candle, glowing at the top. "Found some matches, too."

"Just one?"

"No. A box of eight."

"I don't think it's going to make you appreciably warmer."

"But it's invaluable psychologically. It's the difference between being trapped in a cave and being trapped in something...more like home."

"This filthy abandoned gas station is never going to be homey."

"That may depend upon how long we're here." He gave Dan a sharp look. "This is another fine mess you've gotten us into."

"Says my grumpy companion."

"Grumpy abductee," Ben corrected. "How's your arm? We should redress the wound."

Ben sterilized his wounded arm. Dan did not scream, though it hurt like hell. Once sanitized, Ben wrapped the wound in fresh gauze.

"You're not a bad medic. Done this before?"

"Once or twice."

"I'm getting a warm and fuzzy feeling, now that I know about your caregiving qualities. Have you changed your mind on the value of sharing body heat?"

"No."

"Better than freezing to death."

"I'm not sure."

"You're a bit uptight, aren't you?"

"So my wife says. And...everyone else."

Dan nodded. "Hey...I'm sorry about...you know. Tossing away your phone. I shouldn't have done that."

"No joke."

"I just...I don't know." A crease crossed his forehead. "Wasn't thinking clearly. I'm...worried. Very worried."

"I know."

"But that's no excuse. It was a stupid power move. I bet you'd like to call your wife now. Tell her we're stranded. She could start looking."

"She already is."

"How do you know?"

"I know. And she won't let the snow stop her."

"You know she's got your six. Sounds like a great marraige."

"Best ever. Only reason I'm still around."

Dan scanned the shelves loaded with food, candy bars and chips and such. He had no idea how long they'd been on these racks waiting to be consumed. He'd pass. At least for now.

"Come morning, we can take turns walking to the highway."

Ben nodded. "Bound to see a patrol car eventually."

Dan cleared his throat. "You...might have to be the one who deals with the police. I kinda..." He shrugged. "I was told not to leave St. Petersburg."

"In Florida?" Ben slapped his forehead. "Of course. You're the boyfriend. They would naturally suspect you. And if they know you blew town, there's a warrant out for your arrest."

"A distinct possibility. So I'll let you deal with law enforcement."

"When were you planning to tell me you're a hunted fugitive from justice? In addition to being a kidnapper."

"Look, we're off the grid, and we could go a good long time before we see another human soul in this—"

Dan stopped short.

He was interrupted by a loud knock on the front door.

# CHAPTER SEVENTEEN

DAN AND BEN LOOKED AT ONE ANOTHER. NO ONE MOVED.

Eventually, Dan spoke. "Should we…go to the door?"

"I don't know."

"Seems unfriendly to just sit here."

"We don't know who it is. It might be the guy in the van who tried to kill us. Or the guy in the Reaper getup who tried to kill you. Who may be the same guy."

"Or girl."

"Huh?"

"Don't be so sexist. It might've been a woman firing at us."

"I don't think anyone from the van could be here this quickly. Even if *they* did survive the crash."

He heard the knock again. Louder than before.

"It's very cold outside," Ben muttered. "Our visitor might've seen the light and come seeking shelter."

"But what if it's the Reaper?"

Ben pushed himself to his feet. "Killers don't usually knock."

"*They* could be trying to throw us off."

"By being polite?"

"You never know."

"When you dealt with the cartel before, did they knock politely before entering?"

"Well…"

"Thought not." Ben started toward the door.

Dan grabbed his arm. "No. I'll go. I got us into this mess."

"Can't argue with that."

Dan couldn't see much through the snow-caked front doors. Except for the person-sized silhouette.

If he could see the visitor, the visitor could see him. No use pretending no one was at home.

He slowly opened the door. "Hello?" With the snow and the wind whistling in the background, he was barely audible. He raised his voice. "Hello?"

Mid-fifties, scruffy untended beard, stringy and tall. Ball cap, heavy fur-lined coat. "You okay in there?"

"We're fine. Can we help you?"

"Saw your footprints." He tipped his hat. "Name's Cheyenne Pete."

Seriously? "Nice to make your acquaintance. I'm Dan."

"How long you been walking, Dan?"

"'Bout three miles, I think." Should he invite the man in? Seemed rude to leave him standing outside. Plus, the longer he kept the door open, the colder it would get. "Would you like to come in?"

"Thanks, I will." The man hustled inside, rubbing his hands together. "Cold as a witch's wart out there."

He had a dark, rugged complexion. Native American, maybe? Despite Ben's candle, it was practically pitch black in here, so it was hard to draw many conclusions. Should he have frisked the man? Not that he had ever frisked anyone in his entire life. But it might be a smart precaution.

Too late. Pete brushed snow off his coat. He spotted Ben down the aisle and waved.

Ben waved back. "If you want to hold the candle, I'll let you."

"Does that give off much heat?"

"Nearly none. It's all in the mind."

"The chill ain't in my mind. It's all over."

"Do you live nearby?"

A short pause. "Close enough."

"Can you explain why you're here? You can understand where we might be apprehensive. Since you're visiting our...temporary shelter."

"Ain't yours." Pete pursed his lips. "It's mine."

Dan guided him down the aisle. They both sat on the tile floor. "Are you saying...you live here?"

"Yup. For near half a year now. Since they closed up the place."

"You're homeless?"

"Didn't I just tell you I live here?"

"But I mean—"

"Are you askin' if this is my winter vacation home? Sure, and I got a summer place in Cabo."

"I just meant—"

"Used to live on the rez, but it got too depressing," Pete explained. "People talk about how poor folks are out in India or Nepal. Let me tell you—ain't no one in the world worse off than the American citizens—*First* American citizens—living on our so-called reservations. Squalor and filth like you wouldn't believe. People giving up children they can't afford to feed. Drinking themselves to death because they can't afford a decent meal. I left and got a job at one of those Amazon warehouses."

"Sounds like an upward move."

"Naw. Lost my job during the lockdown. Tried to get on driving an Amazon truck, but they didn't think I was steady enough."

Dan peered at his face. Black circles, red veins. Skin seemed weathered, and not just by the snow.

"I try to find work, but it's hard out there. Prices get higher, wages get lower, and no one needs any more grunts."

"So you've been living here?"

"Not like anyone else was usin' the place."

Good point.

"It's got a sink where I can wash up. Snack food. Water. Bathrooms. And it stayed fairly warm at night. Course that was before you boys busted the front doors."

"We'll be happy to pay for repairs."

"I'm just the squatter."

"You can't stay here forever."

"Don't I know it. Word is there gonna tear the joint down and put in a big chain station. With a Starbucks."

"The surest indicator of the spread of civilization. What will you do?"

"Guess I'll have to move, won't I? And that's hard. Especially for someone in my line of work."

"Which is?"

"Flexible. I been placing ads. Posting online. Craigslist. Dark web. I use the computers at the library in town. Gettin' fairly salty at it, if I do say so myself."

"Posts for what?" Dan asked.

"To find people who might want to hire me."

"But what exactly is it you do?"

Cheyenne Pete smiled, then slowly pulled his hand out of his coat pocket. It held a pistol. "I kill people. For money."

# CHAPTER EIGHTEEN

DAN STARED AT THE MAN POINTING THE GUN AT HIS FACE, WONDERING why he hadn't seen this coming. Of course it was too coincidental that Cheyenne Pete showed up exactly where they were in the middle of a snowstorm. He should've realized Pete was packing. Add that to the thousand other incompetent mistakes he'd made so far, which had not only put them in this situation but left Maria MIA.

Maybe their road trip had reached the end of the road.

"First you were homeless. Now you're a hit man. Which is it?"

The scruffy man grinned a little. "Both could be true."

"He is large," Ben muttered. "He contains multitudes."

Dan kept his eyes locked on Pete. "You always carry a pistol?"

"More useful than a shopping cart."

"I'd like to know who killed me before I die. And why. If that's not asking too much."

"Already told you who I am. You don't need my backstory."

"You mean your name really is Cheyenne Pete? That's what it says on your birth certificate?" Out the corner of his eye, Dan noticed Ben quietly inching away. Pete didn't appear to be paying nearly so much attention to him. Maybe Pete thought Ben was not much of a threat. In any case, he needed to keep the man distracted.

"You don't need my real name," Pete snapped.

"You don't look like a paid assassin," Dan said, trying to keep him engaged. "How do I know you didn't just find that gun somewhere?"

"Your curiosity will be satisfied when you're dead."

"If it's not your gun, you're probably not going to fire it. I don't—"

Pete raised the gun toward the ceiling and fired. The sound was explosive, deafening, especially with a blanket of snow surrounding them.

Dust fell from the rafters, with a helping of snow. Place must not be as secure as they thought. Miracle the roof didn't come down.

"Okay, fine, you're not afraid to fire. That's not the same as killing someone."

The man targeted the gun directly at Dan's face. "Allow me to provide more convincing proof."

"I might be able to help you."

Pete squinted his left eye. "You're about to help me in a big way."

"Look, I've already been shot once today. This is getting old. You said you're getting paid. How much?"

"What difference does it make? That's confidential."

"Whatever you're getting now, I'll double it."

"You might find that puts a strain on your bank account."

"Don't underestimate me. I like being alive. So I'm offering you double. Do you take PayPal?"

"Maybe I should ask for more than double."

Now he had him. "Maybe you should. I have a lot of savings socked away." He didn't mention Ben's much larger bank account. He wanted Pete to forget all about the other man in the room.

"What's your limit?"

"I don't have one."

"Everyone has one."

"Let's cut to the chase. I'll give you a million bucks to not kill me. Is that enough? With that kind of money, you could move out of the abandoned gas station. In fact, with that kind of money, you could rescue everyone you knew back at the rez. How about a cashier's check?"

"You'll cancel it soon as it leaves your fingers."

"You can go to the bank with me."

The man appeared to consider. "Tempting. But who knows what you might try if we go out in public. I'll stick with my original offer. The dude who posted it has a 98% satisfaction rating on the Exchange."

Dan raised his hands, as if that might help stop a bullet. "I can do something for you that your dark web pals can't. I'm a lawyer."

"Now I have two reasons to kill you."

"I can help you out of whatever put you in this situation. Find you a real job."

"I've had real jobs. Didn't like it much. I much prefer the gig economy. One job pays enough to live for half a year."

"Because you're a murderer."

"I prefer to think of myself as a ninja."

"You know you'll be caught if you kill us, right?"

"Don't think so. No one knows who I am or why I'm here."

"Wrong. You forgot one thing."

Pete gripped the pistol tighter. He appeared to be losing patience. "What would that be?"

"You have no way out. You can't go barefoot. And your shoes are ruined."

Pete looked down at his shoes. The instant he did, Dan tackled him.

He knocked Pete into the spinner rack of audiobooks behind him, careful to stay to the left of the gun arm. Pete fired, but the bullet went wide. Cans and potato chip bags scattered in a whirlwind around them.

Pete tumbled to the floor with Dan on top of him. Dan grabbed his gun arm. First and foremost, he had to take the weapon out. He squeezed as tightly as he could, but Pete held onto his pistol. With his other hand, Pete battered him on the side of his head.

Dan winced. Hurt like hell, but a bullet would hurt worse, so he held onto Pete's arm. He banged it hard on the tile floor. The third time, the gun skidded out of Pete's hand.

Now he had a chance. He reared up on his knees and swung for the face. Pete blocked the blow and kicked him hard in the stomach. Dan went reeling backward. Pete followed, hitting him again and again, pummeling his face.

Dan grabbed him by the throat and squeezed. Pete's face scrunched up. His eyes looked like they might pop out of his head.

"I've...had...about enough of this," Dan muttered.

"Likewise, loser," Pete managed to growl. And a moment later, he squeezed Dan's right arm—on top of the bullet wound.

Dan screamed. His eyelids fluttered. He fell sideways, unable to get his bearings. Colors flashed before his eyes. He blinked rapidly, trying to clear his vision.

Pete had recovered his gun. And it was pointed right at him. Point blank.

"Props for putting up a decent fight," Pete said, licking the blood from his lips. "But no one gets the best of me."

"The million can still be yours," Dan replied, gasping. "I'm a man of my word."

"Sorry. Don't much trust you much now. Time to say—"

All at once, his face was transformed into a frozen mask of pain. A few seconds later, he crumpled to the floor.

Ben stood behind him.

Dan wiped the tears from his face. *"Took you long enough!"*

"You're welcome. Glad I could help."

"What were you doing while that man was trying to kill me?"

"Looking for a weapon. You know how hard it is to find a good weapon in an abandoned gas station? Everything's plastic these days."

"What did you use?"

Ben held it up. "Jumbo can of motor oil. The only brand that wasn't plastic." He looked down at the floor. "Pete won't be out long."

"I know." Dan gently massaged his sore arm. "Fortunately, I brought those handcuffs."

"And now you're going to use them on someone who actually needs to be restrained."

Dan pulled the unconscious man's arms behind him and cuffed

him to the dormant hot dog heater. "Okay, thanks. Though I could've taken him."

Ben snorted. "You were two seconds from dead."

"I would've rallied."

"Sure. And the Buffalo Bills might win the Super Bowl."

## CHAPTER NINETEEN

The Grim Reaper ripped off the mask and stared into a mirror. Nothing about this job had gone correctly. Nothing. At this rate, it might not end the way it needed to end. And that was unacceptable.

Granted, any time you bring in hired help, you're taking a risk. But there was no choice. They had eyes on the lawyers, thanks to the man who followed them from the penitentiary. They sent in a cleaner located on the Exchange, a guy called Zava who prided himself on his motoring skills. But Zava lost control of his car and sailed into a tree. He was lucky the impact didn't kill him.

A man should make his own way in the world, should take only what he earned. Politics aside, there were far too many lazy losers lying around contributing nothing for no one. Happy to take a free ride rather than put in an honest day's work. If the nation was going to survive, it had to make some serious changes.

But the plan, like all plans, required execution. Every name on the list. And maybe a few others.

After the crash, Zava managed to crawl out of the car and follow on foot, despite the snowstorm. He saw the tracks and knew where the lawyers must've gone, so he followed them to the station they'd holed up in. But it was now well past the time Zava was supposed to report. Perhaps the lawyers had gotten the best of him. And eased on down the road.

Didn't matter. They could always be found again.

Hiring others was never as sure as handling matters on your own. Long ago, Pappy said there was only one way to get a job done well. Do it yourself.

There was too much at stake here to take any chances.

Look out, lawyers. You may think you've escaped my grasp. But you haven't. You're on a dead-end road to perdition. Case closed.

# CHAPTER TWENTY

DAN WOKE TO FIND THE SNOWFALL HAD FINALLY STOPPED. THERE WAS A lot of snow still on the ground, but traffic was moving slowly. Looked like one lane had been plowed and salted. It might still be hazardous driving, but now that the sun was up, it seemed much safer than it had in the dead of night.

He and Ben bundled up and started out again. He was consumed with worry about Maria but kept it to himself. As soon as he had a signal, he'd call home and see if any progress had been made. In the meantime, they should pursue their only leads, their only chance of getting to the bottom of this. They needed to get to Roswell, then to LA.

He refused to even think about...the most likely explanation for Maria's disappearance. And her failure to reappear. That couldn't happen. Not to her. Not to him. It just...wasn't possible.

They left behind Cheyenne Pete, the broke-ass ninja, despite his protests, promising that they would call the police once they were far away.

Maybe. Ben would have to make that phone call. And come up with some explanation for why he was taking shelter in an abandoned New Mexico gas station...

About half an hour after they went outside, a truck driver gave them a lift to the nearest town which, as luck would have it, did in fact have a rental car agency—a different company than either of the outfits Dan had rented from the day before, which was good, given how both those cars ended up. The painful part was that he was forced to accept a Subaru compact, but at this point, he was glad just to be back on the road. With removable snow chains.

Ben borrowed Dan's phone and called his wife. Dan could only hear one end of the convo, but he thought Ben's wife amazingly tolerant, especially given the story he was telling. Turned out she had been looking for him, and she had lots of others looking as well. Some women might think he'd concocted this outrageous tale about being trapped in a gas station during a snowstorm to cover up something else. Christina took it all in stride.

"You keep an eye on our girls and stay safe." A short pause. "Yes, I'll keep in touch. If my captor allows it."

"He's not my captive," Dan shouted, loud enough that she could hear it. Then muttered, "Not anymore."

---

"YOU'VE BEEN QUIET FOR A WHILE," DAN SAID, HALF AN HOUR DOWN THE road. "I'm assume you're contemplating our situation. Any theories?"

"Christina is sending the cops around to pick up that chump you left at the gas station. Do you think he's the Grim Reaper?"

Dan shook his head. "No. I wrestled with both of them. Not the same people. The Reaper was thinner but stronger. He might dress like a teenage LARPer, but he beat me down. This gas-station clown wasn't nearly as tough. And he had a gun." He paused. "Any new thoughts about the case?"

"Only the obvious. It must have something to do with the *Donovan* case."

"Unless it doesn't. Initial appearances can be misleading."

"Agreed. I don't understand how your cartel fits in. But we don't have much else to work with."

"You said the *Donovan* case is a last-minute attempt to undo a life sentence. Could someone be trying to help the defendant?"

"If so, screwing around with his lawyers seems like the worst possible approach."

"Maybe it's the other way round. Maybe someone wants him to lose."

"Then they should sit quietly and wait. Over 95% of these last-ditch post-verdict motions are dismissed. Usually without a hearing."

"But your guy's already got a hearing. So he's ahead of the curve."

"I suppose." Ben paused. "I called Gary Quince. He's the attorney handling the case. He hasn't seen anything out of the ordinary. Told him to be careful."

"When did you call him?"

"While you were renting the car. They had a phone in the office."

"You could've called anyone. You could've run off."

"Could've. Didn't."

"Then you're committed to helping me."

"I'm worried about Maria. And this case." Ben twisted a bit in his seat. "You would expect the point man for a cartel to be in a larger city, even if the cartel is in shambles. What could possibly cause him to be holed up at a Roswell UFO museum?"

"All good questions. Let's ask him."

# CHAPTER TWENTY-ONE

Dan drove as fast as he could, but the highway was still slick. It seemed to subside the further they traveled west. Still, they didn't make Roswell until shortly after noon.

They were greeted by a large yellow sign with bold red letters: WELCOME TO ROSWELL. With a whirling alien spacecraft overhead.

"Will the captive be permitted lunch?" Ben asked. "I'm starving."

"There was food all over that gas station."

"Months-old stale junk food."

"Beggars can't be choosers."

"I can and I will."

Dan pulled down the visor to shield the sun. "Fine. A quick meal. I'm a bit peckish myself. See anyplace that looks good?"

Ben glanced out the window as Dan cruised down the main drag. "I see a lot of places themed with flying saucers. And little green men."

Dan chuckled. "Yeah. Disneyland for conspiracy theorists." In many respects, Roswell looked like a perfectly ordinary city, not quite large, certainly not small. Five-story office buildings and most of the usual chain restaurants, though many had adopted the UFO theme that made the town famous. The streets were ornamented with life-size statues of bigheaded gray aliens. He particularly like the ET who appeared to be riding the Road Runner—from Warner Brothers cartoons—like a horse. Even the local McDonalds looked like a flattened flying saucer. "Judging by all the wells I've seen, this city also has lots of active oil drilling. And military. Shopping malls. Local branch campus for Eastern New Mexico University."

"And it's a mecca for ufologists."

"I see more people in uniform than in antennae."

"There's an air force base not far from here. That's where the famed UFO crash occurred and why it's called the Roswell incident, even though it was actually closer to Corona."

Dan gave him some side-eye. "You seem to know a little about this."

Ben shrugged. "I'm always interested in anything out-of-the-ordinary."

Dan turned left toward a fun-looking diner with a rotating saucer on its marquee. "Don't tell me you believe in this stuff."

"I've learned to keep an open mind."

"*UFOs*? That's for people who don't understand science."

Ben inhaled deeply. "No. Like most conspiracy theories, it's for people who want to feel smarter than the average bear, even if they maybe don't have the education or gifts to make it happen. Everyone wants to believe there's more out there than the mundane lives we lead on Earth. Everyone struggles to find purpose. This is an easy and relatively harmless solution."

"It's completely lacking in credible evidence."

"Compared to what? QAnon? Voter fraud? Denying climate change? People want to feel like they have the inside track. Helps them fight insecurities about themselves, their accomplishments."

"But UFOs?"

"No one ever shot someone or mounted an insurrection because they believed in UFOs. As long as people aren't doing anything harmful, why not let them have a little fun?" His eyes seemed to go into soft focus. "When you get older, you get less judgmental. More willing to accept the foibles and frailties of others."

"You're going soft, old man."

Ben slowly released his breath. "Sometimes I wish everyone would...go soft. Stop lambasting others because they hold slightly different opinions or look slightly differently."

"*UFOs?*"

Ben turned his head. "We all have to find majesty in our own way."

---

DAN HAD TROUBLE DECIDING BETWEEN THE VENUSIAN IMPOSSIBLE Burger and the Plutonian Pizza, but ultimately decided the burger might be quicker. It seemed to be what everyone else was having. Their waitress was a young woman sporting big green sunglasses with eyeballs dangling from coiled wires. "Greetings, Earthlings." Her lack of enthusiasm suggested she had done this a few times too many. Possibly a thousand times too many.

"You boys going to the UFO museums?" she asked, after taking their order.

"There's more than one?" Dan asked.

"At least four. Some better than others."

He grinned. "Take me to your leader."

She didn't smile. "The big one is the International UFO Museum and Research Center."

"International?"

"That's what they say."

"Sounds important."

"If you're into that sort of thing. But there are things to do around here that don't involve extraterrestrials. I love Pioneer Plaza. Great local musicians. And the wildlife preserve is awesome."

"You grew up around here?"

"Graduated from Goddard High."

"Ever hear anyone talking about a cartel?"

"A what?"

"Drug runners? Sex trafficking?"

"In Roswell? You know how many times we've been received the All-American City award?"

"How many?" Ben asked.

"I don't know. But lots. Order will be right out."

---

AFTER NOURISHING THEMSELVES, THEY RETURNED TO THE SUBARU AND started looking around. Judging from what Dan googled and what they heard in the restaurant, some museums looked more reputable than others. He assumed that anyone connected with a cartel would be at the least reputable one. So he drove there first.

"Still doesn't make any sense to me," Ben muttered.

"What's that?"

"A point man for your El Salvadorean cartel. Holed up in this tourist town."

"Could be a waystation. Like Florida was. Close to the border. And you can hop up to I-40 and go almost anywhere."

"I suppose. Still doesn't seem right to me, though. Actually, nothing about this seems right. We're…missing something."

Dan didn't argue. He'd had much the same feeling himself.

They pulled up to the alleged museum and tumbled out of the car. It did not appear to have many visitors at the moment. He could see two other so-called museums on the other side of the street, so the competition for tourist dollars was cutthroat.

He did notice the cherry-red Ferrari. Mostly because he was jealous. Some skinny kid in a T-shirt and torn jeans was driving a dream car. The kid was…what? Twenty at most? Ought to be a law. Ferraris should be earned, not given.

The front door tinkled as they stepped inside the Museum of Extraterrestrial First Contact. The lobby was filled with full-scale dioramas of various alien settings, like the sexless grays probing people they'd transported to their ship, or having coffee while reading the paper upside-down. The idea, he gathered, was that you'd step into the picture and create your own alien encounter.

A clerk appeared. "Want a photo with the aliens?"

"No thanks," Ben answered.

"Might spruce up your Facebook page."

"I don't have a Facebook page."

"Your next Christmas card."

"Pass."

Most of the exhibits on the wall were mounted newspaper or magazine articles. All well and good, but articles in a UFO magazine weren't evidence of anything. Like so many things in life, Dan supposed, this museum was designed to turn you into a believer—without proving anything.

To his surprise, there was no admission charge. Apparently they made their money in the gift shop. The only other staff member he could see appeared to run the cash register.

Biff—his name was displayed on a nametag—was young, long-haired and much more interested in his phone than either of the two gentlemen in the museum. He also wore white earplugs.

Dan cleared his throat. "Excuse me. Biff?"

He did not look up. "That's not my name."

"But—your nametag—"

"Boss wants everyone wearing a nametag. Says it makes the place seem friendlier."

"No doubt. But—"

"This was the only one he had lying around."

"I see. And your actual name is?"

He looked up from his phone but seemed profoundly irritated by being forced to interact with others. "What difference does it make?"

Point taken. "Is there anyone named...Eduardo Ramos here?"

"Yeah. That's the boss."

"Could I see him?"

"About what?"

"We have a...business proposition I'd like to discuss."

"That's kinda vague."

"It's a private matter."

The kid jerked his head back, which sent that long unkempt hair flying. "He had a visitor earlier. I think he's still with them."

Interesting. "Do you know who it was?"

He gestured toward an office door. "Why don't you ask him?"

Dan didn't wait to be invited again. He and Ben crossed behind the counter and headed for the rear room.

On the way, they passed a life-size statue of Mack Brazel, the man who first found mysterious debris in a trench not too far from town. Later, someone in the Air Force speculated that it came from a UFO, which led to Roswell becoming what it is today. He later recanted, and the official story became "crashed weather balloon," even though the debris looked nothing like a weather balloon. As the plaques explained, some thought it was a Soviet spy satellite. And others preferred to think it was an alien spacecraft. More recently, it was revealed that Robert Goddard had been experimenting with rockets in Roswell since the 30s, which led to speculation that one of his experiments crashed and was discovered before the military could recover it.

Dan reached the office and pushed open the door.

The occupant of this office wasn't merely messy. The place had been torn apart. Like an earthquake confined to this room had struck.

"There was a struggle," Ben noted.

"And it looks like Eduardo lost."

He took a few tentative steps forward.

And found the body slumped behind the desk.

Dan drew in his breath. The stench was unbearable. He wanted to scream, but he held it inside.

He couldn't see any blood, but the skin tone, not to mention the contorted position, was unmistakable. This man was dead and had been for some time.

"I think he's been poisoned."

Ben shook his head. "Shot. You just can't see it."

"Where?"

Ben bent down. He was obviously being careful not to disturb the crime scene. He gingerly took the corpse by the shoulders and twisted it slightly.

"In the back of the head. One bullet."

Dan felt his heart race. "Execution-style."

"Looks that way." Ben gently lowered the body. "Did you notice the star-shaped entry wound? The killer fired point blank. What are we dealing with here, Dan?"

"I don't know. This does seem more like a cartel rubout than anything related to a law case."

"One thing is for certain. Someone is playing for keeps."

Dan's face paled.

Ben raised his hands. "I didn't mean—"

Too late. The thought had already entered both minds.

It was a miracle they were still alive. So what were the chances that Maria was still alive?

Not good.

# CHAPTER TWENTY-TWO

Dan did his best to stay out of sight while Ben convinced the police there was nothing suspicious about two strangers showing up at a Roswell museum just in time to find a corpse. He could tell they weren't buying it. Did he blame them? No. It was all too coincidental. Strangers who have no business in town find an unimportant man in an unimportant museum executed by someone who shouldn't be in this innocent little town. Since they had no idea who might be behind this, the logical move was to hang onto the suspects they had.

Dan was told to not leave town.

Again.

Detective Sergeant Boswick seemed young for his position, but there might not be all that much competition for his job in Roswell. "You say someone is trying to kill you?"

"Definitely. Repeatedly."

"And yet you're still alive. Unlike this poor sucker."

"Only by the hair of our chinny-chin-chin." Boswick wasn't buying it. How long before this guy learned about the guy they left at the gas station? Or that he'd disobeyed the St. Petersburg cops and blown town? Not long.

Boswick flipped his pad closed. "This isn't making sense. I'm calling in my county supervisor. You should get ready for another round of questioning. He's going to expect real answers. Useful answers."

---

AFTER BEING GRILLED SEPARATELY, THE POLICE BROUGHT THEM BACK TO the outside lobby. Dan finally had a moment alone with Ben. "Are you okay?"

Ben shrugged. "My lumbago is acting up."

"I meant after being interrogated by the police."

"Not my first rodeo."

"They are suspicious. You can expect to be held overnight. Maybe longer."

"These guys are pretty reasonable, all things considered. One of them let me borrow his phone." He gave Dan a pointed look. "You'll recall that I recently lost mine."

"Called your wife, I assume."

"And she talked to these officers, then called my best friend, who is also the Chief of Police in Tulsa. He'll sort this out."

Dan pulled a face. "I don't think it will be that easy."

Sergeant Boswick strolled over and spoke to the both of them. "Looks like I'm letting you boys go. At least for now."

Dan blinked. *What?*

Ben rose. "Appreciate this, Detective. I'm going to get a new phone and as soon as I do I'll text you my number."

"I would appreciate that. Just as I appreciate your cooperation."

Dan twisted back and forth between the two. What was going on here?

"We all want this killer brought to justice. Especially my friend here." He clapped Dan on the shoulder. "I can't help but think this homicide is related to the one we're investigating."

"When you figure that connection out, give me a call, ok?"

"Of course. Thank you again for your professionalism."

"No problem. Your wife explained that you have a tendency to stumble into trouble but are rarely the cause."

Boswick faded into the distance. Ben gathered his belongings.

"That's—That's it?"

Ben nodded. "That's it."

"When he was interrogating me, Boswick acted like he was going to lock us up and throw away the key."

"You came on strong. Made demands, argued about legalities. That works in the courtroom. Sometimes. Not so well with police officers."

"I think it had more to do with you having friends. How did a defense attorney ever become pals with the chief of police?"

"He married my sister."

"Ah. Nepotism."

"Not exactly. She divorced him."

"Ouch."

"It's all good. He remarried. A fellow cop. They get along much better."

"And you're still friends?"

"The best. You've got a friend on the St. Pete force, don't you?"

"Jake Kakazu? Yeah, he's the one who told me not to leave town. How do you know about him?"

"I follow your cases. You introduced him to his wife, right?"

"Sorta."

Ben started toward the door. "Here's a good life lesson, Dan. Sometimes, having a forceful attitude and a strong argument isn't the best approach. Sometimes it's good to have friends. Took me years to learn that one. But I did. Eventually." Ben glanced both ways. "Did you see this?"

He pulled a scrap of paper out of his pocket. It was wrinkled and smeared but still legible. A series of numbers ran down the left side. After the numbers—gibberish. Random letters that didn't spell anything. And the top three lines had a line slashed across them.

"Where did you find that?"

"On the floor in the office. Not far from the body."

"The police let you keep this?"

Ben's eyes drifted upward. "Well…"

"You didn't tell them about it."

"It might have slipped my mind…"

"Ben. You're withholding evidence."

"Only if it's evidence."

"That's a felony offense!"

"I don't think it has anything to do with this murder. I think it relates to the case we're investigating."

"It's still evidence."

Ben put the scrap back in his pocket. "Sometimes the needs of the one outweigh the needs of the many."

"Are you seriously quoting *Star Trek* at me?"

"When appropriate—"

"To justify a felony?"

"This is more useful to us than to them. You said the Grim Reaper mentioned a list, right? This could be it, disguised by some kind of code. And I might be able to decipher it. Given time."

"So you stole evidence."

"I wanted to copy it but I didn't have a chance. I'll send the original to Boswick later. Anonymously. Did you notice the kid in the cherry-red Ferrari?"

"Pulling out as we came in? Sure. Great ride. You think he's the killer?"

"I think he's driving a car far beyond his means. Where'd he get it?"

Dan tilted his head. He'd assumed it was a rich kid's Christmas present. But Ben had a point. "Maybe we should ask him."

"That's our next stop. Which we wouldn't be able to accomplish if we were detained at the police station. Or arrested. So it was time to call in a favor."

Dan pursed his lips. "I will admit that I prefer investigating to cooling my heels in jail."

"At last we agree on something." He steered Dan toward the door. "Let's get out of here. We need to find out what's going on. And I don't think these ETs are going to provide any answers."

# CHAPTER TWENTY-THREE

THE GRIM REAPER—OUT OF COSTUME—WAITED UNTIL THE CAR RENTAL office was empty—no tourists, no one in sight but the nebbish behind the counter who appeared to be playing Solitaire on his work computer. He was a lean man with a slight build, a brown skin tone that suggested he might be Hispanic.

The Reaper hated playing dress up. Traveling light was the assassin's credo, so this scam required a stop at a department store and the purchase of their cheapest suit. It was one-time-use, right? And its cheapness might support the cliché that cops dressed badly. Dealing in cultural stereotypes went against the grain. Right-thinking police officers had always been critical to their movement. But when you were trying to mislead someone, it was best to show them exactly what they expected to see.

The Reaper flashed a fake badge. "New Mexico Bureau of Investigation."

The nebbish tore his eyes from the screen. "Can I...help you?"

"I'm looking for two men." The Reaper raised his phone and displayed two photos, one of Pike and the other of Kincaid. "Seen them?"

The kid glanced at the photos. The recognition was instantaneous. But he didn't speak.

"They're wanted in connection with a murder. They're believed to be armed and dangerous."

"Really? They didn't seem dangerous."

"They never do. So you saw them?"

"I think…" He swallowed. "I think they rented a car from me. Well, the younger one did."

"What car?"

"I don't remember."

"Can you look it up? On that game-playing device on your desk?"

The clerk clenched his teeth. "I'm…not supposed to do that. Customer confidentiality. We can get in a lot of trouble if we release personal data."

"Did I mention that I'm with the state Bureau of Investigation?"

"You did."

"Would you prefer to be subpoenaed? Brought in for questioning? Because I can make that happen. All it takes is a phone call."

The clerk gulped again. "Let me see what I can do." He switched to another screen—without terminating his Solitaire game.

"They probably rented under the name of Pike. Maybe Kincaid. But probably Pike."

"Yes, you're right." He scanned rows of text. "Looks like they took a Subaru compact." The corner of his lips tugged upward. "I recall he griped that we didn't have anything more upscale."

"You couldn't rent him a Maserati?"

"It's a small office. We mostly deal with Korean compacts. Not much market for the fancy stuff."

"Did you say it was blue?"

The clerk blinked. "I didn't say that, but it is. How did you know?"

"Seems to be his favorite color. What's the license plate?"

"Okay, I'm really not supposed to tell you that."

"Kid, I could haul you and your computer downtown right now."

"I—I'm not trying to be difficult." His eyes were pleading. "But we could be sued if we give that out and something bad happens. My boss said that I can't release license plate numbers under any circumstances."

"Not even to law enforcement?"

His voice stammered. "No. I'm sorry. Not even to you." Pause. "If it were up to me—"

"It is up to you."

"No, I have to do what my boss says."

"We all have free will. That's what makes us human. It's time we took back our rights. Stopped letting the government and…bosses tell us what to do."

"Look, I don't want any trouble."

Should've worn the Reaper costume. There was no time for messing around with this twerp. "Neither do I."

"Let me call my supervisor."

"We are all free to make our own choices. And you have made a poor one. Despite my best efforts to help you. You should have stayed back in the homeland."

In a space of time so brief it couldn't be measured, the Reaper withdrew a gun, a long-barreled number with a noise suppressor.

The clerk raised his hands. "Hey! Wait a minute!"

"I don't have a minute." A small cry escaped the clerk's lips, quickly snuffed out. The bullet hit him in the dead center of his forehead. Blood splattered against the back wall with a grisly splatter. The clerk fell to the floor in a slow but surprisingly solid crash.

The Reaper stepped around the counter and pulled the screen forward.

Make, model, and license plate number. Time to get crack-a-lackin'.

Roswell was the first stop. Find out what they know, then make sure they didn't cause any more trouble. Then back to the list. Then collect the funds needed to take back America. A real plan, not a half-baked random assault. A blow that would strike at the heart of everything that was wrong with this nation.

Despite all the interruptions, the main job was getting done. The list was getting shorter. When your cause is just, the fates smile on you. Get the job done. Then advance to the next level. Whatever that required. In the large scheme of things, two traveling lawyers really didn't make much difference, although...

This might require another visit to the confessional.

# CHAPTER TWENTY-FOUR

She woke feeling groggy, dazed, disoriented—and staring into the face of Death.

She couldn't help but flinch, even though she'd seen this mask before and it wasn't moving. This belonged to the Grim Reaper. The Halooween refugee who attacked her. Who got the best of her. Much as she hated to admit it.

How much time had passed? Her head was clearing, but she still had no idea where she was. Or when. She wasn't wearing a watch. She didn't have her phone. Her pockets were completely empty. The room was dark. Not pitch black. She could see the hand in front of her face. But dark, just the same.

She slowly stretched her arms and legs. Her head throbbed. Come to notice, her whole body hurt. How long had she been out? How long ago had that ghoul attacked her? Unlike what you saw in movies, in reality any blow serious enough to knock someone unconscious was a major injury, probably concussive, and could have major mental and physical health ramifications. Her head ached, but not enough to make her suspect any long-term injury.

Probably.

She rose to her feet, slowly. Her clothes were wrinkled but intact.

She saw no evidence that anyone had messed with her or her Guccis. She didn't appear to be wounded or bleeding. She hadn't soiled herself. So far as she could tell, she'd simply been...moved.

What was the point of that?

Slowly she drank in the room around her. It appeared to be an apartment of some sort. Maybe a small home or townhouse. Not one she would ever choose to live in. Sparse furniture. No windows, barely a trickle of light seeping in beneath the door. Did appear to have a bathroom and a small kitchen area, but she suspected the Reaper hadn't left her any blueberry muffins.

Slowly she explored the tiny space. She was not particularly surprised to learn that the only door was locked. Metal door. Bolted. Deadlocked. She'd need a key to get out of here. She found few traces of any other lifeform, much less clues to who attacked her. The Reaper had left his mask behind. That was probably supposed to be some kind of reminder. Or warning. Or threat. A creep like that probably had twelve of them in the trunk of the car.

She found some bottled water in the fridge and drank deeply. It occurred to her that this could be some kind of weird Batman trap. Maybe the water was laced with cyanide. But then, if the guy wanted her dead, she'd already be dead. She drank some more and eventually finished the bottle.

She found a box of granola bars which, strangely enough, were exactly the kind she bought. Did the Grim Reaper know? Was it a bizarre coincidence? Or had he been watching her?

She inhaled three of them. She supposed those could be poisoned too. But she was famished.

Okay, food and water in her system. Brain kicking into gear. Assess the situation. Find a solution. Escape.

Except nothing came to mind. She pounded on the door and it didn't budge. Didn't even rattle. No other means of entrance and exit, at least not that she could see. She was not going to MacGyver herself out of this one.

She was trapped.

Maybe someone would find her. She knew someone must be looking, including one person she knew to be extremely resourceful.

An icy hand clutched her heart. The Grim Reaper, the fiend who put her here, was bound to return. Maybe she would overpower him—

Sure. Just like before.

She hunted for a weapon. There weren't many candidates. No silverware in the kitchen. No lamps or fireplace pokers. She couldn't lift the fridge or the sofa. And she wasn't likely to knock him unconscious with a box of granola bars.

What then? Just sit idly until the Reaper returned to finish the job? He must've parked her here for a reason—and she wasn't anxious to learn what that reason was.

There had to be something she could do. Some way to get the word out. To get help. To get away.

She didn't know what that would be. But she knew this. She wasn't going to roll over and die. The Reaper got the drop on her once. But if she got out of here, he was going to wish he hadn't messed with her.

He might have caught her. He might have locked her away.

But there was no way Maria Morales was going down without a fight.

## Part Two

# THE FERRARI HAS LEFT THE BUILDING

# CHAPTER TWENTY-FIVE

DAN COULD THINK OF WORSE THINGS THAN LOOKING FOR A CHERRY-RED Ferrari, which was good, because that's how he'd spent all his time since the police released him. There was no guarantee the kid was still cruising. Then again, what was the point of having a car like that if you weren't going to show it off? Constantly.

Unfortunately, they couldn't find it.

"The Ferrari has left the building," Ben murmured.

Dan stared at him for a moment. "Oh, I get it. Elvis joke. He was a big deal for your generation, right?"

A line crossed Ben's brow. "Elvis was a big deal to every generation. I mean, he was no Harry Chapin. But still."

"If that kid is a hit man, he's got the worst cover in the history of hitmen. Flashy Ferraris are not exactly low-key."

"You're proceeding from the assumption that criminals always do the smart thing, because they themselves are so smart."

"And?"

"My experience suggests otherwise. There are few Lex Luthors in the world. Smart people find some less risky way to make their fortunes."

A legitimate point. "What about that kid? Biff, or whatever? Back at the museum. He might know the driver." His eyes darted to one side. "Wait a minute."

The cherry-red Ferrari was parked just outside Christina's Diner, possibly the only eatery in the area that didn't have a UFO theme. It gave off more of a 50s-diner vibe.

"I'm guessing this is where the locals eat."

"They don't appear to be reaching out to the tourist trade," Ben noted. "In fact, they appear to be avoiding the tourist trade."

"Blue beat-up pickup parked on the side. I saw it at the museum. I'm betting that's Biff's ride." He pulled into a parking slot and turned to Ben. "See? There's an advantage to traveling with someone who's obsessed with cars."

---

DAN CONSIDERED TAKING A BOOTH, GETTING COFFEE, AND OBSERVING the kid from a distance. But the place was not crowded and Biff—no longer wearing the misleading nametag—spotted them the moment they entered. There was no opportunity for subterfuge.

The kid raised his hands as soon as they approached. "I already talked to the cops."

No doubt he did. "That's not what we're here about. Exactly."

"It isn't?"

"No." Dan slid into the booth on the other side of the table. Ben followed close behind. "If your name isn't Biff, what is it?"

"Everyone in town calls me Draco."

Dan squinted. "Like Draco Malfoy? From Harry Potter?"

The kid's neck twisted a bit. "'Draco' is Latin for 'dragon.' It's a cool nickname."

Definitely. "I'd like to know more about that eye-popping Ferrari."

"I don't know the driver. I mean, I've seen him around town the last week or so, but I don't know anything about him."

"You know the car?"

"I've seen it. Hard to miss."

Ben leaned across the table. "Draco, I'm Ben Kincaid. Mostly retired lawyer. We're not after you in any way. But someone is trying to kill us and we'd like to prevent that, if at all possible."

He had the kid's attention. "I doubt I can help."

"When you talked to the police, did you tell them about the Ferrari?"

"No."

"Why not?"

"They didn't ask."

"Did they ask if you knew who committed the murder?"

"Yeah. But I wasn't in his office. I don't know."

Ben tilted his head. "He left the museum just as we were coming in. The possibility that the Ferrari Kid was the murderer must have occurred to you."

Draco's eyes darted. "I don't know one way or the other. And I don't see why I have to answer your questions." He scooted as if he planned to leave, but never actually went anywhere.

Was Draco in on it? Looking at him, that was hard to imagine.

But was it possible? Maybe Draco was more afraid of the driver, and perhaps the driver's bosses, than he was of the police. Or these two lawyers.

He would have to game this interview if he was going to get anywhere.

He looked at the kid levelly. "You know, if you protect the cartel, pretty soon people will think you work for the cartel."

"I don't have anything to do with the cartel," the kid pleaded.

He thought about that. Draco used the definite article, "the," rather than "a," suggesting he was referring to a specific cartel. He wasn't acting as if "cartel" was a foreign concept.

"What can you tell me about the cartel?"

"Nothing. I don't know anything. Please leave me alone."

Draco pushed up on his toes, but Dan grabbed his arm and pulled him back down. "Let me be clear about this. It's not just that my friend and I have been threatened. My partner has been…abducted." I think. "And I'm going to find her. If you think I'm going to let you withhold information that might help me find her, you are sadly mistaken."

Draco gritted his teeth. "I don't know...*anything!*"

"Then you leave me no choice. I'll tell the police you withheld relevant information. They'll give you the third degree for a few days. Lock you up in county and see how you like the company."

Draco looked desperate. "I got to get home to my mom."

"Then you need to tell me about the cartel."

The kid hesitated.

Ben jumped back in. "If you tell us what you know—everything you know—we won't take it to the police. We won't mention your name. Not to anyone."

He looked like a puppy begging to be petted. "Promise?"

"I do." He pushed onward as if they'd made an agreement. "Is this the cartel that used to operate out of Florida?"

The kid shook his head. "I don't think so. I hear they come from Mexico."

That took Dan by surprise. "Sex trafficking?"

The kid crouched down till his chin practically touched the counter. "Narco slaves."

# CHAPTER TWENTY-SIX

A WAITRESS INTERRUPTED, SOMEONE DRACO OBVIOUSLY KNEW, AND they ordered. The waitress reminded them that she served breakfast 24/7, but Dan just got coffee. Draco asked for scrambled eggs. And Ben requested hot Belgian waffles with maple syrup, mile-high whipped cream, and strawberries. Plus a strawberry shake.

Dan's eyebrows knitted together. "Not exactly a healthy meal."

"It's comfort food. I've had a trying day."

Couldn't argue with that. He turned his attention back to Draco. "Tell me what you mean. Surely you're not talking about actual slavery."

"When people are confined, forced to work, and have no options, that's slavery."

"Where is this taking place?"

"The farms started in Mexico. But now they have some in the United States. Lots of them."

"And what are these slaves producing?"

"Mostly marijuana."

Ben appeared confused. "But—marijuana is legal many places now, at least for medical use. Even in Oklahoma."

"Same in Florida," Dan added. "Part of the reason states voted for legalization was that it would supposedly depower cartels and reduce illegal drug trafficking."

"It didn't. Made it worse. Gave the cartels cover. Put one slave farm in the middle of a bunch of legit farms. The cops don't know the difference."

"How widespread is this?"

Draco's voice dropped even lower. "My mother reads Spanish. She goes to Animal Politico, a website that tracks this stuff. They say the Mexican cartels have over 55,000 people working for them against their will."

"Doing what?"

"Kids are forced to work farms or sell drugs on street corners, usually to other kids, kids who can't get a medical marijuana card or want something stronger. Immigrants are forced to carry drugs across the border. Kidnapped migrants are forced to become unwilling hitmen. Women are forced to become drug-peddling sex workers. Tied up, barely fed, threatened constantly. Children carrying automatic weapons to carry out the big boss' dirty work."

"Ok, I got it. It's bad."

"It's slavery. They're coerced with guns. Threats to kill them or their families. I've lived here all my life. And slavery has always been out there. But it's gotten worse. A lot worse."

"You seem very knowledgeable," Ben observed.

"I used to be in college. Till the cartel came after me."

"You went to college?" Dan said. Not to be insulting. But Draco didn't appear to be a college man, and he certainly wasn't working a college-grad job.

"Two years."

"Studying what?"

"Engineering. That was the problem."

Ben's eyes narrowed. "The cartel wanted engineers?"

"They came after many professionals, including engineers. There's a stereotype that only poor people are targeted and manipulated by these bastards. The cartel knows how to get whatever it needs. They're trying to expand beyond the Southwest. Which requires money." Draco spoke in hushed tones. "Five engineers in my department disappeared in a single semester. That was when I decided to get out. Good thing, too. Animal Politico says at least thirty-six engineers have been abducted by cartels and forced to work against their will."

"Why would the cartel want engineers?"

"To build private cellphone networks across Mexico and perhaps in the US. They use these networks to communicate with each other without worrying about eavesdropping by the feds. Or rival gang members."

Dan looked bug-eyed. "Cartels have their own cellphone networks?"

"And most remain completely undetected."

"Why haven't you gone to the police with this?"

Draco made a scoffing sound. "The police are more afraid of the cartels than I am. They are directly in the firing line, after all."

He supposed that made sense. Sergeant Bristow hadn't struck him as a hardened veteran of the cartel wars, or someone who wanted to be. "So this Ferrari guy—is he working for the cartel?"

"He's obviously not a slave. He might be higher up in the organization. Or some bigshot's offspring."

"I wouldn't think the cartel would approve of all the attention that car attracts," Ben said. "Don't they usually try to keep a low profile?"

"Except when they want to instill terror. The sports car sends a message that everyone here understands: You're being watched. It's scare tactics. Make sure no one crosses them. Much less offers any testimony against them."

"Ok, the driver has some connection to the cartel," Ben said. "Do you know where he lives?"

"No idea. Probably not in Roswell."

"Does he have friends? Family? Maybe a girl?"

"Not that I know about."

"What does he do in his spare time?"

"I doubt he gets that much spare time. Probably has a day job on a marijuana farm." Draco snapped his fingers. "He does like to drink. Like many people around here."

"Where does he do that?"

Dan could tell Draco didn't want to say more, but he also seemed to recognize they weren't going to leave until he did, and talking to them was easier than talking to the police. "I saw him once out at Sneaky Pete's."

Sneaky Pete's? Was that run by Cheyenne Pete? "What's that?"

"This bar outside the city limits. Way outside the city limits. Kind of a honky-tonk."

"Frequented by cartel criminals." Ben shrugged. "And I'm guessing bikers. Cowboys. Rednecks."

"You can't use that term anymore," Dan said. "It's considered offensive."

"Spare me the Gen Z vocab canceling. The term refers to people who perform labor outside and thus get sunburned necks. There's nothing wrong with manual labor."

"Nonetheless, people find the term offensive."

"Some people have the same reaction to the word 'lawyer.' I've been living with that for decades."

Dan turned to Draco. "Can you give us directions?"

"I can't guarantee he'll be there tonight."

Ben cut in. "We need to keep moving. Someone is trying to kill us, remember? And we have to get to LA."

"I think we can make a short detour to Sneaky Pete's. I've got a bit of a throat on me."

"Desperate for a drink, huh?"

"Yes. And you can get your strawberry shake or Shirley Temple or whatever is your barroom drink-of-choice."

"Chocolate milk."

Dan winced. "Thank you for your help, Draco. We'll be on our way now."

Ben placed a hand on his arm. "Are you joking? I haven't eaten my waffles yet."

# CHAPTER TWENTY-SEVEN

MITCH NEVER LIKED GOING TO THE DOCTOR'S OFFICE. DID ANYONE?
You always had to wait, you rarely got what you wanted, and it always
cost too much. Seemed amazing doctors could stay in business, given
how little anyone wanted to visit.

Junior year, he took Nutrition—because his friends said it was the
easiest way to meet the science requirement—and in that class he
learned how America's health care system had declined. Once in the
Top 5, America today wasn't even in the Top 50 in terms of life
expectancy and infant mortality and other measurements. Couple
that with the most expensive pharmaceuticals in the world, and you
had a system that was profitable for those in the system but a source
of unending misery for those who were not. Made him glad he didn't
feel called in that direction.

Didn't matter. He wasn't here today for treatment.

Ever since Professor Herwig hauled Mitch into his office—for
reasons that still weren't entirely clear to him—he'd been worried.
After the meeting, he did a little internet research and obtained more
details about David Donovan's second chance. He'd filed something
called a Motion for New Trial and it was slated for hearing next week.

All the online commentators seemed to think his chances of success were next to nonexistent.

What was Herwig concerned about? Was it possible there was more to this case than he realized?

Worse, was it possible that, in the event that David got off the hook, someone was planning to put him in the crosshairs?

The most troubling part was the suggestion that Claudia gave this doctor a lot of money, something she had no reason to do.

Correction. She must've had a reason. He just didn't know what it was. But he wanted to find out.

The doctor was of course running late, so he waited half an hour in the main lobby, then a nurse took him inside to an aptly named waiting room where he sat for another forty-five minutes. By the time Dr. Marilyn Southern made the scene, he felt he had earned this interview.

She slid onto a stool behind a computer screen. She scanned as she talked. "New patient, right? What seems to be the problem?"

Mitch cleared his throat. "Actually, I'm fine."

She arched an eyebrow. Obviously not what she normally heard. "You understand that I'm a nephrologist? I'm not going to give you a physical."

"I believe you were David Donovan's physician."

"And still am." She sighed. "Are you a reporter?"

"Oh no. Just a friend."

"Of David's? He hasn't mentioned you."

"No." A painful pause. "Of Claudia's."

"Oh." Southern pushed away from the screen. "Look, I have patients to treat. And I'm running late. I'm going to have to ask you to leave."

"Just give me a minute."

"Why? You came here under false pretenses and you're stealing time from those who need it."

"Give me five minutes."

She rolled the wheeled stool to the counter where they kept the cotton swabs and antiseptic patches. "You're going to berate me for treating a convicted murderer? Try to scare me off the case?"

"Of course not."

"Well, many have, and I'm getting sick of it. I took the Hippocratic Oath. My job is to treat those who need my help. I don't care what a jury thinks of them. I treat all people equally."

"Even now? After his conviction?"

"Are you kidding? I see him once a week, which means I have to travel to the prison during my day off. He gets dialysis three times a week, and I have to oversee that as well. He's my patient and I try to do right by him. Even if...his time is limited."

"Is it that?" Mitch swallowed. He knew this was about to get rough. "Or was there...money involved?"

"What does that mean?" She seemed outraged, as if no one had the right to question anything she did. "Do you think I need a bribe to treat a patient?"

"No. Judging from what I learned online, you're already handsomely compensated for your work." Pause. "But few people would object to getting...a little something extra. Especially something in the six-digits extra."

"How do you know—" She took a breath, then started again. "What makes you think there was a...a payment?"

"I have it from a reliable source."

"Are you trying to pin the murder on me?"

"I assure you—"

"Do you think I don't know David Donovan is trying to get his verdict set aside? Do you think I don't know people online are accusing me of somehow being complicit in the murder? Even though that makes no sense?"

"Can you explain what the payment was for?" He noted that she had never denied receiving it.

"That is none of your business." She rose and moved toward the door, then stopped. "You want to know what I think? I think the cops are coming after you, and you know it, so you're trying to shift the blame."

"Why would I go after you?"

"The more suspects, the more confusion. The more likely you'll slip between the cracks."

"No one has even accused me. You're deflecting. Or projecting."

"Is that so? Where'd you get your psychiatry degree?" She took a step forward. "You're the guy in the dorm David told me about. Claudia mentioned you too. They both thought you were a creeper. That you had the hots for her."

"She's...not my type."

"What about the violin?"

"I'm a pianist."

"That instrument could pay off a lot of student debt."

Mitch rose. "The only reason I came here was to see if the rumors were true. If you might be involved in this ugly mess."

She opened the office door and pointed. "Get out of my office."

"You haven't answered—"

"Three seconds. Then I call security."

"Suit yourself." He strolled toward the door. "But don't imagine for one minute that this is over. I've got my eyes on you. And I'm not the only one."

# CHAPTER TWENTY-EIGHT

DAN WAS BEHIND THE WHEEL AGAIN AN HOUR LATER, BUT HE AND BEN hadn't reached an agreement on where they were going next.

"This honky-tonk is only half an hour outside of town."

"In the wrong direction," Ben added.

"So we lose an hour."

"An hour plus however long you spend there."

"We might learn something."

"About what?" Ben gazed at the desert landscape, beautiful under the setting sun. "We don't know that this cartel rubout has anything to do with our offices being ransacked. Or the attacks on us."

"Crenshaw sent us to see that guy, And now he's dead. Look, I'll just stop in. If the Ferrari Kid isn't there, we'll move on." He paused. "But if there's a chance he might be able to tell me something— anything—that helps me figure out where Maria is, or what happened to her—I have to take it."

Ben nodded. "You're the driver."

"Come on. You must be enjoying this. At least a little. As soon as we get to LA, you'll be back in a courthouse. Dan smiled. "I bet you owned the courtroom back in the day."

"I was pathetic in the courtroom back in the day." Ben squared his shoulders. "But I improved with time. I was never flamboyant like you. But I was...competent."

"A little flamboyance can go a long way with jurors."

Ben pursed his lips. "Trials are supposed to be a search for the truth. Facts, evidence. Not performance art."

"Ooh. Burn."

"Just making a point. We have different approaches."

"So you say. But I've read about some of your cases. You were a bigshot. You must've had women lined up all the way around the block."

Ben laughed out loud, so hard his head almost hit the dash. "Not exactly."

"Women love litigators. They go for the BDE."

"I've always been...on the reserved side. Especially around women."

"You found a wife."

"She found me. Thank goodness. She's made my life so much better than I ever thought it could be." He arched an eyebrow. "Another benefit of getting older." He gazed out the window, as if he'd spotted something of great interest in the barren landscape. "I apologize if I haven't seemed sufficiently concerned about Maria. I am, and we're going to find her. I'm concerned about the other LCL offices, too. I don't want anyone hurt because they took a job from me."

"You know what Maria said when I saw her last?"

"If it was a booty call, I don't want to hear about it."

"Nothing like that. Not this time." He grinned. "She said she had a surprise for me."

"But didn't tell you what it was?"

"No. Waiting for the right moment."

"Is that common?"

"No. Normally she can't keep a secret for ten seconds."

"And you have no idea what it might be?" Ben gave him a probing look.

"I should've asked. I should've said...a lot of things. But...." He chin set. "We just have to find her, that's all."

"Agreed. Let's do this honky-tonk and get back on the road. As soon as possible."

---

WHY WAS THIS PLACE CALLED SNEAKY PETE'S? DAN WONDERED, AS HE and Ben stepped through the front door and surveyed the joint. Surely they could've come up with something more original. Or more descriptive. Maybe: Beer, Beards & Ball Caps. Because that was what he saw as he cast his eyes around the relatively small saloon.

He also spotted a long phalanx of motorcycles outside, and it wasn't hard to deduce which of the bar's current patrons were the riders. But they'd also spotted the red Ferrari.

Even decades after the Hell's Angels hit the scene, standard honky-tonk regalia appeared to be leather jackets with metal studs and bandannas over hair that hadn't been cut in far too long. Country music played loudly from the jukebox. Garth Brooks, if he wasn't mistaken. Not normally Dan's taste, but he was delighted by the fact that they had an actual jukebox that played 45s.

"Do you smell it?" Ben asked.

Dan took a deep breath. "Urine?"

"No. I mean, that's not what I'm talking about."

Dan tried again. "Sweat? Body odor?"

Ben shook his head. "Fear."

"That's a metaphor. You can't smell fear."

"Maybe *you* can't. Let's take a seat at the bar."

Dan followed Ben's lead. They took adjoining barstools, the only ones still free, which positioned them between two patrons, a woman on Ben's side and a heavy-set man on Dan's side. His haggard face suggested he'd seen better days.

The bartender came by. They both took beer on tap.

"Is it my imagination," Dan asked quietly, as they waited for their drinks, "or are people watching us?"

"Not your imagination. They noticed us the second we walked in. And that's worrying someone."

"Why?"

"Because we obviously don't belong here. Which leads to wondering why we are here." He paused. "Especially if someone recognizes us from the museum."

"You think the murderer is in here?"

"Someone drove that Ferrari."

"You think he recognizes us?"

"I don't see the kid. But I see others."

"The guy who killed the Ramos?"

"Or the guy who's trying to kill us."

That was a sobering thought. "I see a big booth in the back that might be cartel members. They appear to be Latino."

"All Latinos are not in cartels."

"I wasn't stereotyping. May I remind you that Maria is Latina? If anyone in this bar is with the cartel, it's not likely to be the bikers. It's the gentlemen at that table." He snapped his fingers. "Look. It's the kid. Almost in shadow. Two thugs down from the Big Boss." He made eye contact with the man sitting at the end of the booth, a tall, lanky middle-aged bearded dude who wasn't chatting or drinking as much as the others.

"You think we should go talk to them?"

Ben shook his head. "Let them stew a while. Get a little nervous. People don't perform as well when they're nervous. Let's order some food."

The bartender brought them menus—if you could call it that. It was barely as big as a napkin and only listed five items. Which were more snacks than actual food.

Ben smiled. "Where's the prime rib?"

"Are you trying to kill yourself? You don't need arteriosclerosis." Pause. "Especially at your age."

Ben rolled his eyes. "Right. You're a vegetarian."

"Maria set me right."

"Christina has been trying to get me to give up red meat."

"And?"

"She's not here."

Ben settled on a bowl of tomato soup, which Dan suspected came from a Campbell's can. He got some fries. They still hadn't been approached by anyone, so when the food arrived, they ate.

A few minutes later, the bartender brought the tab and Dan grabbed it. "I'll take care of this."

"I think I should," Ben replied. "Technically, I am your boss."

"But I'm your abductor. Least I can do." He tossed a couple of twenties on the tray and nodded at the bartender. "It's good."

Ben nudged him. "Don't leave such a puny tip."

"You want to support the high-class personages here?"

"People who work in restaurants usually don't even get minimum wage. They live off tips. You're rich. Don't be a piker."

Dan threw down another bill. "Next time I'll let you pay."

"I did offer."

"Have I mentioned that you can be somewhat…annoying?"

Ben took another spoonful of soup. "You're not the first."

The lanky man from the booth in the rear rose slowly, gave them both a long look, then headed their way.

"Brace yourself," Dan whispered. "This is about to get real."

"Howdy, boys." The man wore boots and a ball cap. He was Hispanic though his voice had little accent. He was so thin his flannel shirt hung like a drape. "Haven't seen you here before."

"No," Dan said, whirling around on his barstool. "You haven't."

"New in town?"

"Just passing through."

"One of my friends thought he saw you in Roswell."

"That a crime?" He saw Ben roll his eyes. Always a critic.

"Depends. We ain't fond of people who…interfere with our local business."

Dan decided to cut to the chase. "Would your local business include murdering Eduardo Ramos at the museum today?"

The lanky man leaned in closer. "You know what, slick? You need to be more careful about what you say. Throwing accusations around can get a man hurt."

"Especially if the accusations are true, right?"

The man's jaw clenched. "I think it might be best if we continued this discussion outside."

Dan slid off the stool. "And if I decline your generous invitation?"

The man did not flinch. "Then I'll take care of it right here. The barkeep and I go way back. He won't care. Neither will anyone else. We like a good fight here at Sneaky Pete's. And folks like it best when they get to see me mop the floor with some city-boy asshole poking his nose into other people's business."

"What business would you be protecting exactly?"

"One you don't want to be on the wrong side of."

"Did Eduardo Ramos get in your way? What was it? Murder for hire? Narco slavery?

He could see the man's fists tighten. "Took us a long time to get established here. And we're not going to stand around and watch it get flushed down the toilet." He leaned in closer. "If I have to take out a couple of outsiders to protect the operation, so be it."

# CHAPTER TWENTY-NINE

DAN CAST A GLANCE OVER HIS SHOULDER. HE WAS CONCERNED THAT this not-remotely veiled threat might upset Ben, but actually, his companion hadn't shrunk back an inch. He appeared to be scrutinizing the bearded man carefully, as if he might find the answers to their questions through mental telepathy.

"For that matter," the lanky man continued, "you look fit enough. We could use some more workers out at the farm."

Dan locked eyes. "You're not from Mexico, right? Or El Salvador. You're local."

The man fairly snarled. "What's that got to do with anything?"

"Means you're probably not actually a member of the cartel. You're a local they contact when they want something done. An errand boy."

"You sorry son of a—"

"You have the same accent as the people I've been talking to all day. You grew up in the US. You used to live here with your family, a wife at least, though that relationship has ended. Probably due to your poor conversational skills."

The man stiffened. "What the hell are you talking about?"

"You had a good job, but something went wrong. Maybe you got fired, maybe it's just the times. But you're somewhat skilled and held a legit job. Not the typical profile of a cartel gofer."

The man glanced over his shoulder, as if afraid someone might overhear. "I don't have time for this crap. You gonna back off or not?"

Dan grinned. "I love the way you slurred 'going to' into 'gonna.' And you dropped an 'ain't.' You're trying to hide your education." He drew in his breath. "Here's the truth. You've been to school and you had a good job. You have a close-cropped haircut, not the long hair most cartel types fancy. More like an urban professional. But that didn't stop your wife from leaving."

"How the hell—"

"No-brainer. I can see the white ring mark on your finger. Probably your wife used to pick out your clothes because you're poor with colors. You can't tell navy blue from black."

"I've had as much of this as—"

"You've given up smoking recently, too, haven't you?"

The man's eyes widened.

"Good on you. Those things'll kill you. But your flannel still reeks of smoke, and since you haven't lit up since I entered this bar, I'd say you're trying to quit. Was smoking one of the things that caused your wife to walk? Or did it cost you your job? Or were you smoking something other than nicotine? Is that why you're so desperate you've resorted to putting on this big macho show for the absolute scum of the earth? What are you hiding?"

The man slapped his hands down on Dan's shoulders. Dan brought up both fists, breaking the hold. The man pulled back his arm to take a swing, but Dan wrapped himself around the man's torso. They tumbled to the floor.

"Fight!' someone screamed. "*Fight!*"

Was that meant to summon someone to break it up, or to alert everyone so they could watch?

Dan shoved the man off, which took considerable effort. He rolled to the side but soon felt a boot in his ribs. Same guy or a friend? He hoped this wouldn't escalate into a full-out bar brawl, but in a joint like this, there was no telling.

Somehow the lanky troublemaker scrambled to his feet and got in a good kick to the gut before Dan sat up. Which hurt. No ribs broken, but he wasn't going to give the man a second chance.

"We don't need to do this," he grabbed the man by the collar. "Tell me what your Ferrari friend was doing in Roswell today."

"Can't." He shoved Dan away.

"Who killed Eduardo Ramos?"

"Way above my pay grade."

"Ok, who ordered him killed?"

"No idea."

"Why was he killed?"

The man was still in fighting posture. "Don't know."

Dan dodged a swing. "Then why are you hassling me?"

"I don't like troublemakers."

Dan dodged another punch, then managed to land one square in the man's throat. A rush of air poured from his lungs. He staggered from one foot to the other.

Dan got the impression they were both on fishing expeditions and neither had many answers. He didn't mind fighting when necessary, but he did mind fighting when it was pointless. "Why don't we—"

Too late. The man wrapped an arm around Ben's throat, hauling him off his bar stool with a twisted chokehold. No way Ben could breathe with that fat arm around his neck.

"I'd say your friend has about thirty seconds."

Dan raised his hands and took a tentative step backward. "Whoa. No need to hurt anyone."

"Tell me what you two losers were doing in Roswell."

"Someone very close to me has disappeared. I'm trying to find her."

"And why would you think she's in Roswell?"

"I got a tip."

"From who?"

Dan didn't answer.

The man tightened his grip on Ben's throat. "I'm not screwing around here. Me and my boys—"

Before he could finish, Ben grabbed the man's arm, lunged

forward, and flipped him over his shoulders. The man flew almost two feet before he landed hard, capsizing an empty table in the process.

The onlookers in the bar whistled.

Someone murmured, "The old guy has moves…"

Dan peered at him, amazed.

Ben brushed off his hands. "I told you my friends insisted I get some self-defense instruction."

"You didn't tell me you could flip a guy twice your weight."

"It's basically my only move."

Dan raced to the side of the fallen man, who was shaking his head and trying to recover his bearings.

Dan pushed him down to the floor. The man rolled, crashing into a table. The people seated there scattered.

Dan moved in with a kick, but the man caught his boot and twisted it sideways. Dan lost his balance, waving his arms, trying to stay upright, but the man would not let go of his foot. He crashed down, capsizing another table and sending several beer steins flying.

Every eye in the bar was watching the fight.

His opponent crouched down for a punch but Dan leaned in at the perfect moment and delivered a killer head butt. They both careened sideways. Someone screamed. Everyone scattered.

So far, no one had tried to intervene. But he could see the men at the back table were monitoring the situation.

Dan wrapped an arm around his assailant's neck. "Doesn't feel so good when the chokehold is on the other throat, does it?"

The man snarled but didn't resist. "You're a dead man."

"What was Ferrari Boy doing in Roswell today?"

The man blinked twice. Did he expect his cartel buds to rescue him? If so, the rescue was supremely slow in coming.

Dan tightened his grip. "Last chance. Who was it?"

The man spit on the floor. "You're not going to kill me."

"No, but I will continue humiliating you in front of your friends, who I note are not rushing to your side. Then I will strangle you into unconsciousness. Which means, first, your friends will see you melt onto the floor like a puddle of goo, and second, you'll lose control of your bodily functions, so your friends will watch you wet yourself— or worse." Not necessarily true, but at the moment the guy couldn't fact-check him. "That's something people in these parts could be talking about for a looooong time."

The man tried to spit in his face, but he didn't have the leverage. Dan could see that others were shifting anxiously, including the bartender, who was probably afraid he might kill the man. He didn't have much time.

"You know this will get back to your ex. Think how much mileage she'll get out of telling people about her washed-up hubby who soiled himself at Sneaky Pete's."

The man reached, but not for Dan's throat. Instead, he pulled Dan closer so he could whisper. "I don't know why Ramos was killed."

"You're saying this obvious execution-style murder wasn't the cartel?" If this wasn't a cartel rubout—what was it?

The longer he held the man pinned to the peanut-shell floor, the greater the chances trouble would escalate.

He released the man, shoved him away, and smiled. "Good talk." He brushed himself off and turned to Ben. "Ready to get out of here?"

Ben nodded. "I was ready before we came in."

# CHAPTER THIRTY

THE REAPER READ THE REPORT ON HIS PHONE. THIS WHOLE SITUATION was spiraling, if not completely out of control, then certainly wider and wilder than desired. This had seemed like a simple matter. Someone needed an angel of death. A specter who needed cash to fund political activism. It was a win-win.

And to be fair, the first operations had gone swimmingly. Until they didn't. That woman. And now these two legal lunkheads, doing everything wrong and pinning a target on their backs the size of the Great Wall of China.

And yet, they were still alive, threatening to destroy everything. Which meant payment might not be forthcoming.

The Reaper tried to think clearly. What was paramount at the moment was not what was happening in Roswell, interesting though it was. What mattered most was the list.

She looked happy, poor woman. Must've had a good meet with her doc. She was probably seeing the light at the end of the tunnel. An end to the pain and suffering.

Well, there was going to be an end to her suffering. Just not the end she expected.

She was Number 3 and he was working from the bottom up. After this, one more little problem in San Diego and he should be home-free. Assuming LA went as expected.

The Reaper watched as the woman walked to a green Mini-Cooper and pulled out of the parking lot. She headed downtown.

Shopping? Lunch? This was another undesirable complication. She lived alone. Eliminating her at home would be a cinch. Wouldn't attract attention or inspire anyone to connect it to the other killings.

She didn't stop until she reached a strip mall. This one had a coffeeshop, appropriately named Twitchy. Lunch, or just a quick jolt? Didn't much matter. The place appeared empty or darn close. Probably one of the many Mom and Pop coffeeshops that sprang up after Starbucks saturated the nation and made it look easy. If you can create a thriving business by brewing coffee—which a child can do at home in five minutes at a cost of about ten cents—this was an easy way to make a living. Maybe.

The Reaper needed to take care of her as efficiently as possible. But busting in and shooting up the place would escalate the attention this received, and that was exactly what the employer did not want.

Maybe poison was the answer. Slow-acting dose of fentanyl would do the trick. She wouldn't die immediately. About ten minutes would pass before she felt sick, maybe twelve before she was dead. Just enough time to finish her coffee and get into traffic. With luck, she'd lose consciousness, cause a traffic accident, and everyone would assume she'd died from her pre-existing illness—without bothering to perform an autopsy.

After removing the costume, the Reaper entered the coffeeshop and stared at the menu. Didn't take much study. They were all the same, one coffeeshop to the next. Only the names changed. The Howling Howell. The Smithson Slider. Named for regulars.

The barista took an order for a small chocolate mocha.

He caught the eye of the woman he'd followed from the hospital, which was not difficult since she was the only other customer in this boutique java shop.

He nodded her way. "Need a jolt. Just to get to naptime."

"Naptime? I wish."

"People function better when they take naps. Studies have proven it."

"Great. Now if someone would just add two or three hours to the day, I might be able to fit that in."

"A twenty-minute nap is enough."

"I'd rather have three hours." She tilted her coffee cup in a mock salute.

She had not removed the lid or the zarf—the corrugated cardboard that allowed her to hold the hot cup without misery. She had not unfolded her laptop and she was not staring at a phone. She did not plan to be here long.

"I had to get up early this morning for a doctor's appointment," she added.

"Sorry to hear that. Everything ok?"

"Yes. I got some great news. Things are starting to look up for me."

The irony was too thick.

She finished her drink. "If you'll excuse me. I have several more stops to make. Now that I'm properly energized. Have a blessed day."

"Of course."

The poison idea was not going to work. She was leaving.

When did everything get so complicated?

The woman left the coffeeshop and started toward her car. She slid into the driver's seat, put on a pair of sunglasses, snapped on her seatbelt, then grabbed her keys from her purse.

"Wait a minute!" the Reaper shouted, stepping out of the coffeeshop, drink in hand.

She looked up. "What?" She spoke through her still-open car door.

"I think you forgot something."

She seemed puzzled. "I didn't have much..."

The street was clear. "Isn't this yours?"

A split second later the coffee hit the pavement and she felt piano wire around her neck. One of the most useful tools in the world. Easy to carry, simple to deploy. Didn't even require that much strength.

Within seconds, a ring of blood arose around her throat as the wire cut into tender flesh.

Her hands flew to the wire, but she couldn't get a grip on it, and she couldn't have pulled it away even if she had. She was helpless.

Or so it seemed. Until, the woman leaned on the horn.

All at once, the street was split by the piercing noise. Damn! The Reaper yanked her away and then punched her on the side of the face. To her credit, she did not give up immediately. But eventually, after three more blows to the face, she did.

And a few moments later, her eyelids fluttered shut.

No one had come out of the coffeeshop or appeared on the street.

Tough break for her. You get some good news from the doc, then someone kills you on the way home. She would never know who had killed her, much less why.

The Reaper pushed the body down to the floor of the car, locked and closed the door and walked away, ripping off his gloves.

A job smoothly executed. The employer should be pleased.

# CHAPTER THIRTY-ONE

Dan glanced into the rear view mirror. They'd left Sneaky Pete's with considerable alacrity. Nonetheless, someone might have been dispatched to keep an eye on them. Or several someones.

Ben noticed. "Are we being followed?"

"Not that I can tell."

"Which doesn't mean we aren't being followed."

"I know. It's dark." Without even thinking about it, he pushed harder on the accelerator.

"Maybe we should park. Or find a motel. Get some shuteye."

"How would that help anything? I can get us through Arizona. We'll hit California sometime in the morning."

"If you say so. But if you want to stop, we should."

"Not necessary."

"This isn't an Iron Man competition. You don't have to prove how tough you are."

"We may need some tough if we're going to survive this."

"You know what's more important than tough? Smart. If you fall asleep and wreck the car, that's not smart."

"I've pulled pretrial all-nighters that went on longer than this."

Ben borrowed Dan's phone and called his wife. About ten minutes later, he rang off.

"Christina says there's trouble at the LCL office in San Diego."

"What? Why?"

"Don't know. But it seems likely to be related. If I recall correctly, the Donovan case was originally filed there, then transferred to LA. And I believe San Diego is more or less on our way to LA."

"Would you like to make a stop at Disneyland, too?"

"No thanks. Hate the crowds."

They'd crossed into Arizona a few minutes before. They would enter California to the south, but it shouldn't take long to get to San Diego, and from there, unless something new broke, on to LA. Since he was supposedly in charge of LCL, he should know more about this case. But Ben had established seventeen offices in different major cities and they all had multiple cases, so trying to keep track of everything was beyond the capacity of his memory.

Or interest.

"Christina also gave me an update on what's happening in St. Pete, which is basically nothing. No one has found a trace of Maria. Even with Jake Kakazu marshaling his entire department and Mike Morelli sending people in from Tulsa."

Dan drew in his breath. "I have to face the reality that—"

"They haven't found a body. There would be no reason to hide a corpse. If it existed."

Dan didn't reply. Ben was making major logical jumps that couldn't be justified. But it wasn't because he was blind or stupid. He was trying to be kind.

He decided to change the subject. "At least she didn't say Jake has put out an APB on me. He must know I've bolted."

"No substitute for having friends. Mine have saved my bacon time and time again."

"Speaking of which—you handled yourself pretty well back there. At the bar."

"I flipped one guy. Not going to make me an Olympic contender."

"Still impressive for a guy who's—" He stopped short.

Ben arched an eyebrow. "Yes?"

"Who's…sedentary. Intellectual. Book-loving."

"You're trying not to say, 'old.'"

"Age is a factor in hand-to-hand combat."

"There's nothing wrong with being a grownup. I'm in good health and have no trouble getting around or remembering my children's names."

"Of course. But still." He smiled. "Impressive."

"One of the nice things about getting older," Ben added, "is that you stop feeling like you have to prove yourself. I stretch my legs every day, but I don't need to pump iron or run marathons." He paused. "Or kite-surf."

"Hey, kite-surfing is cool."

"Extreme sports are by definition not cool. I mean, come on. What are you trying to prove?"

"Just staying fit."

"Trying jogging. Extreme sports are dangerous."

"If you're responsible and careful—"

"Accidents still happen. Accidents will always happen."

"Are you seriously suggesting that I should give up my favorite watersport?"

"It's not a hint. I'm telling you. Grow up."

"Excuse me?"

"You're not twenty-one anymore. You're not really single. And you're the COO of the LCL network."

"You're the CFO."

"What I'm trying to tell you is, yes, I may be older, but you're not the young, carefree, flashy lawyer who can do anything that amuses him. Walt Disney used to play polo. But after a close call, his brother told him he had to give it up. Bigwigs can't run around endangering their lives for no good reason."

"You should've mentioned this when you offered me the job."

"I'm mentioning it now, because I think you're at a crossroads."

"You mean this case?"

"No. I mean…" Ben took a deep breath, then frowned.

"Just say it."

Another long pause ensued. Finally Ben settled on, "Get some grown-up hobbies. You're pushing forty. And a lot of people depend upon you."

"So I have to take up knitting?"

"No. But you need to be more responsible."

"Fine. Give me an example of an exciting grown-up endeavor."

"Well"—his eyes darted downward—"you could start a family."

Dan rolled his eyes. "You are so predictable. It's the twenty-first century, Ben. Not everyone has to get married and tie themselves down with kids."

"True. And not everyone should. But...you would be an excellent father."

"Thanks for the compliment. But there's no hurry."

Ben pursed his lips, started to speak, then stopped. "You adore that little girl. The one you got your DA friend to adopt. What's her name?"

Dan smiled. "Esperanza. Yeah, she's the sweetest in the world."

"Until you have your own daughter. And then no one else will come close."

"Isn't this all a little pot calling the kettle black? If I recall correctly, you and Christina waited rather late in life before you had children."

"Because I was an idiot. I'm trying to prevent you from making the same mistake."

"Thanks, but if I want your advice, I'll ask for it."

Dan could see Ben was not happy. Why this sudden concern about his lifestyle choices?

They drove in silence for a long stretch. Although he normally enjoyed the desert landscape, it was difficult to savor at night. Especially when he had so many other things on his mind.

"I should return your compliment," Ben said. "You handled yourself well back at the bar, too."

"Took that thug down but good, right?"

Ben waggled his head from side to side. "Certainly you took him down. But what I admired was how well you sized him up. That's what threw him off. You have a keen gift for observation—and for putting those observations together to gain insight. The way he dressed, his haircut, his ring finger. Impressive."

"I was glad to give my skills a workout. It's been a long time since I actually tried a case."

"Administering the LCL is important too."

"Not saying otherwise."

"I always imagined that eventually I would luck into the blowout case that made my fortune. One great jury verdict I could retire on."

"That's not how it usually happens."

"But we all have our dreams." He sighed. "They aren't realistic. That's why we call them dreams."

"Nothing wrong with having dreams," Ben replied. "I remember when—"

A sudden jolt from the rear of the car propelled them both into the dashboard.

"What the hell?" Dan muttered.

He glanced at the rear view. Another car was behind them. He couldn't tell what it was, but it appeared broad and big. Much larger than the rental he was driving.

"*Again?*" Ben asked, craning his neck.

"They came up behind me with no headlights so I wouldn't see them."

"Haven't we already played this road-rage routine?"

"Yeah. But we're not dead yet."

Another slam from behind, this time harder. The first collision was probably just to get their attention. But now the driver appeared to be actively trying to drive them off the road.

"We need to do something," Ben said. "Take evasive action."

"This is a crappy rental car, not the USS Enterprise." Dan swung the wheel hard left, then right. "Speed up? Slow down? Stop?"

"Definitely do not stop," Ben muttered. "Hard to make out details in the dark. But I think the guy in the passenger seat just pulled out a big gun."

# CHAPTER THIRTY-TWO

DAN SWERVED AGAIN JUST AS HE HEARD THE UNMISTAKABLE SOUND OF gunfire somewhere to his left.

Ben peered through the rear window. "I can't see any faces clearly. Too dark. But there are two shooters. At least."

"Get down!" Dan shouted. He grabbed Ben's shirt and yanked him back into his seat.

"They've got more engine power than we do. We're not going to outrace them. We got lucky last time, with snow on the ground. But it won't happen again."

Dan swerved back and forth, trying to cut a curving—serpentine—path so the car behind couldn't get a bead on them.

He turned hard until he was completely in the opposite lane. Dangerous, especially at night, but he didn't see anything coming and the desert road was mostly flat. But the bullets were still flying.

"This is not working," Ben muttered.

"And your suggestion is?"

"I'll take the wheel."

Dan laughed out loud. "I don't think so, Gramps."

"I've still got a driver's license. You're going to get us killed."

"Are you kidding? I live and breathe cars."

"Fancy sports cars. Which this isn't."

Another round of gunfire. They both ducked.

Ben continued. "You lean forward and I'll slide in behind you. If we do this right, the car will only slow for a heartbeat. The second your foot leaves the gas pedal, my foot will replace it."

"And who's gonna steer during this escapade?"

Ben laid a hand on the side of the wheel. "I will."

"This is insane," Dan growled, but his last word was drowned out by another round of gunfire.

Ben unbuckled his seatbelt, then did the same for Dan. "On three. Ready? One."

"This is crazy!"

"Two...*three!*"

All things considered, the switch went smoother than Dan thought possible. He almost impaled himself on the gear shift, but he did make it into the passenger seat. Ben immediately took control.

"Okay, Mario Andretti," Dan murmured, "what's your big plan?"

Ben's eyes were focused straight ahead. "Drive really fast."

"You're already pushing a hundred. I don't think you can drive any faster safely."

"We may have to jettison safety precautions. In favor of staying alive."

Ben started swerving back and forth in short erratic, unpredictable bursts. The car behind them started firing rapidly, spraying a wide field.

Three rounds later, a bullet shattered the back window. Glass nuggets rocketed through the car.

Dan knew that was safety glass, but he could swear he was bleeding on the back of his neck and head. Ben didn't seem to react at all.

"You okay?" Dan gasped.

"My butt's a little cold."

"Not what I meant."

"Don't distract me. I'm trying to get us out of this mess."

"How are you going to do that?"

Ben shrugged. "Improvise."

Dan couldn't tell much about the car behind them, but it appeared to be some kind of sedan, probably chosen for weight, not maneuverability.

Ben jerked the wheel hard to the left, spinning their car right off the concrete.

Dan covered his forehead. *"What the hell are you doing?"*

"Going offroad."

"Does that seem wise?"

"On the highway, we're sitting ducks."

In the distance, Dan could see some kind of mound or mesa. Which seemed like as good a destination as any.

"Did we lose them?" Dan asked.

"Not yet. They're following."

"That is part of your plan, right? You're luring them to one of those Batman death traps?"

"You know, I meant to set up a death trap, but I got busy and it slipped my mind."

"What's your plan?"

"Don't get killed."

"That's a goal. Not a plan. What's the plan?"

"Scare the hell out of them." Braking on a dime and twisting the wheel at the same time, Ben spun the SUV around, doing a complete 180.

Now they could see their pursuers. In their headlights.

The other car slammed on its brakes. It stopped barely ten feet away.

"Recognize anyone?"

Dan squinted. "You mean from the bar?"

"Or anyplace else we've visited since this grand adventure began."

"No."

The two cars faced each other down, headlights blazing, engines revving.

"What now?" Dan asked.

"We see who makes the first move. They may be more anxious than we are."

"Why would they be more anxious? They have guns."

"Because someone hired them. Someone who expects results. Which they would like to deliver without getting killed or arrested in the process."

"We can't just sit here. It's freezing cold with the window shattered."

"Bundle up. It's not getting warmer anytime soon."

Dan rolled down his passenger-side window and shouted. "Can we talk?"

No response.

Dan tried again. "Let's put the guns away and resolve this peaceably!"

Still no words. But he did see someone lean out. Holding a shotgun, appropriately enough.

Ben shifted into reverse, circled, and floored it just as the first blast erupted.

"Apparently they're not big talkers," Dan whispered.

"It was a noble effort."

Once he was out of gunshot range, Ben spun the car around again. The sedan had not moved.

Ben spun around in an arc just wide enough to get behind the other car. The shooter couldn't get a fix.

Dan had to admit that the lawyer from Oklahoma knew how to handle a car.

And then, just when Dan expected him to bolt away—Ben drove straight for the other car.

Dan braced himself against the dash. "Are we playing chicken?"

Ben's eyes were fixed and grim. "No."

Ben smashed into the sedan, clipping it on the left and sending it spinning sideways while he barreled on past. At least two of its tires blew out and the windshield cracked. Their car might not move like a Ferrari, but it had more weight up front, plus they had momentum the stationary car did not.

He turned the wheel hard again to avoid crashing into the mesa, or whatever it was. A few moments later he'd righted the car and headed back for the highway.

"What was the point of that incredibly dangerous maneuver?" Dan asked.

"They won't be following us. They won't be going anywhere soon."

"But we still don't know who they were. Or why they were trying to kill us."

"Would you like to go back and have a conversation? That worked so well before."

"Hard pass."

The car hit the side of the road fast, jolting them up and down. A moment later, they were back on the highway.

"Where did you learn to drive like that?" Dan asked.

"My friend Mike made me take an extreme defensive-driving course, shortly after I almost killed myself in a high-speed chase on the Tulsa version of Deadman's Curve. Spent a week at the Texas Motor Speedway in Ft. Worth."

"What did they teach you?"

Ben arched an eyebrow. "Evasive action."

Dan squinted. "How old did you say you were again?"

"I didn't say. But I'm sixty-three. And just getting started."

# CHAPTER THIRTY-THREE

ONCE THE ROAD WAS CALMER, DAN RETOOK THE WHEEL. BEN CHATTED on Dan's cell phone. Apparently the guy on the other end was the Tulsa Chief of Police—Ben's friend and former brother-in-law. Go figure.

Ben covered the phone with his hand. "Mike thinks the attacks in St. Petersburg are related to other murders in other cities."

"Similar MO?"

"Similar Grim Reaper."

"Then he believes the Grim Reaper exists? Even though he didn't show up on my doorbell cam."

"He doesn't have any footage from anywhere. Just a few eyewitness accounts."

"Have they found—"

"No trace." The voice crackled on the other end, a deep, gruff voice. "Best to Kate." Ben ended the call.

"Learn anything?"

He placed a hand on Dan's shoulder. "We'll find her."

"You don't know that."

"I don't know much about what's going on. But I can see that we're being chased. Hunted. I can see that we're in the middle of something someone doesn't want us in. If they can't capture or kill you, and they still need something from you—they won't harm Maria. She's the insurance policy. Plan B."

"Then why hasn't someone called me? Threatened me? Asked for a ransom?"

"I don't know. They may be busy with all the other murders. They may be afraid you'll mess up the master plan. But their priority is still the master plan. Not you." He paused. "At least for now."

Dan's throat was dry. "I hope you're right." He clenched a fist. "I told you she said she had a surprise for me."

"Right. The surprise." Ben batted a finger against his lips.

"The more I think about it, I don't think it's kitesurfing equipment. That's not so special or expensive. I think it's a boat."

Ben's eyelids fluttered. "A boat?"

"Sure. Maybe a high-powered Criss-Craft."

"A yacht?"

"No. A sport boat. We've talked about it, but never bought one for some reason."

"Because watersports are your hobby, not hers."

"She's very supportive of my passions."

Ben sighed. "Did the possibility occur to you that...the surprise could be something else?"

"Like what?"

Ben's eyes spun in circles. "How is it you and Maria aren't married? You've been together a long time."

"We don't need a piece of paper to validate our relationship."

"Is that something you decided or she decided?"

"Maria has never once pushed for marriage. She's happy with things just the way they are, thank you very much."

"Yes," Ben said softly. "But things never stay just the way they are. Change is built into the tapestry of life."

"Whatever. If the change is a boat, I'm all for it."

"And if it isn't?"

"She might've gotten this outdoor pizza oven I've been drooling over. Installation would be a bear, but—"

Ben shook his head. "I've noticed you're skittish around small children. Like back in Roswell."

"Didn't know them."

"You were an only child, right?"

"As it turns out, I have a sister. Half-sister, technically. But I only found out about her a few years ago. I was raised alone."

"And the rest of your family?" Ben asked, eyes strained.

"You know my story. My father died in prison when I was fourteen. My mom has severe cognitive issues."

"And?"

"And...that's it." Another moment passed.

"Have you and Maria considered starting a family?"

Dan waved a hand in the air. "We have plenty of time."

"No one has plenty of time."

"We're going to enjoy being a couple for a while. Focus on the relationship."

"That's sensible." Ben sat up straight. "But you know what? Sometimes life isn't sensible. Sometimes things just happen and you have to deal with them. And make the best of it." He turned away. "Sometimes the unexpected development is a blessing. Even if it may not appear that way initially."

"I'm starting to get the feeling you're trying to tell me something. Could you explain?"

Ben thought a moment. "When I was younger, I don't recall ever thinking, boy, wouldn't my life be better if I had a couple of daughters? Of course, given how awkward I was around women, I never expected to marry, so why would I expect daughters? Chris changed all that. And my life is a thousand times richer as a result."

"You've lived a very full life."

Ben held up a hand. "You're talking career. I'm talking life. Yes, I've won some cases and helped people here and there. But none of it compares to family. Building a life is good, but building a strong family is a monumental achievement."

Dan grinned. "Well, if I ever get a hint that Maria wants a ring on her finger, I'll bear that in mind."

Ben said nothing.

Dan's phone buzzed. He glanced down. "It's for you. Again. If you keep yakking like this, I'm going to charge you a usage fee."

"Or you could just buy me a new phone. To replace the one you threw out the window in a fit of pique." He set the sound to Speaker. "Chris?"

"Ben? Is everything ok?"

"Sure. You're on speaker. Dan's in the car, of course. What's up?"

"Just got off the phone with Mike, who told me a crazy tale about you and Dan being in a high-speed car chase."

"Well…sort of."

"And a barroom brawl. And someone got murdered in Roswell?"

"It's not as dramatic as it sounds."

"It sounds pretty damn dramatic. Why didn't you mention any of this when we talked a few minutes ago?"

"Because…I was still in shock?"

"Bull. Because you knew I'd chew you out for putting your life at risk. Do I need to remind you that you're not a young, single, devil-may-care adventurer?"

"Was I ever?"

"I want to give Dan a piece of my mind. Dan, are you listening?"

"Indeed."

"Then listen up, Buster, and listen up good. I know what you're going through. But if anything happens to my Ben—"

"I will try not to let anything happen to Ben."

"Not good enough."

"I can't make absolute guarantees when he keeps grabbing the wheel and driving like he's in a James Bond movie."

Christina made a noise that sounded like the roar of a caged cocaine bear.

"Listen, boys, I may have something useful. I was going through the Tulsa office, cleaning up and looking for leads, reviewing the files and such. You remember that guy who was running San Diego till he quit about six months ago?"

"Yeah," Ben replied. "Can't remember his name, though."

"Kevin Helm."

"That was it. What happened to him?"

"We never knew. But he had access to LCL files. And he knew the woman Mike now believes to be the first Reaper victim. She was a social worker in Indianapolis."

Ben's eyes seemed to recede into his head. "Curiouser and curiouser. You think he knows anything?"

"It's worth checking out, don't you think?"

"Yeah." Ben glanced at Dan. "One more reason to go to San Diego. Any idea where we might find him?"

"This weekend?" Christina replied. "I do."

"And that would be...?"

He could hear the smile in her voice. "Keep an eye out for a cape."

# CHAPTER THIRTY-FOUR

DAN HAD BEEN TO SAN DIEGO BEFORE, BUT TODAY IT APPEARED TO HAVE ceased being a coastal beach community and transformed itself into a pop culture phenomenon. For the summer weekend of the famed San Diego Comic-Con, over 130,000 people descended upon the city. This spring event was a smaller affair, but still well attended by cosplaying comic fans and assorted other pop-culture outliers. People flooded the streets surrounding the conference center, including the historic Gaslamp Quarter and the coast and marina.

And far too many of them were wearing capes.

"How does your wife think we could possibly find Kevin Helm in this mess?" Dan was trying to drive, but the streets were packed with colorful pedestrians and traffic moved slowly. "I've never seen so many people. Certainly never seen so many people in superhero costumes. Do you think we need costumes?"

"Oh, stop. You just want an excuse to dress up like Batman."

"Not true. Now my friend Jimmy—"

"Nothing to be ashamed of. Every guy wants to do it."

"Dress up like a rodent?"

"Bats are mammals."

"Rodents are mammals. But bats aren't rodents."

"They're still bats."

"Not dressing up like one. Why would anyone?"

"It's supposed to be fun."

"Dressing up like a rat?"

"Bat."

"Whatever." He paused. "I've always wanted to put on one of those gorilla suits, you know? Jump up and down and wave my arms around like King Kong…"

Ben was looking all ways at once. He had a photo Christina sent to his phone, but the crowd and the costuming, which often involved masks, made it difficult. "According to Christina's source, Kevin comes to this conference every year."

Dan watched people stream out of the glass-windowed conference center. "He's not the only one." Banners were festooned from one lamppost to the next advertising a forthcoming science-fiction movie. The hotels were draped with advertising. Volunteers were trying to keep traffic moving in the right direction, but they were overwhelmed. "Are we going inside?"

"Let's hope not. We don't have tickets. And I doubt we could get any this late in the game."

"I could get one," Dan said.

"How? Gonna roll a five-year-old in a Sailor Moon costume?"

"Yikes!" Dan slammed on the brakes, stopping for pedestrians. Their costumes suggested an interest in truth, justice, and the American Way, but that did not appear to include jaywalking laws.

"*Yikes?*" Ben stared at him. "Because we're at Comic-Con, you've started talking like a cartoon character?"

"Some of the folks we saw back in Roswell would fit in nicely here," Dan remarked.

"How do you know these aren't the same people?"

"I don't think you could fit this many people into Roswell." He scanned the horizon. "Ok, one of those guys is a Smurf, right?"

Ben nodded. "The blue one."

"And that's a Muppet with her?"

"Beaker. Grown to frighteningly large proportions." He raised a finger. "Having children also guarantees you can finally identify the Muppets."

"But who's the woman? The nearly naked one."

"Vampirella." He observed the petite woman crossing the street in so little clothing he wondered if she violated public decency laws. Basically a few strips of red spandex barely covering the essential areas.

"Is Vampirella a good guy or a bad guy?"

"No one's sure. Eye-catching costume, though. I gather you didn't read comic books?"

"No. But I've seen Marvel movies. Does that count?"

"No."

"I need Jimmy here. He knows all about this stuff. Calls me Aquaman."

Ben smiled. "Arthur Curry. King of the Seven Seas. He's in the Justice League."

"With...Iron Man?"

"Wrong team."

"Spider-Man?"

"Please stop. You're just embarrassing yourself."

Dan dodged a long row of food trucks contributing to the chaos. "We need to park. We're never going to find anyone driving around."

"Turn under that wrought-iron trellis. Go south a few miles."

Dan did as told. "Looks like a nice part of town. When there aren't six thousand anime characters crawling all over it."

"Find Croce's. Italian restaurant."

"What was that name again?"

Ben's eyelids fluttered. "Let me guess. You've never heard of the late great Jim Croce?"

"Um...comic book artist?"

"No. Top Ten recording artist. 'Time in a Bottle.' 'Photographs and Memories.' 'Bad Bad Leroy Brown.'"

"I think I've heard that last one. Long time ago. I used to snigger because the singer says 'damn.'"

"And you were how old?"

"I don't know. Three or four."

"God help me." Ben took another deep breath. "Jim Croce died tragically young in a plane crash. His widow Yvonne has a restaurant here honoring his memory. She's moved several times, but it's still serving. She's also a terrific folk singer. They cut an early record together." Ben pointed. "There it is."

No available parking. Not surprising.

"Chris says Kevin eats here every Wednesday."

Dan stopped at a light. A moment later, a big smile on his face, he pointed at a shirtless green guy standing outside the restaurant. He beamed. "Frankenstein! Got one!"

Ben shook his head.

"The Incredible Hulk!"

"Sorry. Martian Manhunter. But he does have a cape." Dan glanced back and forth between the photo and a man on the street. "And I'm almost certain that's our guy. Come on."

---

DAN SOON LEARNED THAT KEVIN HELM LED A PANEL DISCUSSION ON the use of genderbending tropes in the early work of Jack Kirby, and it had been a hit, so most of the people in the room followed him to lunch. Apparently the superhero costume and the green body paint did not prevent them from taking him seriously. He was basking in his fifteen minutes of fame and didn't want to be interrupted.

They stood in the alcove by the maître d' station. Ben introduced himself.

"You're not in any kind of trouble," Ben assured Helm. "I just want to ask you a few questions."

"I don't work for you anymore," Helm said, puffing up his chest, which was easier than usual, because he was wearing an inflated fake chest with sculpted muscles. "You don't own me."

"I'm curious about why you left LCL."

"I have a right to make a change in my life."

"It came at an odd time."

Dan watched a look dart between questioner to questionee. Ben hadn't asked a question, so Helm didn't have to answer. But they were definitely both thinking something.

At last, Helm pursed his lips. "Give me a minute."

He skittered away, presumably to ask his entourage to excuse him for a minute or two.

"Think he's coming back?" Dan asked.

Ben nodded. "He's worried."

"About what?"

"Not sure. But he's afraid we know something he doesn't want us to know. So we have to convince him that we do know it so he will eventually tell us what we don't know. Because he thinks we already know it."

"Could you run that by me again? More slowly this time."

"Martian Manhunter will give it up."

"That's another thing. Who is this Martian Manhunter?"

"Martian Manhunter—J'onn J'onzz—was one of the founding members of the Justice League. He was brought here by an errant teleport ray and he can't get home, so he fights crime."

"Does he have powers?"

"He's strong. Can dematerialize. Telepathic. Flies."

"If he can fly, why doesn't he fly back to Mars?"

"It's complicated."

Helm returned. Several of his friends and followers trailed after him. One large woman wore a Viking helmet and a costume Dan thought he'd seen in a Marvel movie, but he wasn't sure which because they all seemed exactly the same to him. Another guy in a red shirt brandished a very convincing-looking phaser with glowing lights and sound effects. Irritating, but Dan figured that since he was wearing a red shirt, he wouldn't be around long.

"I don't have time for this," Helm said, rubbing sweaty palms together. "This is a big party. And you're crashing it."

"They'll wait."

"They can't wait. William Shatner speaks at two. Everyone will be there. There's a rumor he might play James Tiberius Kirk again. As a video game voice. So it won't be so obvious that he's aged."

Ben's eyes bulged. "Shatner might play Kirk again? Get out of here."

"Swear by the Seven Moons of Rao. If I lie, let my soul be swept into the maw of Cthulhu and never see a moment untinged by excruciating agony."

Ben glanced at his watch. "Did you say Shatner speaks at two?"

Dan scowled. "We do not have time."

"Spoilsport." Ben addressed the man in green. "You knew a woman named Carol Zimmerman?"

"I knew of her. Name came up in David Donovan's medical files. I don't know why the police thought I knew anything about her death."

"And you knew Claudia Wells?"

"For a short time. Before Gary took the case."

"What do you know about her death?"

"Nothing."

"I need to see the files."

"Sorry. They were all stolen."

"By whom?"

"If I knew that, I'd get them back. But the fact that someone wanted them enough to steal from my office suggests it was important. Somehow."

"Or someone was being very careful. Didn't you forward your files to Gary when the case was transferred?"

"Absolutely. Made copies of the essential documents, but not many."

"Did you retain any evidence?"

"Absolutely not. Sorry I can't be more help. What do you need?"

"I was hoping for something that helps my friend find his...girlfriend. You haven't heard anything about Maria Morales?"

"Never heard the name in my life. I only met Claudia because Daivd's case required me to interview Dr. Southern."

Dan's eyes narrowed. "The nephrologist?" He glanced at Ben.

"She's on the witness list for the Donovan hearing. Anything else you can tell us about this case?"

"Sorry. But you know who you might ask? Gary Quince."

"As it happens, we're headed his way." And they were running out of time. "We may be back with more questions later."

Helm snapped his green fingers.

"Hey John Jones!" someone cried from a table in the rear. "We ordered your dessert. *Bananas Foster!*"

A deafening burst of raucous laughter arose from the table, loud enough to catch the attention of everyone in the restaurant.

Helm glanced at Dan. "It's a joke."

Dan squinted. "You don't like bananas?"

"It's a flambé dessert." Helm shuddered. "Martian Manhunter is deathly afraid of fire."

# CHAPTER THIRTY-FIVE

DAN DROVE TO THE OUTSKIRTS OF SAN DIEGO, BUT AS THEY PASSED Coronado Island on their way out of town, he asked Ben if he'd like to take a turn.

They swapped seats, then resumed travel northward. Traffic thickened as they approached Los Angeles, and he felt somewhat guilty about dumping the driving on Ben. But if he'd learned anything from this journey, it was that Ben was a better driver—and a lot tougher—than he appeared.

He pulled out his cellphone and started tapping buttons.

Ben noticed. "You like that little gizmo of yours, don't you, youngster. I been thinkin' about gettin' me one. Oh, wait—"

"Just stop already." Dan pressed the phone to his ear.

"You're making yourself look old," Ben muttered.

But not so softly that Dan didn't hear. "What?"

"The way you're talking into the phone. Showing your age. It isn't a Princess phone. The mic is at the bottom. The cool kids hold it sideways and talk into the mic."

"Do you think I care—" Then he stopped, grimaced, and put the phone on Speaker. "Jaz? Can you hear me? Tell me you've got something."

Static on the other end. Then a female voice. "I'd be lying to you."

Dan whispered to Ben. "District attorney." He raised his voice. "Help me out here."

"Didn't Jake tell you not to leave town?"

"You know I couldn't sit on my butt while Maria was in danger. Come on. You love Maria. There must be something more you can do."

"Without evidence? Or even a lead?"

"You're just saying that because you're afraid you'll get in trouble if you help a defense attorney."

Ben shook his head and made a clicking noise. "I don't think that's what she's saying."

Dan gripped the phone tighter. "If this had happened to you, Jaz, Maria would be moving heaven and earth."

"I know she would. And we're—"

"Excuses are useless. Can't you see how serious this is? She could be hurt. Dying."

Ben leaned sideways so Dan couldn't possibly not hear him. "You're overreacting."

"No one ever got anything by underreacting."

"Wrong."

"Look," Dan said to the phone, "I don't have time to mess around, Jaz. You're either with me or you're against me."

Ben looked at him in despair. "Don't talk to her like that."

Dan punched the Mute button. "Would you stop Monday-morning quarterbacking my phone call?"

"You're doing it all wrong."

"You don't think I know how to talk to a district attorney?"

"I don't think you know how to talk to a woman, that's for sure." He paused. "Or possibly, the entire human race."

"You don't even know her."

"Do you?"

"I've known Jazlyn for years."

"Socially?"

The corner of Dan's mouth turned up a bit. "We did a little socializing back in the day."

"You dated her."

"Just once. Wasn't really even a date. We dined together, that's all."

"While she was district attorney?"

"Before. She was only an assistant DA back then. I told her it wouldn't happen again."

"You friend-zoned her? After you bedded her?"

"I did not—"

"And you can't think of any reason why she might not want to help you?"

"I never said—"

Ben leaned forward. "Just repeat after me." He whispered. "I apologize."

Dan glared at him—but turned off the Mute function and repeated to the phone. "I apologize."

Ben continued. "I had no right to speak to you that way."

Dan looked even angrier. But he repeated. "I had no right to speak to you that way."

"I'm just worried sick about Maria."

Dan dutifully repeated.

The voice on the phone reacted immediately. "I know, Dan. No worries. I haven't quit looking. And I won't. In fact, I'm going to call in some favors with a friend at the FBI. This might be a kidnapping, and it's remotely possible they might know something useful."

Ben just smiled.

"Thanks," Dan said. "Give my love to Esperanza." He ended the call.

Ben continued driving. "Noticed that you gave a shoutout to that adopted girl again."

"Sweetest kid ever."

"So you do like children."

"I like that one."

"Because you spent time with her. Got to know her. But there's no substitute for having one of your own. Seriously, Dan. Don't wait forever. Life is short."

"Deep. Did you come up with that yourself?"

It wasn't the morning, lunch, or evening rush hour—but traffic was still dense and confusing, with too many twisting highways on which everyone drove too fast and changed lanes without signaling.

"Hate this traffic," he muttered. "Worse than New York."

"Agreed. At least in New York City, you've got something to look at. Here it's just big ugly buildings and billboards."

"Isn't it supposed to be swimming pools, movie stars?"

"People in that tax bracket don't drive the highways. They are driven."

Eventually, thanks to Google Maps, he found the building that housed the Last Chance Lawyers' LA office. He parked and they walked to the front lobby.

This office, like all the others, identified itself as EVELYN ENTERPRISES.

"I get that you don't want to advertise the LCL name," Dan said, "given how many whack jobs have a problem with lawyers. But who's Evelyn?"

"My mother. Who always said her children were her most precious gift. Even when we didn't get along." He paused. "I remember when Christina told me we were expecting. It changed everything. Changed my whole life."

Dan smirked. "Did you start crying?"

"Didn't have the luxury. I was dismantling a bomb at the time."

"Whaaaaat?"

"Long story."

The station just opposite the elevator doors looked like a receptionist's desk. But there was no receptionist.

"Maybe they're having a late lunch. Or early Happy Hour."

Since they couldn't find a soul on the ground floor, they invited themselves up.

"Gary's office is on the second floor," Ben explained, as they climbed an interior staircase.

Dan placed a hand on his chest, holding him back. "Maybe we should think twice about this?"

"We traveled a zillion miles to talk to this guy. Now you want to call it off?"

Dan leaned in closer. "Do you remember what happened the last time we visited someone at their office unannounced?"

"You mean in Roswell?"

"We found a guy with a bullet in his head."

"Just stay calm."

"When was the last time you checked in with this Gary?"

"I don't know. I put you in charge of the LCL operation."

They stood outside a closed office door. Eventually, Dan knocked. No reply.

"He's not expecting us," Ben said.

"That much is clear."

Dan drew in his breath. "Okay. Going in." Another deep breath. "Because just because we found a corpse once doesn't mean—"

He pushed the door open.

Even before he spotted the body, he saw the blood.

His eyelids closed like curtains. "We are cursed."

# CHAPTER THIRTY-SIX

DAN INSTINCTIVELY AVERTED HIS EYES. HOW COULD THIS BE HAPPENING again? Had he become some kind of murder magnet?

He noticed his companion was staring straight at the bloody mess. "Look, Ben, I can handle this without—"

Ben stopped him with a curt head shake. "Something is wrong."

"We should call the police."

"Yes. And then search the place while we wait for them to arrive. But something is still wrong."

"Because corpses keep dropping like rain?"

"No. Because this place doesn't smell."

Dan pondered for a moment. "You expected a lawyer's office to be a big stinkfest?"

"Do you recall what the Roswell office smelled like?"

"Not good."

"That's what happens when a corpse has been decomposing, especially in a small closed space. Death has a distinctive smell. Learned that thirty-odd years ago at the Creek Estate Lodge, not that anyone cares." He closed his eyes and inhaled deeply. "But I don't smell it here. And do you know why?"

Dan turned his eyes back to the desk.

Wait a minute. There was a huge blood splatter on the back wall. Or what he took to be a blood splatter. But that corpse...

He felt the air rush out of his lungs. What an idiot he'd been. You see one corpse and then you start seeing them everywhere...

It was a lawyer's doll, a life-size articulated mannikin, dressed and reclining in the desk chair covered with blood or something that looked like it. Upon closer inspection, he saw a knife sticking out of the doll's stomach, and a twist of the left leg that would be impossible for normal human anatomy.

"It isn't Gary," Dan murmured. "It isn't anyone. It isn't real."

"It's real," Ben said. "It just isn't what we thought it was."

"It's...a supremely grisly escape room?"

"No. A re-created crime scene."

"I assume the crime didn't take place here. Who would reproduce a crime scene here?"

"I would."

They both whirled and saw a third man had joined them. He was taller than both of them, wore a well-pressed pinstriped suit, and carried a large catalogue case. Like a briefcase, only bigger. Which proved he was a lawyer.

Ben extended his hand. "You must be Gary Quince."

Gary's lips parted. He seemed starstruck. "Are—Are you Mr. K? For reals?"

Dan chuckled. "You've never actually met the Boss, have you?" He gestured dramatically toward his companion. "This is the man you want. The one and only Ben Kincaid."

"Thanks for outing me." Ben gave Gary a handshake. "Congratulations on all the work you've done running this office. That case you handled last month for the German Shepherd was fantastic."

Gary shuffled his feet. "I thought it turned out well."

Dan squinted. "We have a dog case? You handled a dog case?"

Ben made a tsking noise. "Maybe you need to get more involved with the cases you supervise. Gary fought hard to preserve the dog's fortune. And to make sure he always had a place to stay."

"You defended a dog?"

Gary nodded. "Baxter's late master's wishes were clearly expressed in his will. But greedy relatives were trying to screw the pooch, so to speak. As if they didn't already have more money than they could spend. We set things right."

"Bravo."

"I mean, we normally represent deserving people. But I don't see anything wrong with squeezing in a deserving doggie every now and again. This was a rescue dog. Spent five years at the fire department saving lives. I think it's nice that Baxter and his clan will have a nice place to live." Gary seemed distracted. "I suppose you're wondering about Bernie here."

"Bernie?"

"Just a little joke. You know, like in that movie."

Dan and Ben looked at him blankly.

"Not film buffs? Doesn't matter. I use Bernie to stage the crime scene for myself and sometimes in the courtroom. The cops aren't always so cooperative about allowing defense counsel access to the evidence. And sometimes their photos are unhelpful and they've missed angles that might be useful. And sometimes I like to immerse myself in the scene, you know. Just soak it in. As if I were there when it happened."

Ben nodded. "That's actually kind of brilliant. I wish I'd thought of this. A long time ago."

"I prefer talking to witnesses who are actually alive," Dan said. "I can observe more."

"You can absorb information in a makeshift crime scene too," Gary insisted. "It just takes longer. My client in this case is the victim's family, who insist he did not kill himself, all appearances to the contrary. They want his name cleared."

"Any reason why he would kill himself?"

Gary shrugged. "Talented guy, major agency, hasn't had an acting job for two years."

"Then he might as well die," Dan murmured.

"That's pretty much the thinking in this town," Gary replied. "Show business is cutthroat. You start out being patient, and before long you're starving to death."

"What happened to him?" Ben asked.

"Corpse was found in his office. Receptionist monitored the only door. Says no one went in or out. Cops think he killed himself."

"But you think the receptionist is guilty," Ben said.

"Very logical. But not correct. And it can't be suicide."

"Why?" Dan asked.

"The wound is too high," Ben said quietly.

Gary nodded. "Exactly. No one would stab themselves at that angle. Most people couldn't get a knife through their ribs. They'd stab themselves lower, in the gut. Assuming they were going to stab themselves at all. It's about the most painful way possible to off yourself."

"Much simpler to cut your throat," Dan agreed. "Or there are at least twelve other ways to kill yourself quicker. But if it wasn't suicide, how did anyone get in here without being noticed?"

"I haven't figured that out yet," Gary said. "But now that I've eliminated the impossible…"

"…whatever remains, however improbable, must be true." Ben smiled. "Good work, Sherlock."

"Thanks."

Ben pivoted. "We have to talk about the Donovan case."

A sour expression crossed Gary's face. "Do we?"

"Didn't you file a Motion for New Trial?"

"I've got to get David acquitted. There's no death penalty in California, but he'll get life. He's already dying and a life sentence could make him ineligible for the medical services he needs. So in effect, it's a death sentence."

"I remember. That's why LCL took the case. What's the problem?"

"I've worked it from every possible angle. It's unwinnable. I tried to withdraw, but the judge wouldn't allow it. He's not granting any more continuances. And I don't have anything powerful enough to set aside a jury verdict."

"There's always a way."

"I've received death threats. Pertaining to this case. Someone very much wants me to disappear. Or to lose the case. Or both. I'm afraid they might come after me. Or someone I love."

Dan and Ben exchanged a meaningful look.

"Do you have a partner?" Dan asked.

"Girlfriend."

"Kids?"

"Not yet."

"Call her right now. Send her somewhere safe."

"I've told her about the situation and—"

"That's not enough."

"I could call a friend in security who—"

Dan grabbed him by the collar. "You're not listening to me, Gary. Get her somewhere safe now!"

Gary was startled by the abrupt change of demeanor. Ben tried to intervene between them, but Dan wouldn't budge.

"Okay, I'll call her," Gary acquiesced.

"Better yet, let's take her right now. Somewhere safe."

Gary squirmed. "She's working—"

"I don't care. Tell her to drop everything."

Gary pushed him away. "Would you stop? I'm the one who got the death threats."

"But," Ben said quietly, "he's the one who understands how serious that can be."

Dan raised his hands. "I'm sorry. But my partner has disappeared and...and...I'm worried about her."

Gary's lips parted. "I'm sorry. I didn't know."

Ben inserted himself between them. "Look, let's calm down and get organized. Has anyone ransacked your files?"

"Not to my knowledge."

"Good. Just this once, we may be ahead of the Reaper."

"Who? What?"

"If he hasn't gone after your files then he isn't in LA yet. Gary, I want to know everything you've got on the Donovan case, even if you think it's dead in the water. Apparently our killer isn't so sure or he wouldn't be hassling you."

"But what's his interest in this case? And why hassle me? My chances of success are slender to none."

"But still sufficient to create some worry. First, we hide your girl-friend. Or better yet, maybe you take that long vacation you've been planning. When I hired you, I didn't know I was putting you on the firing line."

"But I still have to show up at the hearing."

Ben turned toward his traveling companion. "Dan, if I'm not mistaken, you've been missing the courtroom, right?"

He shrugged loosely. "Maybe a little..."

"Good. Gary, start packing. Your bosses are taking over."

# CHAPTER THIRTY-SEVEN

As the three of them headed down Grand Avenue, Dan was astonished and delighted by the concept of walking to the courthouse. Back in St. Petersburg, their office was on an island so driving downtown was necessary. But Gary just walked, drinking in the sunshine, waving at friends in food trucks and dodging street peddlers hawking maps to the stars' homes.

"You do this every day?"

"Just about," Gary replied. "Keeps me fit. My girlfriend says it gives me strong thighs. And she really likes that because—"

"Not necessary to explain," Ben said, raising his hands. "We have imaginations."

"You know, it's not just about thrusting power. It's about angle and rhythm and—"

"TMI, dude. Stop."

Dan grinned. "My friend is a bit on the bashful side. Is she somewhere safe?"

"Yes."

"And she's okay with this?"

Gary shrugged a little. "I...indicated to her that...we were going skiing. Sun Valley. She could lead and I'll follow her as soon as possible."

"She likes to ski?"

"Loves it."

"Me too. She'll be safe and happy. Perfect." He crossed the street and, sure enough, spotted the Stanley Moss Courthouse, part of the Los Angeles County Superior Court system.

"Fun fact. Stanley Moss is the largest courthouse in the country," Gary informed them. "More than one hundred courtrooms."

"Sounds like a rat maze."

"At times, it is. Come on, let's take the Hill Street entrance. It'll save us some time."

They crossed at the corner. The stone edifice looked more or less like every other courthouse he'd ever seen in his life—except immense.

Dan noted many people he suspected were lawyers, but much more casually dressed than his norm. Lots of floral colors, Aloha shirts, ascots—even a Looney Tunes necktie. It seemed standards were different on the West Coast.

And to think he got a rep for being eccentric just by carrying a backpack.

"The judges don't enforce dress codes here?"

"Depends on the judge. We have more than a hundred and they're all different. But as long as it's a hearing and not an actual trial, most judges are pretty chill."

"I can't imagine appearing before a judge without a tie."

Gary shrugged. "I've known judges who appeared without their pants. I mean, under their robes. It gets hot sometimes."

"Tell me more about this Donovan case," Dan said. "I don't want the judge to think I'm clueless."

Gary nodded. "Worst case of wrongful conviction I've ever seen. The cops only grabbed David because he had an obvious motive. I didn't handle the trial, but I wish I had, because his lawyer missed a lot."

"And you're trying to fix it after the fact."

"Yeah, and you know what the odds are there. The hearing is set for Monday. The clock is ticking down fast."

"The judge will see your motion as a desperate last-ditch effort to save your client."

"And consequently, he'll expect drama but little genuine legal argument."

"We have to change that."

"We need fraud," Ben said. "Or newly discovered evidence. Something that compels the judge to take a closer look."

"Easy to say," Gary muttered. "Hard to produce." He glanced over his shoulder. "We're a little early. Am I the only one who's hungry? I know a Mexican food truck that's fabulous. Dan, how about you?"

Come to think of it, when was the last time he ate? "Do they have veggie tacos?"

"Dude, this is LA. They have veggie tacos, gluten-free tacos, dairy-free tacos, seitan tacos. I don't even know what seitan is, but people order it."

The man inside the truck appeared more Asian than Hispanic, but the hot sauce was homemade and at the end of the day, all he cared about was how it tasted.

And it tasted very good indeed.

"This is a superb taco."

"And the reason to always come by Hill Street. It has the best food trucks."

While they ate, Gary continued his summary. "This took place at a local music college. Julliard of the West, they call it. Like Berklee, but smaller. Donovan was a student, as was the victim, a young music major named Claudia Wells. Talented violinist. From Cleveland, originally. She was murdered. The cops arrested Donovan."

Ben tried to recall the details. "Claudia had something valuable in her dorm room, right?"

"She was the heir to a huge fortune. Daddy's only daughter and he spoiled her shamelessly. He's big in undergarments."

"Excuse me?"

"His firm makes bras and panties for top retail outlets. Victoria's Secret and the like."

"What did she have in the dorm?" Dan asked. "Jewelry?"

Gary shook his head. "No, it was—"

Ben interrupted. "A Stradivarius." He snapped his fingers. "No. An Amati."

Gary's head turned slowly. "You must've read that in the file."

"No. I doubt she'd keep a diamond necklace in the dorm, but she might keep a violin there if she played regularly. The obvious choice would be a Strad." Ben raised a finger. "But despite the high rep the Strads have in popular culture, they are relatively common. Last I heard there were about 650 Strads, mostly in private hands. But only fourteen Amatis survived the French Revolution."

Dan tilted his head. "Impressive."

"Well, I was also a music major. Music Theory, actually."

"Seriously? Why?"

Ben shook his head. "Long story."

"Give me the short version."

"It made my father crazy."

"Say no more." Dan turned back to Gary. "What's the value of the missing violin?"

"It's been off the market for more than a decade, so it's impossible to say for sure. But the last comparable Amati sold for $900,000."

Dan whistled. "This family wanted nothing but the best."

Gary nodded. "And that might be why Claudia is dead."

"Where did she keep it?"

"She had a safe in her dorm room. Good one. Strong. Digital."

"Had the safe been cracked?"

"Nope. Just opened and emptied. While Claudia Wells bled out on the floor. Neck wound. Carotid artery. Didn't take long."

"Let me guess," Dan said. "Donovan knew the safe combination."

"Worse. As far as I can tell, he was the only person who knew the combo, other than Claudia herself."

"Why would she tell him?"

"They were friends. Students speculated that they were romantic, but he denies it."

"Other suspects?"

"The cops say no. I say, at least three. Another guy in the dorm. A professor, one Claudia seemed to have some contact with outside the classroom. And her physician."

Dan wondered if that was the same doc who was friends with the doc Helm mentioned. "If there are multiple suspects, why was your man arrested? And convicted?"

"Claudia's rich family pushed hard for an arrest, then a conviction. They're all certain Donovan is guilty. And there was some hard evidence against him. He's deeply in debt. Medical bills have destroyed him."

"Could he sell that violin? Seems like any potential buyer would know it was stolen."

"Apparently it can be done. Or so the DA alleged."

"Anything else?"

Gary shrugged. "Claudia and David both had an abiding love for Haydn symphonies. They were seen together at concerts on many occasions by many people."

"Sounds like true love."

"And they both had medical issues. He has kidney problems. She was somewhere on the autistic spectrum. They say her neurodiversity made her an incredibly focused musician." He drew in his breath. "And someone few wanted to work with. They had to draw straws to get someone to do a capstone with her. Other than David, no one wanted to play a duet with that woman. Difficult, exacting, and tended to swear constantly. Might be some Tourette's mixed in there somewhere."

"I'm surprised you don't have the Wells crime scene on display."

"If I'd handled the trial, I would have. But as you know, for this motion, I can't retry the case. I have to find a legal argument that enti-tles David to a new trial."

"What was at the crime scene? Other than a body?"

"A lot of blood. A messy desk. Much unfinished homework. Dirty clothes. A broken pickleball racket. A musical score she was writing. A diary with a lot of passages that make no sense."

"Such as?"

"Inside cover. Only three short words. *Military drumroll surprise.*"

Ben and Dan looked at one another.

"What?" Dan said. "Did you think I was going to solve the mystery in five seconds?"

"I was hoping." Ben looked away. "Sometimes I expect too much of you…"

"The Final Jeopardy music is still playing. Give me some time." He turned to Gary. "Could that be the name of a piece she was learning? A Sousa march or something?"

"Definitely not."

"Some kind of music notation? Like, legato or…glissando."

Gary bit down on his lower lip. "I don't think so."

"Was she in the military? Did she play the drums?"

Gary shook his head. "No one has any idea what it means. Except Claudia. And she can't tell us. But somehow we have to get David a new trial."

Ben nodded. "I work best under pressure. Let's go see the judge."

# CHAPTER THIRTY-EIGHT

DAN EXPLAINED THE SITUATION AS SLOWLY AND CAREFULLY AS POSSIBLE, but Judge Durant did not appear sympathetic. He was an older judge, early sixties probably, with a shock of white hair and a craggy face. He stirred his tea in a porcelain cup that appeared to illustrate a scene from *Tom Sawyer*.

"Don't like carpetbaggers in my courtroom," he grumped. They sat in his chambers, which appeared to be decorated primarily with USC memorabilia.

The assistant district attorney assigned to the case, Liz Chee, spoke. "Your honor, this is just a delaying tactic."

"Excuse me," Dan said, "but we haven't asked for a delay. In fact, we don't want a delay. We want to get this done as soon as possible."

"There's a trick in there somewhere, judge. I guarantee it."

"The only trick," Dan countered, "is that we think this murder was not committed by David Donovan. And it is somehow connected to other murders elsewhere. Give us a chance to prove it."

Chee rolled her eyes. "They're desperate. It's almost embarrassing. Stand aside and let us put the man away forever."

"Forever won't be long," Ben said. "He has serious medical issues.

He was in line for a kidney transplant, but if this conviction stands, his chances of getting it are poor."

"They can't take his name off the list," Judge Durant said. "That would be considered discriminatory."

"But the people who make the decisions weigh many factors. And a convicted murderer isn't gonna rise to the top of the list."

Judge Durant nodded. "You may be right about that. But you're asking for post-conviction relief. That's extremely rare, and for good reason. If we start re-trying every verdict someone doesn't like, every case will go on forever."

"This is a special circumstance. We want to do right by this client. Because we genuinely believe him to have been wrongfully convicted."

Judge Durant twisted around in his chair. "Don't like this. Don't like it one bit. There's an established procedure for these things, and anytime we disrupt the natural order, we're asking for trouble."

"But what if we're right?" Ben asked. "What if Donovan is innocent? Yes, we have established procedures, and all those procedures are designed to attain one goal. Fairness. Hard as we try, we do sometimes make mistakes. And that's why we always leave the door a little bit ajar, always make it possible to correct an injustice." Ben looked the judge straight in the eye. "Like this one."

Judge Durant sat silently for several more moments. Dan sensed not so much indecision—he'd already made up his mind—but a reluctance to do what he knew needed to done.

Durant turned to Gary. "You can vouch for these two?"

"I can, your honor. I've moved that they be admitted to the local bar pro hac vice so they can work on this case. I'll happily sponsor them."

The judge turned to Dan and Ben. "You don't have much time. We are not delaying the hearing."

Dan nodded. "Understood, your honor. It's not so much of a change as it seems. Donovan has always been a client of our firm. We're just making in-house staffing reassignments. We're partners in law."

"More like partners in crime," Chee murmured.

The judge thought another moment, then shook his head, making his jowls tremble. "All right. I'll allow it. Just to be sure we haven't made an unfortunate mistake. But I expect everyone to be ready as soon as I bang the gavel Monday morning."

"Thank you, your honor. You won't be sorry."

"I already am."

---

DAN LED THE PARTY OUTSIDE. "CONGRATULATIONS, TEAM. WE'RE BACK in the ballgame."

Gary followed him through the revolving door. "That went much better than I expected."

Ben winked. "Dan is an extremely persuasive litigator."

"It did feel good to be arguing for a client again," Dan said. "Doing something I'm good at."

An Asian woman stepped in front of him, blocking his passage. She wore a dark suit, dark straight tie, and sunglasses.

"Excuse me," he said. "I'm crossing here."

The woman raised her hand. A second later, two men, similarly dressed, appeared beside and behind her. "You're not going anywhere, Mr. Pike."

Ok, not just a mugger. "You think you and your goons can stop me?"

She smiled thinly, then withdrew a small badge from her coat pocket. "I'm certain I can. FBI."

---

DAN PEERED ACROSS THE CRAPPY METAL TABLE THAT SEPARATED HIM from his inquisitor, who he now knew was FBI Special Agent Courtney Zhang. She was slight in figure but came on like a powerhouse. Her hair was pulled back in a severe bun.

Even though Dan and Ben were perfectly willing to talk at the courthouse, Agent Zhang insisted on bringing them to the local FBI office. She let Gary go but insisted she wanted to talk to Ben and Dan. Separately.

Dan leaned across the metal table. It rocked. He was not surprised to learn that the legs were uneven. He suspected the feds shaved them. Just one more unsettling detail to throw the perp off-balance.

"Is this because my DA friend called an FBI friend?"

"Jazlyn's report did move the case onto the front burner. She was trying to help."

Dan nodded. No good deed goes unpunished...

"Let take this from the top," Zhang said. She was the only officer in the room, though Dan felt certain others were watching through the obvious two-way mirror on the north wall. "What brings you to LA?"

"I'm a lawyer. I work for a firm. My boss wants me to handle a case here."

"And when you refer to your boss, you're talking about Benjamin Jonah Kincaid?"

"Didn't know his middle name was Jonah. No wonder he has such bad luck."

"So you have crossed the US to handle this case at the last possible moment?"

"I started crossing the country because my partner disappeared."

She gave him a look that was...a smirk? A sneer? It was almost as if she was being playful. "You violated a direct law enforcement order to stay in St. Petersburg. Your partner has not been found. But instead of looking for her back home, you're traveling to California to handle a motion for new trial with a near-zero chance of success?"

Dan shrugged. "I specialize in last chances."

"Regular Don Quixote."

"I have tilted at a few windmills in my time. What exactly are you investigating?" He paused. "You know the corpse in Gary's office is just a dummy, right?"

Zhang gave him a withering look. "Yes, oddly enough, I can tell the difference. I've also seen pics of the corpse you left behind in Roswell. And I've read reports of your various car chases, barroom brawls, and gas-station assaults. Seems you boys have made quite an impression during your cross-country jaunt."

Dan felt a thumping in his chest. Agent Zhang knew more than he realized. "The Roswell cops didn't suspect us. They let us go."

"Not that you would've listened if they'd asked you to stay." Zhang opened her briefcase, then removed a file and a few color photos. She spread them across the table and pushed them his way.

"Gruesome scene, wasn't it?"

Roswell. Dan had seen this before and didn't need to see it again. "They thought it was a cartel rubout."

"That's certainly how it looks." She narrowed her eyes. "A little too perfectly, don't you think?"

"Possibly a frame."

"If it was a frame, why did you follow the Ferrari to the biker bar?"

Dan gave her a long look. He could see she was enjoying this, trickling out what she knew bit by bit. "I was thirsty."

"Before or after you decked a guy?"

"Both."

Zhang leaned across the table till they were practically forehead-to-forehead. "Look, we know about the murders. All of them. We know someone grabbed your girl and now is out to get you, which is the only reason we don't think you're the murderer."

"Thank you for that."

"But you could well be associated with this cartel. Gang tries to establish a new location, sends a few boys to set it up, lives get lost. Roswell would be a great location for them. After *Breaking Bad*, drug dealers are afraid to go to Albuquerque. Too obvious."

"I don't know anything about this new Cartel 2.0. I'm just here to represent my client."

"I'm going to stretch my legs a bit. Get some coffee. Have a smoke. I want you to think hard about this situation you're currently in. Whether you'd like to make your court date. Whether you'd like to keep your law license. Whether you'd like to trade your hotel room for the jailhouse."

She pushed out of her chair, which made a nerve-grating screech.

Dan did not budge. "You're lying."

She did a double-take. "Excuse me? That's usually my line."

"You're not going for a smoke. You probably don't smoke, judging by your fingers and teeth. When you leave here you're going to whatever room you've got my pal Ben locked up in. You'll give him the same routine. Try to wear him down. Then you'll grab a friend so you can do good-cop-bad-cop and see who breaks first. Which will be neither of us. Because we haven't done anything wrong."

Her head bobbed. "Not bad, Mr. Pike. You're smarter than you look."

He decided not to return that compliment. "Ben won't crack. He's super-honest. Like, Cub-Scout-leader honest. Why do you think he created this huge legal network for clients who need lawyers? Because he's one of those rare souls who actually cares about others enough to go the extra mile and spend some money to help them."

"Aww, that's so sweet."

"He wants to get to the bottom of this, just like you do."

"Then what do you suggest?"

Dan drew in his breath. "I suggest you let me outta here so I can figure out what really happened. 'Cause you aren't even close."

---

BEN WAS STARTLED BY THE CLANGING OF THE METAL DOOR AS IT slammed against the barren wall.

Courtney Zhang, stood in the passageway, her arms akimbo. After a brief stare-down, she strode to the chair, turned it backward and sat astraddle, leaning toward the table with an imposing glare.

Ben sighed. Bad cop.

Zhang spoke through clenched teeth. "You think you're pretty smart, don't you?"

"If I were really smart, I wouldn't be stuck in your office."

"Do you have any idea how much trouble you're in?"

"Since I haven't committed a crime, I'm going to venture—none."

"No crime? We know chapter and verse about you, buddy. And the string of injuries and crashed cars you've left behind you on this cut-rate Badlands cross-country trek.'

Hmm. She was more aware than he expected.

"You know," she continued, "we talked to the guy you left behind at that gas station."

"Cheyenne Pete?" Ben nodded. "He tried to kill Dan and me?"

"Why would he want to kill you?"

"Someone hired him."

"To take you out?" She stared at him in disbelief. "So you're Johnny Dangerous? 'Cause you look more like a book nerd."

"Both could be true."

Her eyes narrowed. "Was it the other guy? Pike? I don't see you as mob muscle, but that other clown could do the job. Give me the goods on him. I'll make it worth your while."

Ben had to cover his mouth. She probably wouldn't appreciate it if he laughed in her face. "You want me to rat out Dan? You're playing one of us against the other? How stupid do you think we are?"

"Your pal gave me some very interesting information. I gotta tell you—it doesn't look good for you."

Ben just smiled. "Who's lying now?"

She pounded her fists on the metallic table. "Stop screwing around. We've got you on major charges—assault and battery, road rage, maybe even murder. You're looking at serious prison time if you don't cooperate."

"I am cooperating."

"You haven't told me a damn thing!"

"I've told you a lot. It just wasn't what you wanted to hear."

"If you're still claiming you traveled all the way here for some case—"

"It's the truth."

"Did you consider a Zoom call? Would've saved you a lot of time and money."

"You don't take shortcuts when people's lives are on the line."

"Are you talking about the cartel?"

"You know, I keep hearing about a cartel, but I know next to nothing about it. I wonder if anyone does."

"And yet, they want to kill you."

"My friend helped take down a cartel in Florida. This may be retribution. Are you aware that they kidnapped his partner?"

"So he says. But I note that you and your pal are still fine and dandy. It's just everyone around you who keeps disappearing."

Ben pushed back from the table. There had to be a better way to do this. "I've always cooperated with law enforcement."

"Is that why you stopped in McAlester to visit a pal in prison?"

"Dan's pal, not mine. Dan thought he might have some useful information. And he did. He sent us to Roswell."

"How convenient. Did he say who's trying to kill you?"

"No."

"Who do you think it is?"

Ben thought a moment. "I think someone seriously does not want our motion to succeed. Which makes me all the more determined to see that it does. May I make a suggestion or two?"

"I can't stop you from talking."

"First of all, cut the bad-cop act. You're not scaring me."

"Maybe solitary will change your mind."

Ben rolled his eyes. "Second, tough though you are, my wife is sixteen times tougher and I've been living with her for a good long time. So you aren't going to scare me. I'm immune."

"I'd like to meet that woman."

"You may get the opportunity, if you hold me much longer. And you will not enjoy it. So instead of acting as if we're antagonists, why don't we work together?"

"I don't make deals with suspects."

Ben waved his hands in the air. "Your funeral."

"Maybe I should let you stew in jail for three or four days. You might be more talkative afterward."

"You're not going to lock me up."

"You sure about that? You've planted a lot of suspicious seeds. Time for the harvest."

"You don't have probable cause. If you did, you'd have already read me my rights. Let me give you a tip, based upon my years of experience. Not everyone you encounter is an arch-felon. Sometimes cooperation is better than antagonism. And sometimes listening is more valuable than talking."

"Gee whiz, I thought I was interrogating a criminal, but turns out I got a private audience with the Dalai Lama."

Ben tucked in his chin but kept his mouth shut. Wait for it, he told himself. Five, four, three, two…

"Okay, just for laughs, how do you propose that we cooperate?"

"You let Dan and I go. We'll investigate the Donovan case and find out what's going on. If we learn anything about the cartel or the murders or anything else of value to you that does not violate attorney-client privilege, we will relay that information immediately. Basically, you'll be getting two free investigators. It's a win-win."

"I've dealt with lawyers before. Anytime you want something, they claim it's protected by privilege."

"I have an ethical obligation to maintain client confidentiality and if I violate that, even for an FBI agent, I'll be drummed out of the bar. But I won't assert privilege unless it's a valid claim."

"So you say. I don't know you from Adam."

"I don't know you from Eve. But I think you're smart. And I think you know Dan and I aren't murderers. So let us do what we came here to do. If this mysterious murderer is worried we'll get Donovan off, he might make a mistake."

"Or kill you," Zhang suggested, still right up in his face.

"Yes, that would be the other possibility. But I'm not willing to stand by quietly and watch an innocent man die in prison for a crime he did not commit. Are you?"

# CHAPTER THIRTY-NINE

DAN SPENT ANOTHER TWO HOURS AT THE FBI OFFICE UNTIL, WITHOUT explanation, Agent Zhang returned and released him. She gave no explanation at all, but he suspected it wasn't because she found him so charismatic. She took all possible contact info, including their hotel room numbers. Clearly she wanted to stay in touch. If not watch them every second.

Afterward, they returned to Gary's office at EVELYN ENTERPRISES. Gary had already split. They started poring through the files he left behind.

"Did you know the cops also found flecks of skin under Claudia's fingernails?" Dan asked. "The DNA matched Donovan."

"Lots of ways that could happen."

"There's also evidence that Claudia and David got into an angry Twitterstorm."

"If the cops arrested everyone who got into a Twitterstorm," Ben replied, "they would be busy. Like, for years. Getting a judge to overturn a jury verdict requires major-league evidence of misconduct or injustice."

"Yes, thanks, tell me something I don't already know. I'll keep looking. Maybe something will turn up."

Ben took a chair. "Since I'm technically your employer, let me give you a piece of advice. The critical evidence never just 'turns up.' And the cops are never going to give it to you. The only way to get what you want is to get up and start digging."

"Didn't you use an investigator when you were practicing?"

"I did. Best PI ever. But that never stopped me from turning over a few rocks myself. And that's what we're going to have to do now. We don't have time for anything else."

---

DAN ROLLED UP HIS SLEEVES. GARY LEFT THEM WITH OVER FORTY Bankers boxes of documents. They couldn't read them all in a weekend. They couldn't read them all in a week. And they were expected to argue this case in court in only a few days.

It didn't help that Gary's office was what Maria would call a "rat's nest." How he ever found anything Dan couldn't imagine. He probably couldn't, which might help explain why Gary was so certain he was about to go down in flames. The boxes appeared to have no organizational rhyme or reason. He had no evidence notebook, no witness outlines. Worse, his office smelled like tuna fish. Note: Throw away the smelly trash in the bathroom, not the office.

Around eight, Ben suggested that Dan go out for tacos. Dan wasn't sure if Ben was hangry or what, but he did not object to getting out of the cramped office and stretching his legs a bit.

When Dan returned, barely half an hour later, the office was transformed. At first he thought Ben had spent the time housecleaning. No, the joint still smelled like tuna fish. But the boxes were arranged in stacks. Each box was labeled. In half an hour, Ben had turned a nightmare into a professional-looking lawyer's office.

"You've been a busy bee."

Ben nodded, not looking up, still sorting documents. "Hope you don't mind. My mother was a neatnik. Couldn't stand messes."

"And you got her genes?"

"I certainly didn't get it from my father. We never agreed on anything and I never did anything that pleased him. But organization? That's the most important skill they don't teach in law school."

Dan pulled one of the boxes close and scanned the contents. "You've done more than tidying here."

"First I pulled all the court filings. They should've been organized in chronological filing order in a loose-leaf notebook. Now they are. Would be better if they were scanned into digital files, but we don't have time. I put everything the DA sent in those boxes in the far corner. They're stamped and numbered so we have a record of exactly what we were sent—and not sent."

"Far corner?"

"Because I know from experience that they won't contain anything useful. The DA doesn't want to help us, and even if there is anything useful in there, the trial lawyer would've already seen it. We need new information, not old. Gary has taken some interviews and made notes, but they're sketchy at best. There are at least three primary suspects other than David Donovan. I've compiled a box for each."

"You did all that while I was out for tacos?"

Ben shrugged. "Before she became a lawyer, my wife was a legal assistant. Best ever. She knew how to get ready for trial and she could do it fast—which she had to do for me on more than one occasion. She taught me a few tricks."

"So basically, the secrets to your success came from your mother and your wife."

Ben smiled. "Women rule the world. They just keep it to themselves."

"I'm beginning to see that."

"You're familiar with the SODDIT defense?"

Dan chuckled. "Some Other Dude Did It."

"First suspect: Mitch Theroux."

"Very suspicious name. I bet he's the one."

"Roomed in the dorms across the hall from the victim. Gary managed to get a screengrab of texts between the two. They spent a lot of time together for mere friends."

Dan grinned. "The world has passed you by. Kids don't go on dates anymore. They travel in packs. They hang out."

"And hook up," Ben muttered. "I'm not suggesting they were an official couple. But Mitch was working on it. Buying her gifts, inviting her to parties. Even offered to do her homework."

"Ok, he adored her. From afar."

"It's possible they had a drunken fling or something. His texts contain references to 'last night,' which she completely avoids."

"She ghosted him."

"Because she didn't want him to think it was ever going to happen again."

"Didn't the prosecutors portray Donovan as a jealous boyfriend?"

"Precisely. And maybe he had good cause. Or maybe he wasn't the jealous one. Maybe Mitch was pushing for more and Claudia wouldn't give him what he wanted."

Dan picked up the photo of the man in question. Short, stubbled, poorly dressed. Not bad looking, but not in that rich woman's league. "Ok, that might give him a motive for murder. But why take the violin? Did he play?"

"I don't think anyone could play that violin in public, at least not any time soon."

"Did Mitch have the combination to the safe?"

"He says he didn't. But it's possible. He might've watched Claudia get into it. Might've seen it scribbled down somewhere."

"Any other jealous stalkers?"

Ben pushed another Bankers box to the forefront. "Jealous stalker professor."

Dan removed a photo from the box. "Professor Wally Herwig. Bearded. Thick. At least twenty years older. This guy had no chance with her."

"Hope springs eternal in the human breast."

"Translation?"

"To quote an old friend of mine—love makes you do the crazy."

"A crush is not enough to make him a suspect. Got anything more?"

"She was doing a Work Study with him."

"Why does a rich girl need Work Study?"

"I gather it was a chance to advance her career. Make connections. Get inside the classical-music community."

"Does such a thing exist?"

"Of course. Professional musicians put in their ten-thousand hours. They have to."

"Sounds boring."

"Some people would say that about kite-surfing. Playing a violin is far less dangerous. Normally. Her diary records numerous invitations to various outings by this professor."

"Did she call him a creeper?"

"No. She saw the advantages of being his pal. And probably thought she was capable of keeping him at a distance. You haven't had a chance to read her diary and I haven't read much, but she was strong, not stupid."

"And the prof played the violin?"

"True, but a guy on his salary couldn't suddenly pop up with a near-priceless instrument."

"The judge isn't going to release our client based upon conjecture. We need evidence. Who's your third potential suspect?"

"Donovan's doctor."

"Okay. Now I'm confused."

"Me too. We need to talk to our client first thing tomorrow. He saw doctors regularly and sometimes Claudia went with him."

"Sounds like a saint."

"I'm beginning to suspect that, one way or the other, her generosity is what got her killed."

"Being our client's doctor doesn't create a murder motive. More like the exact opposite. Who is this?"

"The same doc our man in San Diego mentioned. Marilyn Southern. Nephrologist. Competent and professional. Excellent career. Educated, smart."

"I sense there's a 'but' coming."

Ben opened a file. "Maybe it's my imagination, but some of this correspondence seems off. In the first place, why is she discussing Donovan's condition with Claudia? She wasn't a spouse. Or a relative. Claimed she wasn't a romantic partner."

"Interesting. But not enough to overturn the case."

"Claudia Wells was talking to Donovan's doc about something. In her diary she wrote that she 'made an offer.' But gives no explanation."

"Offer…for the expensive violin? A bribe?"

"Wish I knew."

Dan pushed the boxes aside and peered across the table. "I don't want to offend, Ben, but you hired me for my legal skills, so I hope you won't mind if I offer an opinion. We do not have enough to win this motion. And I don't think we can dig up enough to change that."

"Which is why I—"

Dan heard a small buzzing noise. "Pardon me. Phone message." He put the cellphone on Speaker and laid it on the table. "Hello."

The long pause before anyone spoke was spookier than anything the caller could have said. Eventually, a voice emerged. It sounded male, but it also sounded like someone was using a voice disguiser, so that didn't mean much. "Daniel Pike?"

"Who else would answer my phone?"

"Is Mr. Kincaid listening?"

Dan felt a chill. Who would know that?

And then the voice started singing. "Here I come to save the daaaaaay!"

Ben and Dan exchanged a look.

"That's who you think you are, isn't it?" The voice laughed loudly. "Mighty Mouse! Or maybe I should say, Mighty Mice?"

"Who is this? What do you want?"

"Don't try to extend the conversation. You couldn't trace this call, even if I were stupid enough to talk long enough. I just have one short message for you two would-be crusaders. You are in over your heads. You have no idea who and what you're tangling with."

"So enlighten us."

"I could. But then I'd have to kill you." More laughter, even louder.

"Really?" Dan said. "What's going to happen if we continue doing our jobs?"

The voice acquired a growling, bitter edge. "You think your little fuck doll is safe? Let me tell you something. She's not. I can do anything I want with her."

Dan's fists tightened. His breathing was deep and uneven. Ben held up a hand, warning him to stay calm.

"I know where to find Christina, too," the voice continued. "And your daughters, Kincaid."

"What is it you want?"

"I want you to drop this case. Go back to Cowboy Country and never return. If you do as I advise, there's a slight chance you and your family might live."

"And if I don't?"

No pause at all. "Then you're going to die for your arrogance. Both of you. And you still won't win. But everyone you know and love will be dead."

# CHAPTER FORTY

I'VE BEEN A CAPTIVE LONG ENOUGH, MARIA THOUGHT. SHE WAS SICK OF it, desperate to be free.

And ready to resort to desperate measures.

So far, no one had visited or harassed her. But she was still trapped in the apartment or whatever it was. Plenty of bottled water, plenty of crappy snacks. But she was trapped. And she knew Dan must be going crazy with worry.

She almost wished the kidnapper would appear. At least she'd have someone to talk to, and might be able to devise an escape. But here, the monotony of captivity was the worst part. She felt like a bored lion trapped in zoo cage.

She didn't know why she'd been taken. But since she hadn't been harmed, she had to assume she was being held for ransom. Or someone was using her for leverage. Probably against Dan.

She had kicked, pried, and beaten on every square inch of this crappy enclosure. Nothing gave. Not even a little. The door was reinforced and deadbolted from the outside. There were no windows. She had tried screaming, as loud as she could manage, over and over again at various times during the day. No one seemed to hear.

And worst of all, she was sick to death of those granola bars.

Maybe the Grim Reaper didn't realize she would be incarcerated this long. She was grateful to have some food, but at this point, a PB&J would seem like a rare delicacy.

She'd maintained her exercise regimen and stayed as active as possible. But given her condition, she should be doing more. She needed to get out of here. Before the Reaper returned.

Was it possible she'd just been…parked? Put out of the way? If so, for how long?

Or was the assassin just too busy at the moment to kill her?

She didn't have all the answers. But she knew one thing for certain. She was sick of sitting around waiting, doing nothing. Especially when Dan might be in danger. At the very worst….

She preferred not think about it.

She couldn't think of a safe way to send a signal to the outside world. But she could think of several unsafe ways.

No matter where she was, smoke could be seen from a great distance. And usually attracted attention from neighbors, police, firefighters.

Unsurprisingly, the Reaper had not left her with a can of gasoline or a box of matches.

But there was a microwave in the kitchen. And a lot of paper towels.

She had to dig around under the sink, but she eventually found one standard kitchen item the Reaper should've removed, but didn't.

Aluminum foil.

She recalled reading articles by critics who complained that the ending of *Rain Man* wasn't realistic because the microwave fire started too easily—and then described what the filmmakers should've done.

She took four granola bars, soaked them in water, wrapped that in aluminum foil, then wrapped that in paper towels. She placed the concoction in the microwave. Then she pressed Start.

The microwave had been humming for less than a minute when she heard the first crackle. She knew microwaves don't like metal, but aluminum foil was thin, so that didn't necessarily guarantee a fire. But she locked water up in the mess and that water was turning into steam, releasing energy in the process. The energy had no release, so the foil heated quickly...

The first flame burst out on the foil. And since she'd wrapped it in paper, the fire spread fast. The package was also wet, though, so she threw a lot more paper on top and below it, effectively creating a trail. She put the granola boxes and anything else she thought would burn on the trail.

A few minutes later, she had an active fire in the kitchen. Several minutes later, smoke filled the apartment.

No windows, but the chimney flue was open. And she doubted the door was airtight.

Smoke signals always worked in Westerns. She was about to see how well they worked in real life.

Only two possible results. This could lead to her being discovered.

Or it could lead to her being incinerated.

Smoke billowed through the apartment, making her eyes water and her throat dry. She knew she couldn't last in this environment long. And it would only get worse.

She wedged herself in the most remote corner, covered her nose and mouth with her blouse, and waited.

---

DID SHE REALLY FALL ASLEEP? HOW COULD SHE BE SO STUPID? SMOKE must be getting to her. When she awoke, she could barely breathe. Her lungs already felt congested and scratchy.

The smoke was so thick she could not see a foot in front of her face. She breathed in short shallow sips, just enough to live, trying to block out the smoke with her teeth, which of course did not work at all.

Her head throbbed. Seemed like an eternity before she realized how foolish she'd been. No one was coming to save her. No one saw. No one knew. She was going to die in flames, a latter-day Joan of Arc, except considerably less saintly. Maybe she hadn't led a perfect life, but she didn't deserve to die. She didn't want to die. Especially now, when the future held so much promise...

Her eyes were fluttering. She knew she couldn't last much longer. She laid on the floor and let her eyes close. She needed to rest. She hoped Dan understood how much she loved him. His name was the last word on her lips and the last thought in her head. She just wished...

And then she succumbed to the darkness...

Which made it all the more surprising when she heard the crash on the other side of the door.

The door bulged but still held. Someone was shouting through a bullhorn. "Is anyone in there?"

A smile crossed her face. She shouted back as loudly as she could.

More pounding at the door. After a few more moments, it practically pulled out of the jamb.

It worked, she thought, as she closed her eyes. Maybe they were too late to save her. But at least she wasn't going to die the Grim Reaper's prisoner.

# Part Three

# PARTNERS IN LAW

# CHAPTER FORTY-ONE

SHELBY PILBARA HAD SPENT THE LAST TWO YEARS HIDING THE PAIN. BUT it got harder every day. Some mornings she couldn't even get out of bed. She stretched out, clutching her gut, hoping that applied pressure might help. It didn't. Even the pain meds Dr. Southern prescribed did precious little. She'd learned to separate her mind from her body, her outward expression from what she felt inside. The world saw a mask, a happy façade she chose to present the world.

Inside, her body was failing her, worse and worse each day.

And the pain was excruciating.

She felt humiliated, but there was nothing she could do about it. No whining! That was Momma's Rule No. 1.

Momma would be disappointed today.

She thought getting some fresh air might help, but it didn't. Griffith Park was wasted on someone who felt this bad and couldn't possibly appreciate it. She spread out across a park bench, curled in a fetal ball, trying not to cry, trying not to feel the inferno blazing within her. Unsuccessfully.

Someone came over to see if she was all right. Not a police officer, not a concerned citizen. A child. A small girl, maybe nine. Pigtails. Jumper. Stuffed panda.

"Are you okay, lady?"

Shelby took a deep breath. "Just need a minute."

"Do you want me to rub your tummy? That's what my daddy does when I'm sick."

"I don't think it's going to work today."

"Maybe a Slurpee? Slurpees make everything better."

"Just—" She drew in her breath, trying to keep it all inside. "I'll be fine. Just need a minute."

"Would you like to hold Maurice?"

Shelby opened one eye, just a little. The girl held a plush panda. Probably something she won or got from the gift shop.

"Hold her for a minute. You'll feel better after."

"Thank you, but—"

"Tammy! Tammy, come back right this minute!"

Her mother, no doubt, dragged the girl—and Maurice—away from this demented homeless-looking person on the park bench. Shelby didn't blame her. A mother's first and foremost job is to protect her child, and right now, Shelby did not look like someone you wanted to be your child's new playmate.

A relief, really. She was not in a conversational mood. And yet, after the girl left, Shelby found she actually missed her. How pathetic was that? Missing someone you'd known for about ten seconds.

She was falling apart.

Which was a nice way of saying she was dying.

She spent more than half an hour on the bench until she felt able to move again. She took the bus home, but it dropped her at a stop about half a mile away. Normally, that would be no problem. But today, she was not sure she could make the journey.

But she did. Momma was right. Skip the whining, grit your teeth, do what needs to be done. Her feet kept moving, one step at a time.

Dr. Southern had warned her there would be days like this. But help was on the way. The doctor made no guarantees but felt certain good news would arrive—before it was too late.

Shelby pulled herself forward, slowly. Her arms were strong even if her legs and everything else below her waist were weak.

She made it home. She opened the front door and stepped inside.

There was no explaining the comfort that came from being in your own space. This room, modest though it was, was hers. She had decorated it to her taste, which leaned toward brightly colored decorative items from Target's Home Decor department. Maybe others thought it was tacky, but to her it was paradise.

Why her? she asked for the millionth time. What did she do to deserve this? She was a good person. She was the healthiest eater she knew. She exercised regularly. No one else in her family had ever had this condition. It made no sense, no rhyme or reason, completely undeserved.

But it was reality. Her reality. If something didn't change fast, she'd be staring death right in the face.

She plopped down into a nearby chair. Television? No. She didn't feel like dealing with twelve different streaming services and figuring out which of ten thousand shows she wanted to watch. Maybe a little music. Chopin usually worked wonders at times like this. Maybe a string quartet. Nothing soothed the soul like being completely enraptured by a piece of music that—

Her head twitched. Did she hear something?

It sounded like it came from the kitchen.

Her heart pounded, even worse than it had before. Her fingertips clenched the padded chair.

Was it her imagination?

She heard another sound. Then another.

Footsteps.

Not her imagination.

Summoning all her strength, she shoved herself out of the chair.

The blade swung around barely a nanosecond behind her, plunging into the back of the chair, missing her by inches.

She jumped out of the way, pivoting as she did.

Barely five feet away, someone stood in a black robe and hood. The Grim Reaper. Death.

When she talked about staring death in the face, she thought she

was being metaphorical. But here he was, live and in person, determined to kill her. Was she hallucinating?

No, Death was definitely in the room with her.

Problem was, she wasn't ready to die. She hadn't fought this hard,
this long, to die like the pre-credits victim in a Scream movie.

A grim voice emerged from the hood. "It will be simpler if you
don't resist. You cannot escape." The Reaper raised a huge scythe, as if
preparing to strike the final blow.

"Forgive me if I don't go quietly."

"Every mortal life must end at the appointed time."

"And what makes you think my time has come?"

"That's my job." The Reaper swung the scythe. She managed to
scoot out of the way but couldn't help but notice that it was sleek and
shiny. Razor-sharp. Honed.

*Think!* she told herself. What did people do in horror movies, the
ones who survived?

They screamed, of course.

So she screamed. As loud and long as she could. Not so much out
of fright as the hope someone might hear. Where was her phone? She
needed to call 911. She raced up the stairs. Maybe he couldn't move
that fast in all that regalia. She tore into her bedroom and slammed
the door behind her.

Her heartbeat pounded like the two-note "Tudum" at the start of a
Netflix show. She could feel sweat dripping down her face. Just when
you think your life can't get any worse....

Only when she was behind a closed door, pressing her body
against it, did she realize how stupid she'd been. She should've run to
the kitchen, and from there, into the alley behind the house. Now she
was trapped. No doors on the second floor.

Only windows.

Gritting her teeth, she pulled her dresser in front of the door.
Probably wouldn't stop the Reaper for long. But it might give her time
to get a window open.

She flipped the lock. It was a long way down to the ground. She might hurt herself, twist an ankle or something, but that was better than being dead.

She pulled on the window, but she couldn't get it to budge. Had someone painted over this, without raising the window? It seemed glued down. Maybe if she—

The sudden noise made her jump and scream, both at once. Someone slammed against the door so hard it jostled the dresser.

Only a matter of time.

She put all her weight behind her weakened legs, using them to shove the window open. She heard the paint crack. Just a little, but she was making progress.

More pounding at the door. Her jewelry case spilled off the edge of the dresser, clattering as it hit the floor.

Come on, she thought, glaring at the window. Open!

This time the Reaper hit the door so hard the entire room reverberated. The mirror atop the dresser cracked.

She saw a gloved hand snake through the crack in the door.

She pushed with all her might. The window finally broke away. Creaking and groaning, she managed to get it up...

Just as the gloved hand wrapped around her throat.

She tried to cry out, but she couldn't. The Reaper pinched her larynx, making it difficult to breath. Impossible to shout.

She could whisper. Barely. "Why...me? What did I do?"

The reply was the most chilling she could imagine. "Nothing."

"Then—?"

"No fault. But you're on the list."

"List? What?"

"Shh. You don't understand. And I'm not going to explain it to you." He pinched her throat even harder and she felt her consciousness ebbing.

"You're...killing me."

"Sadly, that is my role in this drama. You're the next-to-last one. After Monday, my assignment will be complete."

Shelby felt the blackness surrounding her. "Who...gives instructions...to Death?"

The Reaper leaned in, applying the final fatal pressure. "Someone worse."

# CHAPTER FORTY-TWO

DAN SPENT MOST OF THE MORNING AT CLAUDIA WELLS' COLLEGE DORM, but he couldn't help feeling he was wasting his time. The music department seemed to have its own section, with an upscale mahogany-finish interior that looked far nicer than his undergraduate dorm back in Florida. This was more like West Coast Hogwarts.

Eventually he managed to find Mitch Theroux, the student who lived in the dorm and probably had a massive crush on Claudia.

Dan found him in a practice room banging away on a piano, playing from memory, and doing it spectacularly. He thought it was a Chopin prelude, but he was no classical music expert. More of a Johnny Cash guy.

Theroux must've noticed that he came in, but he did not let that interfere with his performance. He kept playing all the way to the dramatic crescendo. Then he paused, took a breath, and swiveled around on the piano stool.

"May I help you?"

"I hope so. I wanted to talk to you about Claudia Wells."

He rolled his eyes. "Thought as much. Your suit gives you away. I've talked to every law enforcement officer on earth and frankly, I'm tired of talking."

"I'm not law enforcement." He was almost offended. "Did you not notice the Air Jordans?"

"The case is over. Go away."

"The case has been reopened." Or at least, that's what he hoped to accomplish. "And I'm not law enforcement. I'm a lawyer. Representing David Donovan."

"The pissant who killed Claudia? Far as I'm concerned, that makes you just as despicable as the murderer."

"Yeah, I get that a lot." Dan took a step forward. "Give me five minutes, okay? Then I'll let you get back to your practicing."

"The mood has been destroyed. I need to walk. Purge your toxicity. Before I can create art again."

Oh, to be a college student once more. Maybe the best approach was to shake him out of his superiority. "How many times did you and Claudia sleep together?"

"I've been over this before. We were just friends."

"Friends with benefits?"

"Yeah. And the benefit was that we're both excellent musicians who liked to play together. Not under the sheets. In the concert hall."

"I've done some reading. Talked to a lot of people." If Mitch wasn't flat-out lying, he was certainly pushing the edges of truth. But he had to get the kid talking. "I'm not the only one who thinks the two of you had more history. Maybe you weren't actually dating. Maybe it was just a one-night fling. Maybe she regretted it. Maybe she woke up sober, felt humiliated when she saw you on the other side of the bed, and did the walk of shame right out of your life."

"Why would she do that?"

"C'mon, look at you. You're a geek and she was a princess. She was rich and you're...not. You've got no game and you had no chance. Unless maybe she was so drunk she barely knew what was happening. Maybe you said you'd help her back to her room and since she was unable to resist, you decide to have a little fun—"

"It wasn't like that at all!"

His words floated as if suspended for the next several seconds.

Dan grabbed a chair and pulled it closer to the piano bench. "Okay. Tell me what it *was* like."

---

BEN POWERED UP GARY'S MACBOOK. A FEW MINUTES LATER, HE figured out how to initiate a Zoom call.

Ben knew he should like Zoom calls. Given his natural awkwardness and social anxieties, any chance to avoid an in-person meeting should be welcome. But somehow, he found Zoom even more oppressive than phone calls. So awkward. And you had to worry about your appearance.

As it turned out, this call was the most delightful thing that had happened since Dan burst into his office and abducted him.

"*Loving*! Is it really you?"

"Live and in person, Skipper." The computer jostled on the other end, making the screen bounce up and down. For a few moments, his head turned sideways. "Sorry. Trudy is helpin'. I could never unnerstand this computer crap on my own."

"It is so good to see you." Loving had always been a large, imposing man. He was a little heavier and grayer than when they last had met, but he still looked strong and vigorous. The years had been kind. Of course, he always got lots of exercise, which was probably better for your health than sitting around reading law books. "Thanks for taking the call."

"Christina said you needed help. That's all I needed to know."

He still remembered when they first met, all those years ago. Particularly memorable, since Loving pulled a gun on him. Not too pleased with Ben's handling of his ex's divorce case. But they worked it out and before long Loving was Ben's go-to investigator, the man who more than once had uncovered the info he needed to protect an innocent client. Loving was, as he liked to say, a man of the people— which Ben was not. He could go places Ben couldn't and talk to people who wouldn't give Ben the time of day. He might have rural roots but he had proven himself plenty resourceful in the Big City.

"You look great, Loving."

"Wish I could return the compliment. But as my beloved granny used to say, you look like you've been rode hard and put away wet."

"It's been an unusual few days. And the next few are threatening to be even worse. I need—"

A pop-up box appeared on his computer screen. Someone else awaited permission to join the call.

Ben tapped the red button. A few moments later, another familiar face appeared.

"*Jones*! Now this is an official office reunion!"

"Good to see you, Boss." Jones had been, first his assistant, later his office manager, for many years. He was persnickety, fussy, and tended to whine. But he was also an early adopter of computers, and his digital resourcefulness had been critical on many occasions.

"Jones, I haven't seen you since…"

"Since you needed help getting Oz off the hook."

"Right, right. Why is it we only get together when there's work to do?"

Loving didn't hesitate. "Because you have poor social skills and prefer to be left alone."

"Well, I don't know about—"

"That's what Chrissy told us. She says when you started work at that law firm where the two of you met, most people thought you were unfriendly. Or stupid. But she liked you and she knew you'd never get anywhere unless you warmed up a bit. So she made you her project."

"Her…project?"

"Took you under her wing. Helped you fit in better."

"When I started my own firm, she was the first to join."

"So she could keep an eye on you. Make sure you didn't get yourself killed."

"This seems to have been a long chat you had with my wife."

"*She* stays in touch, Boss. Hint, hint. She looks after you. She even bought you a cat."

"Now what?"

"Remember? Giselle? For your thirtieth birthday. She could tell you were a cat person."

"I'd never had a cat before in my life."

"Immaterial and irrelevant, as you lawyers like to say. You needed someone you could love on. So she got you a cat."

He cast his mind backward. Come to think of it, Christina was the one who gave him that cat. But he always thought it was because she didn't know him well and couldn't think of a more personal gift...

And now they lived with Giselle's daughters.

"Look, I'm sorry to end the chitchat, but I need help from both of you. And I need it fast."

"Like always." Loving shook his head. "Drop everythin' in your real life and help me now."

"I would never ask you to do that."

Loving chuckled. "Since when?"

Ben inhaled deeply. "This case has dropped into my lap at the last minute. And someone really wants us to lose. Unless I'm mistaken, that someone has killed numerous people for unknown reasons. But I would never ask you to put yourself in danger."

"Since when?"

"I'm serious!"

Jones grinned. "Hey, Loving, how many times have you been shot at while you were working for Ben?"

"Lost count 'round fifty." He chuckled. "But to be fair, only two of the bullets hit the target."

"That's a good batting average."

"Still got a limp in my left leg, but who's complainin'?"

"You gripe about your leg constantly. But I had it worse. Remember that time some blatherskite broke into our office—and messed up all my files!"

Loving nodded, a grim expression on his face. "You were in therapy for months."

Jones sniffed. "PTSD is serious. Doesn't go away with a snap of the fingers."

"Maybe we should get to your wish list, Skipper. I got to warn you —I stay busy these days."

"The PI business is thriving?"

"Oh gosh. Nah. Christina hasn't filled you in?"

"Evidently not."

"I gave up my PI license years ago. I'm an entrepreneur now."

"Good for you! Private security?"

"Haute couture."

Ben blinked. "Excuse me?"

"That's a French term for fancy clothes."

"Did Christina teach it to you?"

"No. Had a client who got in over his head, needed a new partner. I had some bucks saved. Turns out, I've got an eye for fashion."

Ben felt as if he needed to go outside and clear his head. Loving, his rough-and-tumble, no-holds-barred investigator, was working in the garment industry? What next? Jones performing open-heart surgery?

"You heard of LuluLemon, Skipper?"

"Of course. Christina loves that stuff."

"Well, our company is OkiePeach. And we don't specialize in exercise gear. We specialize in silk."

Ben batted his eyelids. "Silk?"

"Comes from worms."

"I know that, but—"

"We make all kinds of attire. Dupioni. Brocade. Satin silk. Chiffon is my favorite."

Ben was still adjusting to a world where Loving was knowledgeable about silk...

"We're filling a niche," Loving continued, then grinned. "That's another French word."

"Barely."

"Our clothes are custom-made, exclusive, bespoke, one-of-a-kind. Handmade from start to finish."

Ben looked at Jones. "Did you know about this?"

"Of course."

"Do you—actually—have some of his silk garments?"

"Are you kidding? I can't begin to afford that stuff. I've seen it, though. Take a trip to Utica Square. Half the people there are decked out in Loving Silk."

"That's the name?"

Loving beamed proudly. "With our signature store near Saks. We're making money like you've never seen. And I keep gettin' invited to all these shows in Paris and Milan. Mostly I just show up, throw out haughty glares, and keep my mouth shut. They think I'm the next Christian Dior."

Ben was tempted to pinch himself. "What are you doing these days, Jones? Nuclear physics?"

Jones waved his hand dismissively. "Nah. My life has been far more predictable."

"Office managing?"

"Oh, God no. What am I, twelve? As you know, I've always been good with computers. I was one of the first coders in my class at UT. My company is on the cutting edge of AI programs designed for the modern workplace. You've heard of ChatGPT? DALL-E? Our programs are much better. We tailor-make apps for various industries to eliminate the necessary but boring or repetitive aspects of the work. Like writing ad copy. Creating graphics for social media. Calendaring major events. With built-in controls to ensure that the AI doesn't, you know, take over the world."

"You have your own company too?"

"I call it Red Delicious."

Sounded like they made pornos. "Because…"

"Because we're the little Apple. But growing fast."

Ben pushed away from the screen. "Why do I feel like I was holding you two back? Winding down my Tulsa practice was the best thing that ever happened to you."

Loving shook his head. "I wouldn't be where I am today without you, Skipper. I wouldn't be anywhere. You could've had me arrested. Instead, you gave me a job."

"Ditto that," Jones added. "You pulled me out a bad place, gave me a shot, and got my life restarted. It's what you do. Give people a second chance."

"Which is the reason we're here," Loving said. "And why I've cleared my calendar for the next five days. What do you need?"

"I've emailed you the details. We have three possible suspects. And since our client insists he did not commit the murder, it's possible one of these people did. So be careful."

"Understood."

"I know the police have investigated them thoroughly. But I also know you two have a knack for turning up secrets others want buried. I doubt you'll find much dirt on the student. Mitch Theroux. He's too young to have many skeletons in the closet. Dan is talking to him. But the doctor and the professor—all kinds of possibilities."

"And Christina says there might be a South American cartel involved?"

"Maybe. The FBI is also in the mix. Point person on the case is Courtney Zhang, who gave us the third degree, wasted a lot of time, and is probably still watching us."

"Okay," Jones said, "what about me?"

"I thought while Loving searches the physical world you could explore cyberspace. Social media posts. Blogs. TikTok videos. Facebook. Threads. See if you can find something relevant. Did the professor have a hankering for his student? Did the doctor have a hankering for a priceless violin? And why is someone so anxious to convict our client who, according to Gary, is already dying?"

"Curiouser and curiouser."

"If we don't win this motion, Donovan stays in prison for a crime he didn't commit."

Loving glanced at a notebook. "Okay, my multi-million-dollar fragrance retailer can wait. I'll see what I can dig up that might be useful at your hearing." He grinned again. "So we're all actually going to work on a case together again?" He raised his hand. "Fist-bump! The Over-the-Hill Gang rides again!"

Jones sniffed. "I'm not as old as you are..."

"I'm going to be busy prepping for trial," Ben said. "If you can't get me on the phone, just email or text the info."

"To you? Just you?"

"Yeah."

"Aren't you going to tell Dan we're working on the case?"

"No. I'm going to show up with new evidence and let him think I'm a miracle worker." He raised a hand in the air. "Fist-bump!"

A red alert appeared on the screen. Christina was asking to be admitted to the call.

That was odd. He pushed the button and admitted her. She didn't waste a second.

"Ben, this is ridiculous. You've got to get a cellphone."

"Dan threw mine—"

"I know. Get a new one. I can't get Dan on the line either."

"He probably silenced it. He's interviewing—"

"I don't care what he's doing. He needs to look at his phone."

"When he's finished he'll—"

"No. Right this second." She took a deep breath. "They found Maria."

# CHAPTER FORTY-THREE

Dan had to wait two hours before he saw the doctor, two hours he could not afford to waste. He tried to use the time efficiently, reading files, checking email on his phone, but this was not the best use of his limited time. He hoped the interview proved worth the wait.

Seemed like you always had to wait for a doctor. Even when you weren't a patient. He didn't know if it was innate untimeliness, poor planning, or pure arrogance, but it seemed to be the one medical certainty left in the world.

Eventually, Dr. Southern entered her office. No explanation for the delay and certainly no apology. "I have to warn you up front—I don't have much time. I can give you maybe ten minutes."

The physician as power broker, establishing from the get-go that she was more important than you.

"You're going to take the stand at David Donovan's hearing on Monday?"

"I was subpoenaed. Should I have my lawyer present for this?"

"Totally up to you. I'll be happy to wait if you want to make a call. But I know your time is precious."

Southern glanced at her watch. "Let's see what happens. I don't know why I'm testifying anyway. I don't know anything about the murder."

She slid onto a stool and masked herself partially behind a computer screen.

"Can explain that huge sum of money Claudia Wells transferred into your bank account?"

"That was...medical in nature."

"And yet, deposited to your personal bank account."

"You know, I think I am going to call my lawyer."

"Because you have something to hide?"

"No. Because I've been all over this with the police and I don't care to do it again."

"Forgive me," he said, "but the police are not always forthcoming with information. I've been all through the documents provided by the DA. It's possible I missed something, given how fast I had to work." He paused. "But I don't think so."

Southern pursed her lips, obviously debating whether to proceed. "I assume you've discussed your client's medical condition with him."

Was he going to admit that he had not met his client yet? No. "Some kind of rare kidney ailment, isn't it?"

"He has ESRD—end-stage renal disease. It's permanent. He's been on dialysis three times a week to remove wastes and other toxins from his blood."

"And a kidney transplant will fix that?"

"For twenty years or so."

"I understand he's waiting for a kidney?"

"God willing. I don't know exactly where he stands, but no one has been able to guarantee that he'll receive a kidney anytime in the next month or so. And if he doesn't..." Dr. Southern remained unemotional. Phlegmatic. As sterile as this office, with its glistening floors and anticeptic glass jars.

"But doesn't explain the huge payment to your bank account."

"Claudia and Donovan were close. And she came from money."

"She was trying to...buy him a kidney?"

"To put it bluntly."

"But why pay you?"

"Because organ trading is illegal in the US, in most circumstances. But I have contacts in Australia. I had to keep this off the books. I didn't want to implicate the hospital in any way."

"Why Australia?" Hadn't Australia come up before in this case?

Southern glanced at her watch. "I don't have time to educate you. You must have some research skills. Or an intern who does."

"Give me the CliffsNotes version."

She frowned. "Only one nation on earth currently permits the unrestricted buying and selling of organs."

"Australia?"

"Iran. Oddly enough, most Americans don't want to travel there. But both Singapore and—you guessed it—Australia recently legalized compensation for living donors. The idea is that you're not buying the organ. You're compensating the donor for their trouble and expense. In Australia, donors get nine weeks' paid leave from work."

"And a hundred grand might get Donovan a kidney?"

"That was the idea. Federal law here forbids selling organs, but a few states allow compensation for travel and other expenses. So technically, that's what the payment was for."

"But actually, Claudia was buying a kidney. From a living donor."

"Money talks."

"Seems...unethical." He prevented himself from saying, "disgusting."

"As with all ethical questions, it's a matter of opinion. Most believe people have an inherent right to govern their own bodies. I think there's a famous law case about that, isn't there?"

Dan nodded. "*Schelgendorff*. Justice Cardozo. 'Every human being of adult years and sound mind has a right to determine what shall be done with her own body.' That hasn't stopped states from criminalizing abortion."

"Why are kidneys so hard to come by?"

"What happens anytime there's a shortage? Of anything? Prices go up. So the wealthy are more likely to purchase."

"I seem to recall reading something in the files about a Uniform Anatomical Gift Act."

"The purpose of the Act was to ensure that those who take money or make promises actually deliver. But it's totally ineffective, in part because it was left to individual states to enforce and most have more pressing concerns, so they end up siding with the next-of-kin, even when the deceased donor expressed other wishes."

"Easier to appease the living, I suppose."

"The dead can't file lawsuits."

"So you took money from Claudia Wells. But you still haven't found a kidney?"

"Obviously. Which is why that pile of cash is still in a separate bank account, totally untouched. I'm basically holding it in escrow. Until the organ arrives." She paused, and for the first time, Dan thought he detected a trace of an actual emotion. "If it does. And he's still able to receive it."

Her story made sense, even if it was a sad commentary on how the global medical community handled—or failed to handle—a critical problem of enormous importance to hundreds of thousands of people. "How would this give Donovan a motive for murder? Seems like he'd be grateful, not vengeful."

"Donovan brought the check to me and explained her enormous generosity. I never spoke to her about it."

"Are you suggesting he could've forged the check?"

"It looks like her handwriting. I believe the police theory is that he forced her to write the check. Then killed her."

And apparently the DA was able to sell that story to a jury. With the help of this physician.

"May I ask you a question?"

"Just one."

"Do you think Donovan killed her?"

"I know what the jury decided."

"Which we're trying to undo. And I'd like to have your help. You wouldn't want a grave injustice to occur. Would you?"

Southern took a long breath before replying. "Donovan hasn't been able to find an organ. Without one, he isn't going to live long. He's barely living now. So…"

Dan glared at her. "So what difference does it make?"

She sighed. "I'm a practical woman. I'm extremely busy and I never have enough time to do everything I want to do. The idea of running around trying to save a man who probably only has a month to live…" She folded her hands. "Not at the top of my list."

"I don't have the liberty of being…so practical. I have an obligation to my client."

"I understand. We all do what we have to do."

"And I don't believe Donovan killed Claudia." He almost surprised himself, saying it out loud. "Are you aware that someone has been threatening me?"

"I'm aware that lawyers are universally despised."

"In the medical community, perhaps."

"I have a lot of friends who would like to knock off a lawyer or two. Maybe it would be best if you quit this case while you're still able to talk about it."

———

DAN WAS STILL MULLING OVER THE UNHELPFUL CONVERSATION WITH Dr. Southern when it finally occurred to him to check his messages.

He gasped. Why hadn't Ben—?

He already knew the answer. Because Ben didn't have a cellphone and probably didn't know Dan's cell number. He couldn't convey the news.

He clenched his eyes shut. Tears crept through the cracks. He felt as if an enormous burden had been lifted from his shoulders.

Maria was alive. And unharmed. And headed for California.

# CHAPTER FORTY-FOUR

BEN WAITED ALMOST AN HOUR BEFORE THE JAILHOUSE GUARD TOOK HIM back to the visiting chambers. Time he didn't have to spare. Dan had texted him about his interview with the physician, which appeared to be equal parts frustrating and unhelpful.

Truth was, interviewing his client was probably about the least useful thing he could do. He'd already read the witness statements and the trial transcript. He knew Donovan's story. But going to court without meeting your client beforehand seemed wrong. And it was always possible Donovan knew something useful that wasn't in the record.

The guard seated him in a small room with a locked door. No Plexiglas screen this time. It would appear that in LA, they let visitors sit in the same room with the convict they're visiting. Or at least, they let lawyers do it. He wouldn't miss the germ-infested phones or the smeary screen that impeded true communication.

People always looked bad after a stay behind bars. The harsh fluorescent lighting didn't help, but the main cause was unhealthy diet, crappy clothes, lack of exercise or sunlight, and fear.

In all his decades of lawyering, Ben had never seen a client who looked as terrible as David Donovan did.

It must be the disease, he told himself. This guy has a kidneys that've shut down and the strain is tearing him apart. He's getting dialysis three times a week, but that's barely keeping him alive. Add in the fact that his freedom is restricted. He's probably bored to tears half the time and scared to death the rest.

Ben extended his hand. It was an important gesture, showing his new client not only openness but that he wasn't afraid to touch him. "I'm Ben Kincaid. I'll be handling your hearing on Monday."

"What happened to Gary?"

No need to go into the details. "Gary had to leave town. He wants you to get the best representation you can. He thought it might be best to bring in some experts."

Donovan looked him up and down. "And you're one of the experts?"

"I do have some experience with criminal law."

"What's your win-loss record?"

"I've never kept statistics. We're not collecting baseball cards. We're trying to see that justice is done."

Donovan made a snorting sound. He lowered himself onto the bench. "Not doing a great job of it. I've been in jail for months. And I did not kill Claudia. Why would I? She was an angel. She cared about me. Best friend I ever had. Did my parents help when I got sick? Hell, no. Did the university care? Only to make sure I got my tuition paid up before I died. Claudia was the only person who gave a rat's ass about me."

"Sounds like she was a wonderful, generous person. Why would anyone want to kill her?"

"I don't know. It wasn't me."

Donovan seemed genuine. But he'd been fooled before. He wished Christina could be here. She had much better instincts about people than he did. "What about that other guy in the dorm? Mitch Theroux."

"Creeper. I told her to stay away from him. But he kept showing up."

"He had the hots for her?"

"I don't think he's into women. He had the hots for her violin."

"The Amati."

"You know anything about music?"

"I play the piano and I was a music major. Why do you think he's a creeper?"

"He was always lurking. And incapable of interpreting social cues, because believe me, she was not encouraging him."

"I hear Mitch plays the piano. But you play the violin, right?"

"I didn't want her violin."

"Even if you don't want to play it, you could sell it."

"I don't need money that badly."

"Don't you, though?" Ben gave him a direct stare. "Money buys organs, at least some places."

"Claudia volunteered to buy a kidney from some outfit in Australia. If they could find a match. And that's a better plan than trying to secretly sell a priceless violin on the black market."

Ben couldn't escape feeling there was something he was missing. Over the years he had learned to listen to those nagging instincts. "What about the professor?"

"You mean Herwig? They should investigate him. Unlike me, he had all the motives. He wanted Claudia *and* her violin."

"When you say he wanted her...I'm guessing you don't mean he wanted her in class."

"He wanted her in bed. He was always playing up to her. Cutting her slack. Giving her grades for assignments she hadn't completed. I heard him invite her to his home once."

"I'm sure there was some legitimate pedagogical purpose."

"Yeah. Getting into her panties."

"Did she complain about him?"

"Big time. But I couldn't get her to file a formal complaint. If she had, he'd have been out on his ass for sexual harassment."

But since she didn't, this was all hearsay. Even if he could get it in under the "deceased declarant" exception, it still wasn't enough to overturn a verdict. "I can't imagine anyone committing murder over a violin."

"People have committed murder over fifty-dollar parking tickets."

Well, true…

"And have you read the description of how her body was found? Half-dressed. Skirt over her face." His voice choked. "When I—When I think about what that man may have done…" Donovan covered his face. A few moments later, Ben saw tears.

Ben couldn't begin to claim he had this case figured out. But the one thing he knew for certain was that David Donovan loved Claudia Wells.

Which, sadly, did not eliminate him as a suspect.

"Have you thought of anything new? You've had a lot of time in here to think about things. Any revelations?"

"I know that on at least one occasion Herwig came to Claudia's dorm to see the violin. She might've opened the safe while he was present."

"And he might've peered over her shoulder and snagged the combination?"

"It's possible, isn't it? It's a digital lock. All you do is type in three numbers in the correct order."

"Definitely worth looking into. In the extremely limited time we have before the hearing begins." He snapped his fingers. "Which reminds me. You've never formally agreed to let Dan and I represent you. We've filed the proper court papers, but ultimately, this is your decision."

"And Gary is out?"

"Gary is way way out."

"Would the judge appoint a lawyer to represent me?"

He tried not to be offended. "For a motion to reconsider? Probably not. And even if he did—and I have utmost respect for public defenders—it probably wouldn't be the best move for you."

"I guess beggars can't be choosers."

Not flattering. But he'd take it. Donovan smeared his signature on the dotted line. "Are you okay? Anything I can do for you?"

"I've been in here so long I've almost forgotten how people live on the other side." He hesitated. "Maybe a new book to read."

"I can arrange that."

"The guards don't allow—"

"I'll tell them it's part of your defense and they can't interfere with your preparation. What do you like? Science fiction? Mysteries?"

"Actually, my favorite author is Trollope."

Ben's eyes widened slightly. He spoke quietly. "Mine too. But I thought I was the only one."

"Have you read *The Way We Live Today?*"

"Best novel ever. Bleak. But amazingly insightful. Prescient."

"I never finished the Palliser novels."

"I'll have all six of them delivered today. With luck...you'll be free before you finish them."

"You—You think there's a chance? I mean, truly? Don't lie to me. I need to know where I stand."

Ben had been on this case for exactly two days. He hadn't spoken to all the witnesses. He'd breezed through the files. He was totally unqualified to answer that question.

But he did. "Yes. I think there's a chance. I don't want to make any promises I can't keep. Judges are not always predictable. But Dan and I will do everything possible to get you out of here."

"That would be so...wonderful. I mean, sure, I want to clear my name. And I want to find out who killed Claudia. But some days...I think I'd cut off my bowing fingers for a slice of hot pizza."

"That settles it then." Ben rose. "The pizzeria will be our first stop. Once we get you out of here."

# CHAPTER FORTY-FIVE

DAN KNEW ONE OF THE PRINCIPAL DETERMINING FACTORS FOR courtroom success was knowing the judge. In some cases, like this one, it might be even more important than knowing the facts of the case. A bench hearing, at which you have only one person to convince, is an all-or-nothing affair. You either persuade the judge or you lose. Back in the day, his colleague Garrett used to research and report on judges. Everything was potentially useful. Sweet on cats? Dogs? Daughters? Football? Cop shows? Tom Cruise? BTS?

Once Dan knew the judge's soft spots, he could touch on them whenever useful. The sports fan got sports metaphors. The comic book buff got superhero analogies. The bookworm got references to Proust or James Joyce. The client could drop references as well. This didn't guarantee a win, but particularly in a close case, it didn't hurt. Garrett would also review judges' past rulings and decisions. Who elected or appointed them. How they dressed. What car they drove. Secrets revealed by their Facebook vacay photos. All Gary had managed to tell him about Judge Durant was that he was "over-worked, underpaid, and cranky toward defense lawyers."

Fine. Not to be excessively stereotypical, but he assumed any judge over sixty would be cranky. He assumed any judge appointed by a

Republican politician would be conservative. But that didn't necessarily mean he would he would hostile to this motion...

"Why are you carpetbaggers still wasting my time?" Judge Durant said as he entered his chambers from a back door, probably a changing room. "Do you think I don't have enough to do already?"

"It's in the interest of fairness," Dan said. "You did agree to hold the hearing."

"Your client was convicted by a unanimous vote? The jury only deliberated for three hours." The judge glided into his seat behind an outsize cherrywood desk. "Three hours, then they convicted. I mean, that's barely enough time to read the instructions and vote."

Dan glanced at Ben. The plan had been for Dan to take the lead, since the courtroom was supposed to be his specialty, but now he was reconsidering. Ben was older and capable of being just as cranky as Durant. Maybe he should take the lead.

Ben shook his head. Translation: Your problem. Enjoy.

ADA Chee sat in one of the overstuffed chairs, currently silent, smiling. She didn't have to do anything. The judge had already put them on the defensive.

Dan cleared his throat. "Your honor, I can assure you that we would never waste your time—"

"You already have."

He started again. "We filed this motion because—"

"It was actually Gary Quince who filed the motion. I know and trust Gary. But I notice he isn't with you."

Dan tried again. "Your honor has graciously agreed to allow us to appear before this court. We thought three lawyers for a single motion would be overkill."

"Don't need the local boy anymore, huh? 'Cause you bigshot out-of-towners are superior to us locals."

Boy, did this guy get up on the wrong side of the bed. "It's nothing like—"

"Or maybe you thought that with Gary absent, you could criticize everything he's done."

"That's not our strategy at all." Well, it wasn't Plan A. "We've uncovered evidence that law enforcement either didn't uncover or didn't reveal—"

"Now you stop right there, mister." The judge stretched his robe-sagging arm across the desk. "I won't tolerate that kind of talk in my courtroom. You don't have to tear down our appointed officials to help your client. In my courtroom, it's more likely to have the exact opposite effect."

This was going to be an uphill battle. "We will argue that the police had an obligation to investigate the crime, not simply arrest the first suspect who tumbled into their laps—"

"Who was then convicted by a unanimous jury in less time than it takes most people to have dinner at a nice restaurant."

"The prosecutor has an enormous amount of power."

"And the defense has all the procedural advantages," the judge shot back. "Don't whine about the justice system to me, my friend. This is our world and we have to live in it. Your man was convicted. I'm not likely to restart the whole process unless you can show me something so surprising that"—he clutched a hand over his chest—"it's heart-attack inducing. Complete gamechanger. You got something that good?"

Dan kept his eyes locked on the judge's. "Yes, your honor. We do."

Judge Durant leaned back in his chair. "Well, I admire a man who has the courage of his convictions. Even if I don't believe a word he says. Show me what you've got, Florida-boy. Put your cards on the table."

---

Dan knew the judge wouldn't want a long opening statement. He was somewhat surprised the judge gave him a chance to speak at all. But given the opportunity, he would take it. He wouldn't talk long enough to bore the judge or make him regret his decision. But there were a few seeds he wanted to plant.

"I know the court's time is valuable," he began, "so I won't waste it." Given what he'd heard in chambers, this seemed like the most sycophantic way to open. "Yes, we urge the court to re-open this matter and order a new trial. Not because of any misconduct by the trial court." So we won't be attacking you, your honor. "But because the law enforcement community did not do their jobs, and sadly, that includes the district attorney's office. The jury did not have the opportunity to view critical evidence. Or hear from critical witnesses. We will argue that this evidence was not revealed earlier due to failures by the police and the DA, and before you start rapping that gavel, let me assure you that I would never suggest such a thing if I didn't have proof."

Fine. No gavel. He paused, letting that sink in.

"We will call three witnesses, your honor, all of whom have important information to share. And after the court hears what they have to say, you will realize that this is about much more than a mere violin."

The judge maintained his professional composure. If anything, he looked a little bored. "You'll be happy to hear that we should finish our part of the case today. I have no idea what the DA plans..." He paused and let that hang in the air for a bit. "...but I doubt it will take much longer."

A glance over his shoulder told him his opponent was not enjoying his opening. In fact, Chee looked angry.

Good. Angry lawyers tended to get too emotional and argue irrationally.

"Because what can they say? It will be obvious they missed important evidence, and that is sufficient cause for a new trial. They were determined to put my client behind bars...and as a result, a few minor details...like truth and justice...fell by the wayside. And then, after our show of proof, because justice demands it, we will ask this court to set aside the verdict and order a new trial. Thank you."

Once he was back at his seat, he checked his phone. He'd delivered that in fewer than five minutes. Surely that was quick enough.

He glanced at Ben, who gave him a big thumbs up and mouthed the word "Perfect."

He hoped Ben was right.

ADA Chee walked to the podium, shaking her head and feigning bafflement. Dan hadn't said ten words to her since they first met, and he disliked her already.

"You know what I think, you honor? I think we've got a couple of drifters who think they know more about how we ought to do our jobs than we do."

Dan felt Ben's hand clamp down on his wrist. "Stay seated," he whispered. "Let the woman have her fun. Then bury her under a mountain of evidence."

Chee continued. "Even though I was not legal counsel at the trial level—anymore than they were—I was personally involved with the preparation and presentation of the state's evidence and I am grossly offended by the suggestion that there was any misconduct, unintentional or otherwise. We did our job, which is to investigate crimes and prosecute criminals. I hope we don't have to do it over and over again. I understand that the defendant is facing a harsh sentence. That's what happens when you murder someone. Let's not create an infinite regress, examining and re-examining cases over and over again."

Judge Durant nodded. Chee was singing the song he wanted to hear.

"As for this newly uncovered evidence—I can't comment. The defense lawyers do not have to share anything with us, and as a result, they don't. I think these two out-of-state boys are going to throw a lot of alternate culprits at you—a bunch of SODDITs," she said, winking. "They are simply stirring the water and hoping something will float to the surface."

Chee paused. "I will remind the court what it already knows. This case was fully and fairly presented to a California jury. The jury voted unanimously to convict. And too often...what floats to the surface after you stir the water isn't the truth. It's pond scum."

# CHAPTER FORTY-SIX

After Chee finished her opening, Ben requested a break, then disappeared.

Dan waited not-patiently in the hallway, tapping his toes and drumming his fingers. And then a familiar figure came racing down the hallway.

And everything changed.

Before they even spoke, Maria wrapped her arms around him and pressed her face into the crook of his neck so tightly it took his breath away. Who needs air, anyway? He had the only thing he wanted.

He buried his face in her hair. Just feeling her beside him made a host of anxieties melt away.

"So good to...have you back where you belong," he whispered.

"I feel the same way." She squeezed him so hard she practically became a part of him.

"I have a million questions. Are you hurt?"

"No. A little groggy. Sleep-deprived. But I'm fine."

"He didn't...take advantage..."

"No. Barely saw him. I was trapped, not tortured."

She felt so good in his arms he never wanted to let go. He'd been so worried. This was a gift. One he did not intend to squander. "How did you get here so soon? I thought the police would want to talk to you, and the FBI, and—"

"They did. For a while. That agent who interrogated you—Courtney Zhang, right?—she held me up for hours with a lot of questions I couldn't answer. And she still acted like I was lying."

"Sounds like Zhang. What happened?"

"Someone intervened."

"Ben?"

She shook her head. "Someone far more formidable."

"Who—"

He didn't have to finish the question. A few feet away he saw Ben in exactly the same pose. With his arms around his wife.

Ben glanced up. "Dan, let me formally introduce you to Christina. Live and in person."

She was several inches shorter than Ben, with a shock of strawberry-red hair and a light dusting of gray. She had eschewed the traditional female power suit for a jacketless puffed shirt with ruffled sleeves. Not that he was one to criticize other people's style choices, but to him, she looked more like a pirate than a lawyer.

He wiped his eyes dry then took her hand. "A pleasure to finally meet you."

"The same. I hear you pulled my husband's fat out of the fire, so thanks."

"It was nothing."

"I know better. Having done it myself several times."

Dan slapped himself. "Where are my manners? Ben, this is Maria."

"I know. I've worked with her longer than you have, remember? But we've never actually met face-to-face." Ben took her hand. "Thank you for coming. And...congratulations."

Dan did a double-take. "Congratulations? What?"

Ben waved a hand, cutting her off. "Later. We have to focus on this hearing. I understand Maria has uncovered some disturbing evidence."

"You found evidence while you were held hostage?"

Her smile faded. "As I turns out, I was being held in an isolated condo outside the city."

"The killer broke into someone's house?"

"It was rented. Airbnb. Paid by PayPal transfer from an anonymous account."

"They could trace the IP address and—"

She shook her head. "Burner laptop."

The renter must've given a name."

"Indeed. David Donovan."

"That's not possible. He's been in prison."

"Doesn't mean he doesn't have internet access."

"Why would he do that?"

Dan closed his eyes. "This changes everything."

"No," Ben said, reaching across the table. "It changes nothing."

"How can you say that? We may be representing a guilty man."

"Even the guilty are entitled to the best possible defense. And I don't believe he rented that condo."

Dan looked away. "I wish you hadn't told me."

"You have a right to know." Ben glanced across the table to Christina "Let me tell you a little story. Many years ago, Christina and I were in Arkansas."

"Camping trip," she explained. "Lots of fun. Ben is quite the outdoorsman."

"You're joking."

"Yes, I am." She paused. "But he does have a certain….*je ne sais quoi.* Back when—"

"But the point of this story," Ben said, "is that we got dragged into a local case. A white-supremacist militia group was harassing a Vietnamese immigrant community. Someone died, one of the militia types was arrested. No one would represent him."

"Understandable," Maria muttered.

"So Ben jumped into the fray," Christina explained.

Dan stared at Ben with widened eyes. "You repped a white supremacist?"

"It was the only way he was going to get a fair trial. And it entailed...considerable personal sacrifice."

"But you did the right thing. I get it. You're—"

"There's more to this story." Ben took a deep breath. "Less than a year after Chris and I were in Arkansas trying this case...the Oklahoma City bombing happened." He took a deep breath. "Chris was in OKC that day, in the courthouse across the street from the Murrah building."

"Scariest day of my life," she said quietly. "No one knew what happened. People were running, panicked. Bloodied. And so many dead."

"Scariest day of my life, too," Ben said. "I couldn't get anyone on the phone who could tell me if she was okay for hours. And it has haunted me." He closed his eyes. "You know the rest of the story. The police found the bombers quickly. Both were arrested. And guess what?" He averted his eyes. "That guy I got off the hook? He was pals with them."

Dan's lips parted. "No."

"Yes. They'd visited several militia camps together, including the one in Arkansas."

"Did your former client have anything to do with the bombing?"

"No one has uncovered any evidence of that. But...it's possible. We know they talked. Maybe they conspired. Maybe..." His voice broke. "Well. That's what I had to say."

"Do you regret what you did?"

Ben took another deep breath. "No. I was young and idealistic and..."

"Stupid," Christina added.

"As you may have guessed, Christina opposed my involvement in this case from the start."

"Because you only have book sense. And I have common sense."

"Whatever. I don't have regrets but it has...haunted me. And you're about to put yourself in a very similar situation, Dan, so...I think you have a right to know the circumstances. All the circumstances."

The table fell silent for a long time.

# CHAPTER FORTY-SEVEN

INSIDE THE COURTROOM, DONOVAN SAT AT DEFENSE TABLE. THE marshals had removed his cuffs and allowed him to wear street clothes. But there were still two in the courtroom, maintaining a discreet distance but ready to jump in the second Donovan made a move.

Dan sat beside him. As soon as he did, he got a queasy feeling inside. "How do you feel?"

He looked tired and worn. "Like my whole life hinges on what happens during the next couple of hours."

Which was entirely accurate.

"Anything you need to tell me before we get started?"

"I'm a bit peckish. Could we have that pizza delivered during the hearing? I mean, just in case we aren't celebrating later?"

"In the courtroom? No."

"Could you get me a better cell? The one I'm in now sucks."

"Maybe you should rent an Airbnb."

Dan watched his face carefully. Donovan's only reaction was confusion. "I don't think the prison guards will allow that."

"Anything else I can do for you?"

Donovan gave him a raised eyebrow. "Win."

"That is always my intention." And it still was. Sort of. He hoped. If he wasn't representing a big fat liar who was manipulating him to get out of jail...

---

DAN WATCHED AS JUDGE DURANT RE-ENTERED THE COURTROOM. AFTER a few preliminaries, Dan called Mitch Theroux to the witness stand. Mitch looked nervous, but almost everyone did when they were called to testify. He'd shaved, but not all the way, leaving a veneer of stubble. Which still looked better than the scruffy ungroomed look that seemed to predominate on college campuses these days.

Hard to imagine this guy stealing a book from the library, much less murdering someone. Dan had his work cut out for him.

He ripped through the introductory questions. He knew the judge didn't care about Mitch's life story. He needed to move to the part involving fraud or newly discovered evidence as quickly as possible.

"So you lived two doors down from the victim, Claudia Wells. And you exchanged texts with her."

"That was our primary means of communication."

"Your room was ten feet away from hers. Why not talk face-to-face?"

Mitch shrugged. "Ok, Boomer. Whatever."

Dan's teeth ground together. Mitch was truly obnoxious. And come on, he wasn't nearly old enough to be a Boomer. Gen Y maybe. "You liked Claudia, didn't you?"

"Of course. As far as I know, everyone did."

Well, there was one person who didn't. "Yes, lots of people liked her...but you especially liked her, didn't you?"

"I've already said that."

"Would you say you loved her?"

"You and the police. Always trying to invent facts when you don't have any real ones. Yes, in fact I did love her. But not in a romantic way. We were close friends who cared about one another."

"One of the texts makes reference to 'what happened last night.'"

"So of course, you assume that meant sex. In fact, we'd both been to a party the night before. We drank way too much and had spotty memories the next morning. We got together later and swapped notes. But we did not swap bodily fluids."

"She wrote, 'That was a one-off. It should never happen again.'"

"The same words spoken by anyone who ever woke with a hangover."

"So you claim you weren't pining for her."

He shifted around in his seat. "I was perfectly happy with our relationship the way it was."

"And you weren't at all jealous about her relationship with David Donovan."

"Why would I be? I don't think she cared that much about him. He was just...convenient."

"What does that mean?"

"She didn't want a long-term relationship. But she liked sex. So she used him. But I don't think she liked him that much."

"Maybe that's what you wanted to think. Because you were jealous. You had visions of you and Claudia playing together with that priceless violin, following a sensual performance in bed—"

"You are so far off the mark." Mitch moved past irritation into anger. "I don't know why I should be subjected to questioning by someone who so clearly knows nothing about her. Newsflash, dude. Not that it's any of your business. I'm gay."

Dan took a moment. Okay. Hadn't seen that coming.

Since Dan didn't immediately ask another question, Mitch continued. "Haven't you heard? Women feel safe around gay guys. They can be friends without worrying about secret agendas or sublimated passion. Lots of coeds have gay best buddies. Including Claudia."

The fact that he said it didn't make it so. But it would be futile to dispute the point. Prove you're gay? That wasn't going to happen. He'd probably get canceled if he tried. "Are you in a relationship now? I mean, with a man?"

"Yes. Not serious. But I am seeing someone."

"Who?"

ADA Chee rose, but Mitch beat her to the punch. "That is totally none of your business."

"So you're seeing someone male, but you also spent a great deal of time in Claudia's room."

"Not all that much time in her room. We usually went out. Not dissing her in any way, but Claudia tended to be...untidy. I have OCD issues. I can't stand messy, cluttered environments."

"Let's talk about violins."

"I play keyboards. Never played a violin in my life."

"But you knew Claudia kept a valuable violin in her dorm room."

"Lots of people knew. She played it on campus, in class."

"She kept it in a safe?"

"Right. And how many people have safes in their dorm room? Anyone who entered her room would know there must be something valuable there."

He took his best shot. "You knew the safe combination, didn't you?"

Chee shot to her feet. "Objection. Leading."

"Permission to treat the witness as hostile." Which meant he could ask leading questions, among other things. "I thought that was understood."

Judge Durant nodded. "It was. Your request is granted and the objection is overruled. The witness will answer."

Mitch drew himself up. "You know what? I'm tired of hiding. I did know the combination, but not because I wanted the violin. Because she trusted me with it. Because we were close. She probably thought someone else should know the combination in case she forgot it. She was afraid to write it down, except maybe in code. And she knew I didn't want the violin. So she gave me the combination."

Dan took a moment to think. So far, he hadn't laid a glove on this witness. He needed to push harder. "You've admitted to having opportunity, and I think you had motive. Even if you personally did not want the violin, could you sell it?"

"I suppose I could try. But I didn't. The police would've caught me if I had." He fell silent, then before Dan could resume, added more.

"I'm not going to leave it at that. Because the fact is, I didn't want the violin, I couldn't play it, and I didn't need money. But you know who did? Your client."

Dan ignored the last part. "Please tell the—"

"Plus, in my own way, I loved Claudia and she loved me. But your client would've killed his grandmother to get that violin."

"Objection!' Dan said.

The judge nodded. "Sustained." But that didn't mean Durant didn't hear it.

Dan continued. "I think you loved Claudia and hated my client. You decided that if you couldn't have Claudia, no one would. And after you killed her, you stole that violin—not for money but because you wanted to incriminate Donovan. Which worked. The police bought it hook, line, and sinker. And here we are today. Because you stole a violin you couldn't play."

"Total fabrication. Didn't happen. I loved her."

"Did you still love her after you read her diary?"

Mitch's lips tightened. "I would never read her diary without her permission."

"You're telling me your haven't read the portions the police released? They've been published all over the media. Do you have a Twitter account, Millennial?"

A slight smile. "I did read those. Since Claudia was gone, I didn't see the harm."

"In one diary entry she wrote, 'Mitch is starting to be a problem.' Did you see that one?"

"I did. I can't remember what that was about. She probably thought I was drinking too much at parties."

"The complete quote was, 'Mitch is starting to be a problem...I may need to switch to a different dorm.'"

"Those were two different thoughts. Two different sentences on different pages that you've combined to create an unintended meaning."

"That's not how it reads to me."

"The so-called 'problem with Mitch' was that although I had done her homework on many occasions, I wouldn't take her online final in Music History. She was planning to switch to a more expensive dorm because she thought there was too much riffraff in her current one. She was probably worried about the violin. But she wasn't worried about me."

"And what's your spin on the entry dated March 6? She wrote, 'Mitch can be helpful, but needs to learn to keep his hands to himself.' Can you explain that away?"

"Yes. She was HSP."

"Excuse me?"

"Stands for Highly Sensitive Person."

"That sounds made up."

"It's a clinical diagnosis. She was more sensitive to physical, mental, and social stimuli. Some people don't like loud sudden noises. Awkward phone calls. Cringey situations. And typically, they don't like to be touched. Even a harmless fist bump or high five. Once I knew her issues, I stopped. And that was long before she was murdered."

One last thrust and then it was quitting time. "You know, the crime scene was wiped clean. All that cleaning would take a long time. Who do you think did it?"

"The murderer, obviously. Donovan."

"And he stayed in her room for hours, cleaning up the mess?"

"Apparently."

"But you were only two doors down. And you knew her habits. And you knew the combination to the safe. Did you have a key to her door?"

"No."

"And why would David need to spend hours cleaning up the mess? Sure, his prints were all over the room but since they were dating, that's not particularly incriminating." Dan leaned in closer. "Who would do all that cleaning? Someone who wasn't dating her, and thus shouldn't be leaving prints around her desk. Or her bed. Or her safe. Maybe someone who can't bear to leave a mess behind. Like someone with OCD. Which you just confessed to having."

# CHAPTER FORTY-EIGHT

DAN APPRECIATED THE FIVE-MINUTE BREAK JUDGE DURANT CALLED after Mitch was excused. He knew from experience that a five-minute break would become a ten-minute break if not twenty, and at this juncture, he was not in a hurry. He needed time to think. He'd barely laid a glove on Mitch and he'd certainly not done enough to inspire the judge to overturn a jury verdict.

He still the distinct feeling he was missing something. Something important. He'd been paying attention—watching, listening, inter-twining facts, but somehow, his renowned ability to "connect the dots" wasn't working.

He pulled Ben aside. "How did that examination play?"

Ben shrugged. "Not as well as I'd hoped. But it wasn't your fault. I don't think Mitch is our killer."

"You're sure about that?"

"No. But we don't need personal beliefs to postulate a SODDIT."

"I thought he was lying."

"So did David, who I had the misfortune of sitting next to during the questioning."

"What did he say?"

"Something about Mitch being a "pervy stalker wannabe.""

"Milder than I expected."

"There was more. Expletives deleted."

"You're very Nixonian."

"I hope not."

"You used the phrase—"

"I was alive in the '70s. Don't rub it in."

Dan glanced at his watch. Time was fleeting. "Any suggestions?"

"Get more out of the next one. If we have two weak witnesses in a row, the judge will stop paying attention."

"Easy to say." Dan spotted David wandering aimlessly up and down the courthouse hallway, his two marshal babysitters following him from a distance. Didn't seem to be any purpose to his movements. Maybe it was just the novelty of having freedom of movement. Somewhere other than a prison yard.

He waved David over. "Don't worry. We're just getting started."

"I couldn't tell that you'd started yet."

"We don't think Mitch is the killer."

"But he's still a pervy stalker. Couldn't you do more to bring that out?"

"Despite what you may have seen on television, judges tend to frown on bringing up irrelevancies to smear the witness. And since he says he's gay, that could be misinterpreted as homophobia."

"I think his stalker status is directly relevant to the case."

Dan smiled. "That's why you have lawyers."

———

DAN HAD BEEN PLANNING TO CALL THE PROFESSOR NEXT, BUT THE doctor was already at the courthouse, and he thought it might be smart to change things up. Follow Mitch with a professional woman. Granted, he was only putting her on the stand so he could accuse her of murder. But still. He didn't want the judge to think all his witnesses were pervy stalker losers.

As efficiently as possible, Dan established that Dr. Marilyn Southern was a nephrologist with offices at St. Bartholomew's Hospital, which was not far from campus. She was Donovan's doctor, but she had also been in touch with Claudia Wells, even to the point of discussing his case. She'd been practicing for over fourteen years and, at least according to her, was one of the leading transplant surgeons in the country. She went to med school at Johns Hopkins and completed a residency at Yale.

"We don't need a great deal of detail, Dr. Southern, but could you give the jury some information about the medical condition my client currently suffers from?"

"He has end-stage renal disease. That's the most common cause for transplants, although they can also be needed in some instances for diabetics and those suffering from extreme hypertension. He's currently getting dialysis three times a week to remove wastes and other toxic substances from his blood. His creatinine levels are well over 1.9 and have been for a long time. He needs a transplant."

"Is that going to happen?"

"Not if he remains in prison. Kidneys are in short supply. And although some feel it's inappropriate to make value judgments about who should get them—I can't imagine a convicted murderer getting an organ when so many children and non-felons need one."

"In that sense," he said, looking at the judge, "this hearing is a life-and-death proposition."

"I suppose you could say that."

"How long have you been treating my client?"

"Over four years now."

"How did you come to know Claudia Wells?"

Dr. Southern recrossed her legs. "As I think you know, she was dating David. They may have been engaged."

Really? He hadn't heard that before. Not even from his client.

"She often came with him for doctor's appointments and dialysis. She seemed very supportive."

"Did you like her?"

ADA Chee rose to her feet. "Objection. Relevance."

Dan's brows knitted. "We're exploring whether people had a motive for murder. Asking about the witness' relationship with the victim is directly relevant."

Judge Durant licked his lips. "'Directly relevant' might be pushing it. But I'll allow the question."

The doctor answered. "Yes, I did. I love music and I've always had a great admiration for musicians. I could see that her support was keeping David alive." She paused. "Even now...despite the circumstances...I can see how much he misses her."

And thus would never think about killing her? He decided not to push his luck. "You texted Claudia several times."

"Yes."

"Is that appropriate? Talking to third persons about your patient's medical history?"

"David explicitly authorized it. In writing."

"See any signs of stress? Arguing? Fighting?"

"Can't say that I did. I thought he loved her deeply. And I could see why."

"In your experience, do men who love women deeply typically murder them?"

Chee was back on her feet. "Objection. Argumentative. And not relevant."

"No, let me answer," Southern said, her arm outstretched. No one said anything, so she continued. "I do think David loved her. And depended upon her. But that doesn't mean he was incapable of committing a crime. He was under a lot of stress, both because of his medical condition and his financial condition. I think she was helping with both."

"Surely you're not suggesting—"

"All I'm saying is that when people are stressed, they sometimes become unpredictable. They lash out against those trying to help them. And David was on a lot of medication."

He remembered what Ben had said earlier. Love makes you do the crazy. "Did you ever see my client act in a dangerous or threatening manner toward Claudia?"

"I did not."

"Good. Let's not make any suggestions that aren't based on what you've actually seen or heard."

She shrugged. "You asked the question."

Time to change the subject. "Were you aware that the victim kept an extremely valuable violin in her dorm room?"

"Is there anyone who doesn't know about it at this point?"

"But before the murder."

"Yes. She'd mentioned it. More than once."

"In what context?"

"She contemplated selling it to help pay for her boyfriend's medical expenses."

He didn't see that coming, but it was helpful. David had no reason to steal the violin if she was planning to sell it to pay his bills. "Didn't he have health insurance?"

"Yes, but that isn't enough, as most Americans know. Especially when major surgery is needed. I absolutely forbid her to sell that instrument and told her we wouldn't take the money if she did. There had to be other ways."

"As I think you know, the violin has vanished."

"Are you suggesting I might've stolen the violin?"

"Someone did. You knew about it."

"I didn't steal it."

"That would be perfect, wouldn't it? Stage a theft so she can file a claim with her insurer. While you keep the violin and sell it quietly on the black market to pay for a kidney."

"Why am I being accused?" She craned her neck to look at the judge. "I've done nothing wrong. I don't need money. Claudia found a way to help David without selling the violin."

"How much do you make?"

Southern's neck stiffened. "That is none of your business."

"I'm told Claudia's violin could fetch close to a million dollars from the right buyer. That would improve anyone's bottom line."

Southern began to look irritated and indignant. "I don't need it. Or want it."

"Maybe you'd like to start your own clinic. And need seed money."

"At this point in my life? No thank you."

"Did you know the combination to Claudia's safe?"

"No. But your client did."

Now she was fighting back. "Why do you say that now? You never said it before."

"I don't recall that it came up before. But they talked about it at one of the dialysis sessions. They take a while and she usually stayed with him, usually held his hand. And once I heard her ask if he would get the violin later and bring it to her. So he must've known the combination."

"Why did she want it?"

"Not sure. I think she had some kind of performance scheduled. I can't remember the entire conversation. But she winked and said, 'Go back to my place and play the Military Drumroll Surprise.'"

Back at the defense table, he saw Ben sit up. He'd read those cryptic words before. In Claudia's diary.

"What did it mean?"

"No idea."

"To summarize, you knew about the violin and you knew there was a combination safe in Claudia's dorm room."

"But I'm not stupid and I don't need money."

"Then why did Claudia give you a check for over 123,000 bucks?"

Southern slowly eased back into her chair. "As you already know, she was trying to get your client a kidney. From a foreign country where the buying and selling of organs is legal under certain circumstances."

"Or maybe it was hush money?" He didn't believe that, but if he suggested something worse than the truth, maybe it would make her more likely to admit the truth.

"Hush money? For what?"

Chee was back on her feet with another objection. "Your honor, this is uncalled for."

Dan didn't even blink. "Is that an objection?"

"He's basically accusing the witness of committing a crime."

Dan looked up at the judge. "Your honor, this is, in effect, cross-examination."

Judge Durant nodded. "The objection—if that's what it was—is overruled. The witness will answer."

"It was not hush money. What in God's name would she be trying to hush?"

"Maybe something that got her killed."

"I'm not keeping anyone's secrets. Or hiding any of my own."

"But she paid you all that money."

A long hesitation. "I'm a physician. I work at a Catholic hospital. We do things by the book. But it's well known that organs can be obtained...other ways. There are a few places that allow people to flat-out buy a kidney. But even that becomes complicated, when you've got Customs and foreign governments involved. There are simpler alternatives."

"You're saying Claudia paid you to get a black-market kidney?"

"No. I was just the...conduit."

"Doctor, I've reviewed your bank records, and I know that money hasn't gone anywhere. You've written no checks nor made any withdrawals."

"No. I told you already. I'm holding it in escrow. We never found a kidney."

"Then shouldn't you return the money?"

"To whom? It came from Claudia's trust fund. I believe she would want me to continue looking. Now more than ever, given the circumstances. I don't think David is getting a kidney the usual way and he doesn't have much time left."

They'd bantered long enough. It was time to get mean. "You know what I think? I think you're a smart, determined woman, and if you'd wanted to find a black-market kidney, it would've already happened."

"It's not that easy."

"I think that you want money. Maybe to change your career. Maybe so you can retire. I know you're carrying a lot of debt and the mortgage on that Brentwood mansion is costing you over nine thousand bucks a month."

Even Judge Durant's eyes widened.

"Isn't it true that Claudia wanted the money back?"

"How did you—"

"It's in her diary." Although he hadn't understood what it meant until just this moment. 'Asked doc to return the booty. Refused.'"

Southern took a long, slow breath. "Since I hadn't found a kidney, after a time, she asked me to return the money."

"But you didn't."

"I was going to. I just didn't—didn't—"

"Want to."

Her voice rose in volume. "It's not that simple."

"Seems pretty simple to me. You write a check. Takes about five seconds."

"We had to disguise the transaction. For tax purposes. I didn't want it to be perceived as income. Or a gift. And before I could figure out how to handle it, she was dead."

"I think you blackmailed her. Pay me some money or your boyfriend dies. So she paid you off. And then you stole the violin. Or maybe she gave it to you to keep you quiet or compliant. Or maybe you kept it against her will because you were greedy and you wanted more."

"That's ridiculous. You can't prove any of—"

"Here's what I can prove. You deliberately withheld this information about refusing to return the money from David's defense team and the police."

"It had nothing—"

"Therefore, by definition, this is newly discovered evidence that casts doubt on the trial-court verdict. A jury can't be expected to reach a correct conclusion if it doesn't have all the critical facts. And you withheld facts."

"It was no one's business but—"

"Try telling that to David. Do you know how many days he's spent in prison for a crime he didn't commit?"

Her face flushed. "I did not take that violin. And I certainly did not kill Claudia."

"That's a question for the jury. Which is exactly why you made sure they didn't know everything there was to know."

# CHAPTER FORTY-NINE

DAN WONDERED IF JUDGE DURANT HAD REACHED THE POINT IN LIFE when bathroom visits became more urgent and more frequent, because they seemed to be taking breaks at least every hour or so. Maybe he had some pressing desk work. Or maybe this case bored him to tears.

Or maybe the weight of knowing he was determining the length of someone's life made this uncomfortably stressful. Was it possible Durant was not entirely convinced of David's guilt? Was it possible he was less hostile toward this motion than Dan imagined?

He could but hope. Because right now, he had no idea where they stood.

"How do you think that one went?" he asked Ben, in the courtroom hallway.

"Definitely better...."

"But?"

"You know the standard of review." He glanced at their client, who was probably feeling the stress worse than any of them. "We have to present newly discovered evidence that might—"

"He did that," David insisted. "The cops didn't know Claudia tried to get her money back. I didn't even know that. Doesn't that mean the trial was flawed?"

Ben answered. "The Constitution says every defendant is entitled to a fair trial—not a perfect trial. Because there's no such thing."

"I'm not seeing the distinction."

"It's not enough to dig up new evidence. We have to show that, had it been introduced at trial, there's a reasonable probability that it would have impacted the jury's verdict. In other words, it can't just be some rando fact we dug up. It has to matter. In a big way."

"I think knowing the doctor got a big check and wouldn't give it back matters."

"Look at it from the judge's standpoint. Sure, that should've come out. But what difference does it make? The doctor is not on trial."

"Maybe she should be."

Ben nodded. "We have to convince this judge that someone else committed the murder. If we can do that, Durant might feel motivated to order a new trial, even if our evidence is last-minute and not as strong as we'd like. He a decent judge and he's been on the bench for a long time. He'll try to make a bad situation right."

"Do you think the judge is convinced?"

"I'm not a mind reader. I think we've got his attention." He paused. "But we haven't given him the smoking gun."

"But we will," David said. "Right? With the next witness?"

Dan shoved his hands into his pockets. "I hope so. Because this is our last shot."

———

WHEN DAN RETURNED TO THE COURTROOM, HE FOUND FBI SPECIAL Agent Courtney Zhang, their interrogator from a few days before, waiting for him.

"This is unexpected. Have you come to apologize?"

Zhang looked at him as if she had an unpleasant taste in her mouth. "No. I have more questions."

"Not interested."

"You should be. I'm trying to make the lame story you two boys told make sense."

"Maybe later. We're in the middle of a hearing."

"I'm supposed to stand around twiddling my thumbs while you lawyer boys play lawyer games? I don't think so." She whipped out her badge. "I'm taking you into custody. It's much simpler than asking nicely."

"I'm telling you—"

"Or I could make it an arrest. Would you like that better? If I decide to place you under arrest, there's not a thing you or anyone else can do to stop me."

*"You are greatly mistaken."*

All heads whirled. Judge Durant had re-entered the courtroom. And he looked angry.

Zhang stepped forward. "Sir, I'm a federal agent investigating—"

"I don't care. We're in the midst of a hearing and you are not going to interfere."

Zhang offered a small patronizing smile. "Your honor, I'm a federal agent. This is a federal matter. And—"

"And this is my courtroom."

"A state courtroom. District court. The federal government has jurisdiction—"

"Not in my courtroom. Here, what I say goes."

"Sir, I don't want to pull rank—"

"And you won't, because you don't outrank me. Not here."

"Sir, if necessary I will—"

The judge spoke to his bailiff. "Barney, if she speaks or attempts to interfere with this hearing in any way—restrain her."

"Understood, your honor."

Zhang watched, eyes squinted.

"And if you resist arrest, I'll hold you in contempt of court. For an indefinite period of time."

She scoffed. "I don't think Barney—"

"There are over fifty security officers in this courthouse. I don't care if

I have to call every one of them. You will not interfere with the business of this court. Do whatever you want afterward. But we're proceeding with the matter at hand." Without another word, he settled in at the bench.

Dan and Ben shared a wide-eyed expression. Damn. Who'da thought? Judge Durant turned out to be a white-haired asskicker.

---

EVEN THOUGH HE HADN'T HAD A CHANCE TO MEET OR TALK WITH Professor Herwig, Dan still chose to call him last. Dan whipped through Herwig's background and credentials. He knew the judge didn't care about Herwig's academic publications. He wanted to hear about the murder.

"You had Claudia in some of your classes, correct?"

Professor Herwig wore black round owl-eye glasses he probably thought were stylish—and might have been, fifteen or twenty years ago. The rich-girl hottie who played the priceless violin was so far out of this guy's reach that any pairing seemed inconceivable.

"Two. During two different semesters. And I advised her. I'd known her for a while."

"Good student?"

"Superb. She practiced night and day. She had relatively small hands with a touch of early arthritis and sometimes couldn't duplicate the fingering suggested by the composer. So she developed her own approach that worked amazingly well. She'd taken advantage of her problem to innovate, to make something wonderful. I know other students who have now adopted her approach. It's amazing, really. While still a student, she developed something that may linger long after her passing. Her death was a tragedy—but her life was a triumph."

More than Dan expected, but he could roll with it. "So you liked her?"

"Everyone liked her. Certainly the faculty did. Instead of the typical sophomore drifting along aimlessly, this was a young woman with serious musical ambitions. And I think she could've achieved them. I mean, look how much she did in the time she had."

"You were…involved with her, weren't you? Quite a bit."

Herwig adjusted his glasses. "You'll need to define what you mean by 'involved.' An unscrupulous person could twist that word around to mean something inappropriate."

Oh, well played. This Ph.D. was no dummy.

"How much did you work with her?"

"In addition to those classes, she played in the student orchestra. She did the annual Southland concert just a few weeks before she died. And she held a Work Study position with me."

"Did you ever hear her play the 'Military Drumroll Surprise?'"

"No."

"Nickname for the violin?"

"I don't think so."

"Piece of music she was focusing on?"

"Not to my knowledge. And I would know. She was working on a capstone project and chose me to be her advisor."

"So you were seeing a great deal of this one particular young woman. Who died under mysterious circumstances."

Herwig took a deep breath but maintained his composure. "I know nothing about her death. I wish I did. The police told me David Donovan did it and I assumed that was correct."

"But you don't have any actual knowledge about that."

"No. I don't."

The direct approach was not going to work with this guy. He was too intelligent.

"Why do you think she chose you to be her advisor?"

"Claudia had a great fondness for the work of Haydn." If he recalled correctly, both she and David shared that fondness. "Haydn, as it happens, was the subject of my dissertation and several published articles. She wanted to analyze his symphonies and define the common structural patterns that underlined all his large-scale composing. I was the obvious choice to work with her."

"Did you think she was onto something?"

"Honestly? I don't know. It was a big project, very ambitious for someone at that stage of her career. Especially given what she was dealing with at home. She was totally estranged from her mother, though her father tended to indulge her. But even if this project failed, something else would eventually succeed. She had that kind of drive. She was no quitter."

"Any other reasons to choose you?"

"I don't want to toot my own horn, but I am well-known in the classical music community, which here in LA is quite large. I have connections. Students who work with me get jobs."

"Did she need a job?"

"I don't know anything about her financial situation, but I know she wanted to play professionally."

"Did you ever see her afterhours? At night?"

Only the slightest hesitation. The man was too smart to be caught in a disprovable lie. He knew what was in her diary. "Yes."

"For what reason?"

"I often invite students to my home—with my wife—for informal gatherings. Sometimes I play choice bits of classical music. And of course we talk."

"Drink?"

"Not to excess."

"How many students?"

"It varies. Ten or twelve."

"Was Claudia ever at your house by herself?"

A slight pause. "Not that I recall. If so, it would've been briefly. Like if she were the last to leave."

"Do you think she liked you?"

"I prefer to think so."

"And did you like her?"

Herwig took in a deep breath. "Yes, I liked her. But only in a completely acceptable and appropriate way. Don't try to make it into something more."

"Did you ever touch her?"

"No."

"Kiss her?"

"It would hard to kiss someone without touching them."

"Any other kinds of contact?"

"Give it up already. There's no *there* there."

"You play the violin, don't you?"

"I play six instruments very well and four passably well."

"And one of those is the violin?"

"That's my best instrument. I used to play with the Pops, you know. Played concerts at Gehry's fabulous Disney Concert Hall. And that's another reason why I was the best choice to mentor her."

"You knew she possessed an extremely expensive Amati, right?"

"Everyone did."

"Antique?'

"Obviously."

"Rare?"

"Very."

"Did you know she kept it in her dorm room?"

"In a big safe. She talked about it. I thought it seemed unwise myself, but she insisted there was no point in having a treasure if you never enjoyed it."

"Did you ever play the Amati in question?"

"Yes. Twice."

"Was it all it was cracked up to be?"

"More. It's an incredible instrument and she has taken excellent care of it. I felt absolutely transported. One of the great experiences of my life, actually."

"I bet you wished you could play that violin every day, didn't you?"

Herwig gave him a long look. "I wish I could solo at Carnegie Hall, but I don't think it's going to happen any time soon."

"But this violin was within your grasp."

"It wasn't. It was locked up. I didn't know the combination. But your client did. End of story." Herwig pushed himself up, as if he were done and ready to leave.

"I don't see it that way. I think you wanted the violin and you wanted Claudia. And since you couldn't get either voluntarily…you forced the issue."

"You need to be careful what you say."

Dan ignored him. "You spent a weirdly unnatural amount of time with a single student. You were not the only choice for her capstone. In fact, you pushed someone else out of the way to get the position. She was unqualified for the Work Study position and didn't need the money though others did. But you gave it to her. Because you wanted to get close to her."

"Objection." Chee had heard enough, it seemed. "The witness has already denied this. Asked and answered."

"That's true," the judge said, rapping his desk. "Let's move forward."

Time for the main thrust. "If everything was so hunky-dory with you two and nothing inappropriate ever happened—why did she break up with you?"

Herwig's face twisted. "Break up? Not a phrase I would use…"

"But the exact phrase Claudia used. In her diary." He glanced down at his notes. "Herwig went too far. We're breaking up. Will suck it up and deliver bad news Friday."

"She may have been contemplating dropping out of the student orchestra. She was very busy."

"Pardon me, sir, but that's complete baloney. No one in the history of the world ever talked about 'breaking up' with an orchestra." He leaned in closer. "The only way you can break up with someone is if you have a relationship with them in the first place."

"A professional relationship."

"What did she mean by 'breaking up' with you?"

"I don't know. She never said anything like that to me. And of course…she died before Friday came. Maybe she was contemplating switching advisors. Maybe she wanted a different perspective."

"You're tapdancing as fast as you can, trying to shuffle-ball-change around the obvious explanation."

"I was never in any kind of inappropriate relationship with Claudia."

"You were in love with her. And I'm not the only one who thinks so. Some of the other students thought your devotion to her was creepy. And eventually, she did too."

"You're wrong."

"I think you invited her to your home when no one else was there. Especially your wife. I think you made a pass and she shot you down hard. After that, she knew she couldn't work with you anymore and wrote it in her diary."

"Total fantasy."

"What's more, I think you realized she was likely to file a sexual harassment charge, and these days universities take that sort of thing very seriously. At the very least, you'd be suspended, probably without pay. But once they knew what you did, you'd be fired. You'd never work in academia again. You had to stop her."

Herwig leaned forward, looking outraged. But the sweat trickling down his cheek told Dan he was worried. "Lies. All lies. Every word of it."

"Your honor..." Chee said, trying feebly to intervene. No one was paying attention. The drama was on the witness stand.

"You killed her to save yourself. And while you were there—hey, why not take that violin? You'd earned it, right?"

"This is a complete fantasy. I did not hurt that girl. I would never hurt her."

"Without a good reason. Which you had. Because she was breaking up with you. And you would've been destroyed."

"I did not kill her!" Herwig shouted. "I had no reason to. It was... just a misunderstanding."

Dan's head jerked around. "What was the misunderstanding?"

Herwig looked as if he were about to explode. "I was...trying to help her."

"And got a little handsy in the process?"

"Never!"

"You probably resented her as much as you crushed on her. Why should she have that enchanted violin? She hadn't earned it. You were the talent. You probably thought it was wasted on her. She only had it because Daddy had money."

"None of this is remotely true."

"And that was the real problem, wasn't it? She thought the violin belonged to her because her daddy bought it for her. But you thought it belonged to you, because you had the talent and experience to play it the way it deserved to be played."

"Well I did!" he shouted, suddenly rising. "Claudia was talented. But this was an Amati! For God's sake, Paganini played that violin! What in God's name was it doing in this little girl's dorm room, lying around with the empty pizza boxes and dirty laundry? Was she one of the best violinists in the world?"

"No. But you think you are," Dan said quietly. "And that's how you justified doing the most terrible thing imaginable. And letting my client take the rap for it."

## CHAPTER FIFTY

HERWIG CONTINUED TO PROTEST HIS INNOCENCE AND DAN KNEW HE always would, so he ended the examination. Had he made Herwig look suspicious? He thought so. Made Dr. Southern look pretty bad too. But when it came to identifying a murderer, he hadn't proven anything, at least not to any degree of certainty.

For once, the judge opted against taking another break. He gave them each ten minutes to close, then indicated that he would rule from the bench. He did not want this motion to drag on another day.

Ten minutes to save a man's life. No pressure there.

"Your honor," Dan began, "I know we have the burden of proof. I know we have to show misconduct, new evidence, or some procedural error grievous enough to mandate a new trial—even if no one at the trial was necessarily at fault." He opened this way for a reason. He was trying to signal Durant that it was possible for him to order a new trial without suggesting that he had committed any legal errors. "I don't know if the DA and the police overlooked or suppressed this evidence. There are two possibilities. Their investigation was so superficial and selective that they missed important details. Or they ignored these details so they could convict an easy target—David Donovan. It demonstrates either negligence or corruption, and either is sufficient reason to order a new trial."

The judge wasn't nodding. But he wasn't frowning, either. He was listening.

"I realize that we probably haven't presented enough information against any of these suspects to get a conviction. But that isn't our job today. There are many possibilities that were not thoroughly—or in some cases, even superficially—investigated. Are you willing to let this conviction stand, to literally end this man's life, when there are so many unanswered questions? If I may remind the court, the defendant has no prior record, was well liked, well respected, had no violent tendencies, and basically is now having his life threatened because someone else killed his girlfriend. Which you might think would make him an object of sympathy. But to the police, he offered a shortcut. The crime got a lot of publicity, the pressure was on to charge someone, so they arrested him. But did they catch the right guy, or as sadly happens far too often, did they catch the most conveniently available guy?"

He raised a hand before he drew an objection. "Could they concoct a motive for my client? Of course. That violin. But the violin would be valuable to anyone, and everyone knew where it was. During daylight hours, getting into that dorm was a piece of cake. Just follow a student with a pass and you can do whatever you want. Claudia frequently left her door unlocked. Anyone could get in.

"I will respectfully suggest that David Donovan is not the most likely suspect but the least likely suspect. Someone cleaned up the room—to avoid leaving evidence of their presence. But David had no reason to do that. He was her boyfriend. They hung out together. He spent the night in her room on many occasions. But who might want to eliminate all traces that they'd been there? Mitch Theroux was two doors down. Professor Herwig had a faculty pass."

He took a small step forward. "Claudia had already paid a large sum of money to get a kidney, and there's no reason to think she wouldn't continue dipping into her trust fund as needed. But Dr. Southern's handling of the money from Claudia is bizarre. And she still has that money. Who knows what else she might have received—and doesn't want to lose?"

He took a small step forward. "Your honor, the exact same case the DA made against David Donovan could also be made against each of the three witnesses we put on the stand. And the case would be just as strong."

He knew the court was impatient, so he wrapped it up. "Here's what we learned today. Mitch Theroux adored the victim and deeply resented the fact that she chose my client over him. Mitch had access to both Claudia's room and safe. Dr. Southern received a secret payment from the victim and her explanation for it, even if true, proves she was engaging in unethical activity. Why would she admit to that? To mask something even more damaging?"

He paused. "And then there is Professor Herwig, who so obviously saw the victim as a giant object of desire. He coveted not only her but her instrument. To be fair, he probably was more deserving of that fine violin. Did that give him the right to take it? No. Did it give him a reason to murder her? Obviously."

For the first time, the judge cut in. "But he didn't know the combination."

"So he claimed. She might've told him."

"Why would she tell her professor?"

Dan tried to come up with a good answer. "Maybe he forced his way in."

The judge shook his head. "The safe was not damaged. Someone knew the combination."

"They were working on a project together."

"They both loved Haydn. That doesn't mean she gave him the combination."

"When people spend a lot of time together…things slip out."

The judge frowned but did not reply.

Dan continued his closing. "There is far more uncertainty in this case than certainty, which should be the surest sign the conviction was a mistake. The standard we use in criminal cases is that guilt must be proved 'beyond a reasonable doubt.' How can we possibly say that burden was met in this case? Any one of these people could have committed this crime. That's why the court should order a new trial. So a jury can be presented with all the relevant evidence and reach an informed conclusion about guilt. Thank you."

Normally, when he sat down at the table after a big speech, he checked his client's expression to see how he did. But this time, he checked Ben.

Who was not smiling.

"That bad?" he whispered.

Ben seemed lost in thought. After a moment, his head jerked up. "Hmm? What?"

"I asked how you think my closing went."

"Oh. Fine. Best you could do under the circumstances. But something the judge said…"

Dan felt confused. "What?"

Ben shook his head.

Chee followed with her summation, which was exactly what Dan expected. A rehash of the standard of review. Denigration of the new evidence. She didn't seem able to work up much enthusiasm despite the fact that her office had been seriously impugned.

And that was frightening in its own way. Chee was just going through the motions. Because she was certain the judge would rule in her favor.

"There's not much I can say that hasn't been said before, your honor. This is a desperate rehash. I commend the court for not simply dismissing this summarily, as most courts would've done, but I will warn that we don't want to encourage this sort of thing. If we start holding a hearing every time someone wants the trial court to reconsider a verdict, we'll have double the dockets for every judge, most of whom already have more cases than they can handle."

Now the judge was nodding. A bad sign.

"I notice defense counsel keeps criticizing the police for not investigating enough. But I also note that he has no evidence to support this argument. Does he know what law enforcement did or did not do? He just joined the case a few days ago. The truth is, the police were aware of all three of these witnesses—but the evidence pointed to Donovan and still does. Maybe the police didn't specifically know about every single detail. That doesn't prove anything."

She lowered her head as if finished, but soon lifted it. An afterthought, or at least that's how she wanted it to play.

"It's not enough to show that some angle or another wasn't discussed at trial. All parties were represented by counsel and they decided what they wanted to emphasize or ignore. Why are these arguments being made for the first time now? Shouldn't we assume that the previous defense attorney ignored them because he didn't believe they were helpful? Was it an omission or a strategy call? The jury received the evidence that mattered and reached a unanimous verdict based upon it. End of story."

She paused. "Or at, that should be the end of the story. Let it end, your honor. Dismiss this frivolous motion."

And with that she sat down.

# CHAPTER FIFTY-ONE

DAN WAS SURPRISED WHEN THE JUDGE CALLED FOR ANOTHER BRIEF break. Durant said before that he planned to rule today.

Which led Dan to one conclusion. The judge had already made up his mind. He just wanted a few moments to compose his thoughts.

Dan and Ben strolled into the outside corridor. Maria and Christina were waiting for them.

"Congrats on the last witness," Christina said. "That was a powerful cross."

Dan shrugged. "I hope it was enough."

"You knew this was going to be an uphill battle."

"True."

"No judge likes to set aside a verdict. Instead of getting something off their docket, they end up with something that stays on their docket for several more years."

"But realistically, this is Donovan's last chance."

"He can appeal."

"Already did. But as you know, appeals are limited to legal errors. And there really weren't any."

"Then let's hope the judge sees the light."

Maria took his arm. "I thought you did a great job, Dan. Especially for someone who's been out of the courtroom for a while."

"I should've let Ben handle it. I just thought it required some..."

"Panache?"

"More like...grittiness. Willingness to roll up your sleeves and get dirty."

Christina grinned. "Let me tell you something about my husband. Yes, he's quiet. But I've seen him rip a witness' throat out with his teeth." She glanced at Ben. "Metaphorically speaking."

"What do you think, Ben?" David asked. "You've barely spoken."

Ben's lips were pursed. "I'm free-associating."

David looked baffled. "Is that a...lawyer thing?"

"Something is tugging at the back of my brain. But I can't quite tease it out."

"I have the exact same feeling," Dan said. "Did you see something on the stand? Hear something?"

"Yes. And it's driving me crazy."

Dan laid a hand on his shoulder. "Give it a rest. The hearing is over. Wouldn't matter, even if you thought of whatever it was."

"I suppose. David—how are you?"

"My stomach is roiling. My head throbs. I'm so nervous I can barely breathe. But other than that..."

"Let me say something while we can. I am one hundred percent certain that you did not commit this crime. Even if we lose today, we won't stop fighting."

"I heard what Dan said. This is our last stand."

The court clerk poked her head outside the courtroom doors. "The judge has returned."

Dan and Ben exchanged a grim look. "Showtime."

---

JUDGE DURANT WAS ALREADY SEATED WHEN THEY RETURNED. DAN TRIED to apologize for making him wait, but he waved it away. It was obvious he had something to say and he was ready to get it done.

"First of all, I want both sides to understand that I came to this hearing with no preconceived notions. I listened to what you said and I considered your arguments. Let me also say, without being too specific…that you shouldn't assume the court is always hostile to motions for new trial. They get dismissed frequently because they are typically thrown together quickly without much thought so lawyers can say they did everything and check off an imaginary box somewhere."

His shoulders rose. "But I've been sitting behind this bench for a long time. And many a jury trial. Those twelve in the box are the ones who decide whether the prosecution has met its burden of proof. And more than once I've encountered instances when the jury thought it did—but I didn't. While I'm always reluctant to set aside a jury verdict…I am willing to prevent a gross miscarriage of justice."

Dan looked at David. For the first time, he saw a little light in his eyes, a tiny flickering of hope.

Till the judge continued. "But that does not necessarily mean I will always agree with the defense arguments, and in this case, I simply do not."

Dan's lips parted. David's face fell.

"True, the defense has presented alternative suspects, but it did not prove any of them committed a murder. Not even close. And frankly, even if Mr. Pike had pulled a Perry Mason and gotten someone to confess—it still wouldn't necessarily mandate a new trial. We're not retrying the verdict. The question before us today is whether the newly discovered evidence is of such magnitude that the defendant did not obtain a fair trial. And in this case, the defense has not presented evidence of that magnitude."

To his side, he saw Ben place his hand on David's wrist, steadying him.

"The State was right to note that the defendant was represented throughout this process, including at the trial court. Any improprieties should have been raised then, while there was still time to remedy them. There has been no argument of ineffective counsel."

Which Dan considered but decided against, in part because it might not look good if two out-of-staters started maligning local lawyers.

"Absent such claim or fraud, the fact that counsel was represented at trial makes this motion all but impossible to prove. I will not set aside a jury verdict based upon speculation about other parties. There will always be other parties. But in this case, the jury found it had enough evidence to convict. I will not set aside their decision.

"Motion dismissed." The judge rapped the gavel.

The sound seemed deafening. And it reverberated far too long.

# CHAPTER FIFTY-TWO

DAN WATCHED IN SILENCE AS THE MARSHALS TOOK DAVID AWAY, BACK to his world of coveralls and fatty food and constant danger. The sadness in his eyes, the abject terror, were unmistakable. He was already at death's door, and now he would get to spend his final, painful days behind bars.

They had failed him.

Which would hurt in any case, but never more so than now, because like Ben, he'd become convinced that David was innocent.

They returned to Gary's office, their new home away from home. Dan slumped into a chair, head in hands. "We blew it. We totally blew it."

Maria wrapped her arms around him. "You lost. You didn't blow it. No lawyer wins every case."

"We should've won this one."

"Ben, talk to him."

Ben's head jerked up, as if she were retrieving him from a deep reverie. "What? Oh. No, thanks. I'm with Dan. We blew it."

"The judge didn't want to set the verdict aside."

"We should've convinced him. Made him feel he had no choice."

Christina jumped in. "You've lost cases that should have gone your way before, Ben."

"Have I ever been happy about it?"

She smiled a little. "No."

"And this time, we blew an innocent man's last chance. He'll never get a new kidney and he'll die in prison. Soon."

"You did your best."

"Did I? I know there's something I haven't figured out. But what is it? It involves...someone. I...don't seem to be able to recall names as quickly as I once did. Stupid."

"That's not stupidity, Ben. That's getting older."

Ben ignored her. "It triggered something when the judge mentioned...it starts with an 'H...'"

Dan rolled his eyes.

Maria tried to guess. "Hancock. Hart. Harris. Holden."

Ben snapped his fingers. "No. *Haydn.*"

"Claudia's favorite composer. And apparently a fave of Professor Herwig, too."

"And mine," Ben added. "Haydn has many underappreciated piano pieces. Victim of his own success. He wrote symphonies so well that other deserving works slip through the cracks. I think his work for the piano rivals Chopin's. His preludes are considered the definitive piano show pieces."

Dan didn't know nor care about classical music. But if this mental diversion distracted Ben from the awfulness of what had happened, fine. "There's a piano downstairs. Maybe you could play a little Haydn for us."

"Not in the mood."

"Do you have to be in the mood to play the piano?"

"Of course. Piano is about interpretation. Energy. Feeling every note. All music is, I suppose."

"I used to play a mean kazoo," Maria said.

Ben continued, as if he were talking to himself but talking out loud. "Haydn is best remembered as a prolific composer of symphonies. Everyone has heard them, even if they don't know it.

He's famous—"

All at once, Ben's lips parted. "OhmiGod. OhmiGod."

A crease formed between Dan's eyes. "Was is it?"

Ben held up a finger. As in, *let me think.*

Christina's eyes narrowed. "Ben, I've seen that look on your face before. You've thought of something."

He spoke, tentatively at first, in barely more than a whisper. "I...I think I know who killed Claudia. And...I know how it was done, too. How the safe was opened."

"Ok. Spill."

Ben slammed his palm down on the tabletop. "We need to get out of here."

"Why?"

"To recover the violin."

"You know where it is?"

"I think so. And it probably won't be there long. It can't be played in public right now, but it could be sold on the black market, a deal I suspect has already been arranged. Most Amatis are either in museums or private collections. It could disappear for as long as it needs to before the new owner acknowledges it. So we need to move fast. If we find the violin, we find the murderer."

"And how do you know this?"

Ben allowed a small smile. "We were told. During the hearing."

Dan's neck tightened. "I'm pretty sure I would remember that. Where the violin?"

Ben was already halfway across the room. He grabbed the keys to their rental car. "It's easier to show you."

Christina stepped in front of him. "Is this going to be dangerous?"

"Why would you think that?"

"Because for decades I've watched you plunge foolishly into danger and barely survive."

"I'll take Dan with me."

"I'd rather you took a big dog. Or a big stick. And why are you assuming Dan wants to plunge into danger with you?"

Dan shrugged. "I mean, hell, we've come clear across the country together. Might as well finish the hero's journey."

Ben nodded. "Saddle up, pardner. Looks like we've got one more roundup before we ride off into the sunset."

# CHAPTER FIFTY-THREE

Dan sat in the driver's seat. Ben called shotgun. Both stared at the modest house halfway down the street. They'd parked in a spot that allowed them to watch discreetly without attracting notice. Unless someone wondered why two adult men were sitting in a car doing nothing, which would be hard to explain. They scrunched down low, especially when they saw a car coming by.

A green SUV shone its headlights their way, then drove on.

"Think he saw us?" Ben asked.

"Who knows? Someone will eventually. If our target doesn't come home soon." He glanced at his watch. "You know, we could just…accidentally slip into the house."

"You're talking about breaking and entering."

"Occasionally I've had to resort to things that…weren't exactly by the book. I know. You're appalled."

"You might be surprised." He laughed. "In the early days, Christina and I broke into an office. More than once."

Dan's eyes widened. "You? Mr. Law and Order?"

"I fought for my clients. Just like you. And sometimes that meant pushing my luck. Especially early on, when I had no staff and no money for luxuries like private investigators. We did what we had to do."

"I'm shocked."

"Really? Does the Last Chance Lawyers seem like an outfit that toes the line and recites the law school credo?"

"Well...it is...unusual."

"For a reason. Everyone else can practice law the way it is. I wanted to practice law the way it should be."

"A bold statement."

"Christina calls it visionary. She loves the LCL concept. She loved it even more when you took over. Though I always suspected that was because I had more free time and could finally take her to France."

"Please tell me that you did."

"Two weeks. Floated all around the country. Saw the Eiffel Tower. Ate lots of baguettes."

"She must've loved that."

"Her exact words were, 'It's like the France pavilion at EPCOT. Except without clean bathrooms or ice in your drink.'"

Dan couldn't help but grin. "But the important thing is, you got her there." Dan glanced at his watch again. He didn't want to seem impatient. But sitting around doing nothing was not his style. "We should've gotten a subpoena."

"Tip our hand? No. We're not breaking in. We're waiting till someone opens the door for us. Then we'll tell a big lie, get invited inside, and look around."

"You seriously think we'll be welcome?"

"I'm counting on your charisma."

They passed another twenty minutes with similar chitchat until finally they saw a car swerve around the corner and pull into the driveway. If the driver took notice of them, Dan saw no evidence of it.

"Good. We may still have the element of surprise." Dan watched as the car sailed into the garage. "Let's wait ten minutes."

"That's too long. Two minutes. Just long enough to hang up a coat."

"Bathroom break?"

Ben shook his head. "The more uncomfortable the better."

As it happened, they waited only a minute before they arrived at the front door.

Dan rang the bell. A catchy series of notes sounded.

"Haydn," Ben murmured. "Naturally."

Another few moments and the door opened. The face on the other side took only a moment to recognize them. Then started closing the door.

Dan stepped forward and put his shoe in the opening. "Just give us five minutes."

"I'm not giving you five seconds."

"We just want to talk."

"I have nothing to say to you. The case is over."

"An appeal is pending. But if you'll just answer a few questions, we may be able to clear your name." Or not. Depending upon what he said.

Frown. Hesitation. Deliberation. "And it will finally be over?"

"Perhaps."

"Fine." Professor Herwig opened the door.

Dan and Ben stepped inside. His home was furnished as might expect for an unmarried intellectual. Books everywhere, randomly flung on shelves. Dirty dishes on the coffee table. A cabinet filled with records, mostly classical.

"I hear vinyl is making a comeback," Ben said.

"It's the only way to listen to music for the true audiophile. Vinyl, with a good sound system, has enormous power. Digital music is cold. Doesn't have the same oomph. It's like listening to monophonic background noise."

"Harsh."

"Sorry. We musicians see the world differently."

"I'm a musician," Ben said. "And I can't get nostalgic about something that was so flawed the first time around. I don't miss the skips, pops, and crackles."

Herwig made a tsking sound. "You must take better care of your records. But let's talk about why you're here. What is it you want?"

"We know we can't get David off the hook. But we might be able to get a reduced sentence. We've hired a mitigation specialist."

Herwig blinked. "A what?"

"New thing in the legal world. They look into someone's background, find out if they had a rough childhood, abuse, drug problems. Or an impossible financial situation. Anything that might make them more sympathetic."

"And you think I'm going to help? Sheesh. I need a drink." He strolled toward an open bottle of red wine. "Anything for you boys?"

Ben raised his hands. "Unless you've got chocolate milk, I'll pass."

Dan winced. "I'm more of a whisky man, but if that's what you've got, sure."

Herwig poured two glasses. Dan noticed his hand shook, almost imperceptibly. But still it shook.

Herwig appeared calm. "Mr. Kincaid? If you don't care for alcohol, I've got some Red Bull in the fridge."

"God no. I want to sleep tonight."

Dan winked. "No caffeine for Grandpa after noon. Look, we're hoping you might be able to tell us something that will help the expert."

"Why me?" Herwig picked up his wine glass and sipped.

"You know David. You knew Claudia. You had them both in your classes."

"Yes, with about two hundred other people. I don't have time for heart-to-hearts about students' troubled childhoods."

"I recall you testified that Claudia didn't get along with her mother. But Daddy controlled the purse strings."

He waved a hand dismissively. "I heard her mention that once in the green room before a performance. It's not like I was quizzing her about her life story."

"Did you hear anything about David?"

"No. Didn't speak to him that much."

"You paid more attention to the pretty rich young woman?"

Herwig's lips tightened. "Am I still on the witness stand?"

"No, no. I'm sorry. Bad habit. Here's the thing. We've heard that David was subjected to a lot of bullying. Like daily. And as everyone knows, that kind of harassment can lead to depression, poor decisions, insecurity. Even suicide."

"He didn't kill himself."

"But he made some poor decisions. Did you see any instances of bullying?"

"Sorry, no."

"Did you hear about anything second-hand?"

"Again, no."

"We heard it was particularly bad at...the Southland concert. Which you mentioned."

"That was a great performance. My student orchestra shone. And we raised a ton of money for the department."

"Did David seem...disturbed?"

"Not that I recall."

"Did you take any photos?"

"Sure, with my phone. I always do."

"Could we look at them?"

"Oh, I don't know. I wouldn't feel right—"

"Even if it saves a man's life?"

"I think David deserves to spend his life in prison."

"That will be a short life."

"I still don't think—"

"Please. How can it hurt? Just let us see the photos."

Herwig sighed heavily. It was clear he wanted this to be over and wanted these people out of his house. "Fine." He looked around, then patted his pockets. "I must've left my phone upstairs. I'll be right back."

"Thank you so much. I appreciate it."

They watched as he clumped up the stairs. And as soon as he was out of sight—they sprung into action.

"Found it yet?" Dan whispered.

Ben had been scanning the whole time Dan engaged Herwig in

conversation. "Think so. The key is understanding the depth of this man's obsession with Joseph Haydn. And his delusional assessment of his own talent. He was convinced he could be one of the greatest violinists who ever lived—if he just had the right instrument."

Ben walked to the nearest bookshelf. "See this row of vinyl records? All perfectly organized. Alphabetized by composer. Then the symphonies by each composer are organized by chronological or numerical order."

"The man is obviously sick. I thought Mitch was the OCD one."

"Except one LP doesn't fit. The one on the end. Look." He pointed. "Marlis Petersen's famous recording of *The Seasons*. By Haydn. Except it doesn't look like the others. There's something...bland about the spine. Something not quite right."

Dan reached toward it. "There is something...different...."

"The others are real." Ben pulled out one of the other albums to show him. "See? Perfectly normal record. But this one...." He tried to pull it out.

Didn't budge. As if it were locked into place.

Then, instead of trying to pull it out, he pushed it in.

They heard a clicking sound, as if a hidden latch had been tripped.

Then a bump. And the shelf swung out a few inches. "*Voila.*"

Inside the revealed alcove, resting on a stand, was a violin.

Dan's lips parted. "You were right."

"I never believed the threat of a sexual harassment charge would be enough to make this milquetoast commit murder. But the violin might. He can't sell it, at least not now. He just wants to possess it. He wants to play it."

"Badly enough to kill someone?"

"Maybe someday in the future he planned to sell it, then use the money to get another violin, something of supreme quality but not stolen so he could play it in public."

"What do we do now?"

Ben snapped a pic with his phone. "We take the violin and get the hell out of here." He held it gingerly with both hands. "I can't believe how old this is. It's like playing one of Bach's harpsichords. Let's—"

He froze in his tracks.

Herwig stood just behind them. Holding a pistol.

"I really wish you hadn't done that," he said.

# CHAPTER FIFTY-FOUR

DAN FELT HIS SPINE STRAIGHTEN. THE EXPRESSION ON HERWIG'S FACE was so dark he couldn't predict what might happen next.

"Aren't you the little ninja?" Dan said, glowering.

Herwig stretched out his arm. "I was onto you two liars from the start."

"Just as we were onto you."

"How did you figure it out?"

Ben shrugged. "When the judge referenced your testimony, your affection for Haydn, it triggered something. Something that had been lurking in my subconscious but hadn't quite congealed. This afternoon, I visited the Licorice Pizza in Culver City."

"If you'd been one of my students, that wouldn't have been necessary."

"It wasn't necessary. I have a memory. And a cellphone." He glanced at Dan. "A new one. But as a lawyer, I've learned to confirm my facts."

Herwig's lips were clenched. He still had the gun outstretched. "And?"

Dan understood what Ben was doing. There was no reason to explain everything to a man threatening to kill him. But Ben hoped that if he kept the man preoccupied, Dan would concoct a way to get them out alive.

Like what? He could try to rush Herwig, but bullets are faster than people.

"There's that phrase that kept popping up in this case. Military Drumroll Surprise. Claudia wrote it on the inside cover of her diary. Mitch Theroux mentioned it. But what did it mean? Claudia was not a likely ROTC candidate. No one in your classical music classes was likely playing Sousa marches. So what was that? And then, all at once, it hit me. It's about Haydn."

"You do know your classical music," Herwig said, beads of sweat appearing on the sides of his face. "I will grant you that."

"Haydn wrote 106 symphonies," Ben continued. "Or 108, if you count two works he called symphonies but really aren't. The point is, there are so many that some of the most popular have come to be known by nicknames rather than numbers. I remember in grade school when our music teacher, Mr. Blackwell, played the famous Surprise symphony. Everyone loves that one, with the unexpected volume surges. And guess what? There's also a Military symphony. And a Drumroll symphony."

"So?"

"The Surprise Symphony is #94. The Military Symphony is #100. And the Drumroll symphony is #103. Claudia used a digital lock. No dial-turning. You just have to enter three numbers in the proper order. Which in this case means the combination was 100, 103, and 94—Military, Drumroll, Surprise. Your extensive knowledge of Haydn, coupled with overhearing the phrase Claudia invented as a mnemonic, made figuring out her combo a cinch. You used your faculty pass to get into the dorm, found her room unlocked or forced it, opened the safe and stole the violin. Being charitably minded, I like to think murder wasn't originally part of the plan. Claudia walked in on you and you panicked. A fight ensued. Maybe there wasn't a blunt instrument. Maybe she fell and banged her head on the desk."

Ben paused. "But I could be wrong. Maybe you planned it all along. Maybe you saw a way to get the violin and remove the risk of a sexual harassment claim that could completely destroy your academic career and might lead to criminal charges. Or maybe you tried to come on to her in the dorm room and she resisted. So you took her out."

"You don't know what you're talking about." Herwig's voice was high-pitched and wobbly.

"I didn't expect you to admit anything. This isn't *Murder She Wrote*." Ben paused. "And yet. Here's the violin."

"You know what? I'm not only going to kill you—I'm going to enjoy killing you."

"Will you, though?" Ben raised the violin and held it directly in front of him. "Do you want to kill me so badly you'll risk damaging this?"

Herwig's teeth ground together. "Put down the damn violin."

"No."

Herwig readjusted his aim, but every time the gun moved, so did the violin, in front of Ben's face, then his chest, then his face again.

"Fine. I'll shoot you in the leg."

Ben raised the violin high. "The impact will cause me to drop the violin. Wonder what it'll sound like after that?'

Herwig looked as if he were about to explode. "You wouldn't dare!"

"To save my life? I'd drop a dozen Amatis."

"I do not intend to spend the rest of my life in prison. I wouldn't last a week."

Ben kept moving the violin. "If you damage this instrument, your whole criminal enterprise was for nothing."

"I don't care!" Herwig ran at Ben, trying to get close enough to shoot without putting the violin at risk.

Which gave Dan the opening he'd been waiting for. He grabbed a stack of records and threw them at Herwig's head.

The side blow took Herwig by surprise. When he saw the LPs tumble to the floor, he screamed—then fired. The bullet went into the ceiling. He started to fire again, but Dan was on top of him. He grabbed Herwig's gun arm and twisted it backward, practically wrenching it from its socket.

Herwig cried out in pain, then fired again. The bullet hit the record stash. Dan twisted the man's wrist until he dropped the gun.

Dan raised his fist. "Are you going to lie still? Or do I need to beat you into submission?"

Herwig raised his hands to cover his face. "Please…don't…"

"Tempting." Dan whipped off his belt and tied the man's hands behind his back. "Ben, would you be so kind as to call the police?"

"Already on it."

"Then call ADA Chee. Tell her we want to reopen the case. Again."

"She's not going to want to hear that."

"Tell her we found the violin. Something they never managed to do."

Herwig was sobbing, choking, unable to wipe away his tears with his hands immobilized. "I never…meant for this to go so far…."

"I think you did. You may have been horrified afterward. But you knew what you were doing. This was a cold, calculated operation." Dan snatched the gun from the floor. "But it's over. You're going to prison. Claudia's family will get the violin back. And against all odds, Ben—we're both still alive. All we need to do now is—"

A harsh voice disrupted the tranquility. "Drop the phone."

Dan spun around.

The Grim Reaper stood directly behind him.

# CHAPTER FIFTY-FIVE

Dan froze. The Reaper held a shiny metal scythe that looked as if it had been honed to a razor-sharp point.

"I mean it. Drop the phone. Now."

Ben complied.

"We meet again," Dan said.

He couldn't see the Reaper's smile. But he felt it.

"I knew Herwig wasn't the Reaper," he explained. "Among other reasons, I've fought with both of you. You're smaller but stronger. The costume makes you appear much more frightening than you would be otherwise."

Ben wiped his hands on his slacks. "Was that you back at the gas station during the snowstorm?"

The Reaper's metallic voice replied. "Just an emissary. Obviously."

"Why obviously?"

"Because if it had been me, you'd be dead."

"And back in Roswell. You killed that poor guy?"

"Another emissary."

Ben took another step forward, hands raised in a demonstration of harmlessness. "Look, there's no need for more violence. We know Herwig took the violin. Did you put him up to it?"

"Does that seem like something I would do?"

"Depends on who you are. Take that mask off and ask me again."

"I'm not here to confess. I'm here to kill you."

"You can explain what this is all about first. Since we won't have a chance to tell anyone."

"You mean you haven't solved the whole case? You tracked down Professor Dumbass. I thought you were some kind of super-sleuth."

"No," Ben replied. "Just humble attorneys."

"Who solve crimes."

"I've been lucky once or twice."

"Till you got to me?"

Ben smirked. "Oh hell no. I figured you out days ago."

Dan's head whipped around. When did this happen? And why did he never mention it? Had he been holding back? Or was this a gigantic bluff?

"Bold move, Mr. Kincaid. I'm impressed. Even if you're lying."

"I'm not lying. But I had to prioritize the hearing. Saving David Donovan. By the way, I've already called the police. You need to make tracks."

"I don't think you have," the Reaper replied "Because you're nervous. I can see it. Your neck is tight. You keep shifting your weight so I can't see that your knees are unsteady. You wouldn't feel that way if you knew the cavalry was coming."

"Maybe I'm faking. Putting on a show to keep you off guard."

More laughter, which coming through the voice disguiser, was seriously creepy. "I like you, Kincaid. You've got some flint in you. But you still have to die." The Reaper aimed the scythe at Ben's head.

"Seriously? You're going to decapitate me? Both of us? And then what? Pin it on the professor?"

Herwig remained handcuffed but broke his silence. "Don't be an idiot. I've seen too much. He's going to kill me, too."

The Reaper turned. "At least one man understands what's happening."

When the Reaper pivoted, Dan ran like a linebacker, pushing the cloaked figure against the wall. The Reaper brought around the scythe. Dan was too close to be impaled, but the blade scraped inside his jacket.

"Damn!" That hurt. Especially since it was near his earlier gunshot wound. Dan slammed the Reaper against the wall.

The Reaper shoved back hard, but this time, Dan had the advantage. They struggled like two boxers in the ring with their arms locked around one another so neither could take a swing.

Dan headbutted him, bouncing the Reaper's skull off a metal door frame. While he was momentarily stunned, Dan grabbed his wrist with both hands and twisted the skin.

The Reaper cried out. The scythe clattered to the floor.

Out the corner of his eye, Dan saw Ben retrieving his phone.

"Get the scythe!" he barked.

Ben tried, but the next moment the Reaper roared back with a vengeance. He shoved Dan into Ben, knocking both men to the floor. The Reaper kicked Dan in the gut for good measure.

Dan tried to clear his head. Ben was stuck beneath him.

The Reaper took the gun from Dan's coat.

"You two gents are definitely making this challenging." The Reaper laughed again, the same cheerless, terrifying chuckle. "But this has gone on too long. Say your prayers. Or maybe lawyers don't believe in God? That would explain so much."

Ben pushed up on his arms. "Who's the kidney for?"

The Reaper seemed to hesitate. "What?"

"I know about the list. My friend Jones found it. This has all been about kidneys, right?"

No reply from the Reaper.

"That was a Top Five list of potential kidney recipients in line for the next organ that comes available. Those lists are constantly shuffled and reprioritized according to patients' changing conditions, age, situation." Keep talking, Ben, he thought. Keep the Reaper distracted. "Right now, all organ procurement in the US is controlled by the United Network for Organ Sharing, but they've been heavily criticized for mismanagement and inadequate funding. They don't even have a modern computer system. Meanwhile, there are over 104,000 people waiting for an organ. That can take years, plus there are huge disparities based upon race and location, and although 47,000 transplants happen each year, seventeen people die every day while waiting."

The gun wavered but the Reaper did not fire. "What's your point?"

"Someone wasn't going to get a kidney in time. So you decided to eliminate everyone who might conceivably get one before the person you wanted to get one." He paused. "Who's the kidney for?"

Dan barely understood what Ben was talking about, but he kept his mouth shut and let it roll. Ben was keeping them alive.

The Reaper sounded smirky. "That would be telling."

"What do you have to fear? You're going to kill us anyway."

"I get it. You want me to monologue."

"No, I just..."

"You want me to start babbling egomaniacally about my evil plan until finally your stronger friend figures out a way to take me down. Guess what? I'm not stupid."

"I know that. I can admire a clever person who brings off a complex plan, even when they're on the wrong side of the law. How did you get the list?"

The Reaper hesitated a moment and then, apparently seeing no harm in it, spoke. "Hired someone to hack the website."

Dan pushed up on his arms. The Reaper whipped his gun around and pointed toward his head.

"I'm getting very tired of this conversation. You two boys have about one more minute left to live. Maybe you should spend those brief moments praying for forgiveness. I don't feel like talking anymore."

But Ben continued to press. "It's for you, isn't it?"

"What?"

"The kidney. It's for you. That's why you've done all this. You've probably done something that disqualifies you. Criminal record. Medical complications. Drug addiction. Something that decreases your likelihood to survive. Something that made you unlikely to get a kidney the usual way. So you tried to buy one. And when that wasn't working fast enough, you decided to steal one."

The Reaper head seemed to twitch.

"But think ahead for a moment. What's going to happen when Donovan's lawyers disappear? Won't there be an investigation?"

"Maybe of the murders. Not the kidney."

"Are you sure? Perhaps law enforcement is smarter than you realize."

"That has not been my experience."

"I believe most cops are persistent, dogged—but fair."

"That's because you're a rich white boy."

"Eventually they will figure it out. And that's when you go down."

"You'll go down first." Dan started toward him, but the Reaper stopped him with a twist of the gun. "Time's up, boys."

# CHAPTER FIFTY-SIX

DAN KEPT HIS MOUTH CLOSED. IF THIS WAS HOW IT ENDED, HE WAS NOT going down screaming. His side still hurt from where the scythe had cut him, but he had no trouble ignoring that in face of a much larger looming danger.

"You two led me a merry chase. Clear across the country. But all good things must come to an end." The Reaper pulled back the hammer.

An instant later, the wail of sirens split the night.

The Reaper took a step back.

Ben shrugged. "I did tell you the police were coming."

"You didn't have a chance. I watched—"

"Two steps ahead," Ben said. "The only reason I'm still alive. All I had to do was send an emoji to my wife. She knew what to do."

The Reaper snarled. "You son of—"

"You're about to be caught and you don't need two more murders on your rap sheet."

The Reaper hesitated, then threw the gun down and raced through the kitchen toward the back door and flung it open.

Maria stood on the other side.

*"What?"*

"Good to see you again, asshole." Maria grabbed the Reaper by the collar of the robe. "You caught me by surprise last time. Not again." Her hand was taped. She wore brass knuckles.

And she slugged so hard the Reaper teetered backwards and crashed.

"You put your filthy hands on me," Maria said, hovering over him. "Without consent. You tied me up and left me alone for days."

"I—I—planned to come back. But—I had to chase them—my first priority—"

"Save it. I don't want to hear any more of your BS. You hurt me. You used me. And most unforgivable of all—you took my phone."

"It was nothing personal."

"It seemed very personal to me!" she shouted, then kicked again for good measure. "How can you say it's not personal? Because all women are just meat to you? To be used as you see fit?" Her voice spiked. "If I hadn't gotten free, I'd be dead now."

The voice was so soft as to be almost inaudible. "I let you escape."

"What?"

"I didn't leave you alone. I left you so anyone with half a brain could escape."

"You're saying you wanted me to get away?"

"I never wanted you in the first place." The voice was still altered, but the mechanism must've been broken during the fight, because it squealed and crackled. "You got in the way while I searched the files. I knocked you out and put you in the trunk of my car. I used your face to get into your phone, then used your monitoring app to delete all the doorcam footage that showed me. I thought holding you would be enough to keep Pike out of my way. That turned out to be wrong. It made him more determined. So I had no reason to keep you any longer."

They heard footsteps on the porch.

Ben took Maria's arm and gently led her away. "Don't let the cops see you violating this scumbag's constitutional rights."

"If you insist."

"Besides, all this strenuous physical activity isn't good for you."

Dan's eyes narrowed. What?

The front door slammed open and two police officers entered, guns unholstered and at the ready.

Christina was a few steps behind them.

Ben and Dan raised their hands. "We're not armed. The guy in the Halloween costume is the killer."

"Keep your hands up," the lead cop said. "And keep your distance." It seemed he wasn't trusting anyone yet. And that was a smart move on his part.

Dan leaned toward Ben. "You really did signal Christina."

"In fact, I did not have time."

"You can thank me for this rescue," Christina said.

"How did you know we'd end up in over our heads?"

"I've been with Ben for over thirty years now. I've detected a pattern."

Ben wrapped his arms around her.

The cop looked at them, gun still out, obviously confused. "Could someone please explain this?"

"I can," Ben said. "But first—wouldn't we all like to know who the center of attention here is?"

Ben lowered himself beside the Reaper.

"Stay away from me," the Reaper said, twisting from side to side.

"No way in hell." With a sudden jerk, Ben ripped the mask off.

The Reaper was a woman.

"Zhang," Ben whispered. "Thought so. FBI Special Agent Courtney Zhang."

"Small wonder she was so suspicious of us. Tried to scare us off the case."

No response from the Reaper.

"But her actual name is…?"

Ben stared at his phone, scrolling. "Exactly that. She really is in the FBI. Which might explain why she's such a formidable fighter."

Christina's eyes widened. "This Reaper routine was an FBI assignment?"

"Don't think so. An extracurricular activity, I'm betting. She's probably on sabbatical right now or something like that."

Dan leaned into Zhang's face. "Why?"

Without the voice disguiser, her voice seemed thinner and much less frightening. "'Behold, a pale horse....Put in your sickle and reap, for the hour to reap has come, for the harvest of the earth is fully ripe.'"

He recalled her using that phrase before. "And you're in charge of the...cleansing?"

"America is a mess. I want to put us back on course. Put power back in the hands of true Americans."

"Which would be what? People like you are tearing this nation apart."

Zhang's eyes flared. "You are such a tool. Do you believe everything the lamestream media tells you?"

"I believe this." His entire body trembled. "You hurt my Maria. And now you're going to pay for it."

# CHAPTER FIFTY-SEVEN

DAN WAS GLAD TO RETURN TO THE LA COURTHOUSE. TRUTH TO TELL, he always felt a bit of a buzz when he entered a courthouse, but this was even better—because he hoped for a much better result than he got the last time around.

David was at the table again, dressed in street clothes and accompanied by his ever-present marshals.

"How are you holding up?" Dan asked.

"Fine. I'm meditating."

"Why?"

"Because I've been in this courtroom before. Each time I've gotten my hopes up. And each time I've been…"

"Disappointed?"

"Crushed. I can't do it again. I'm pretending this is just a dream." He paused. "Of course, when I wake up, I'll be back in that ten-by-seven cell."

Dan's heart went out to him. If anyone was entitled to whine, it was David. He'd been through the wringer far too many times for someone in ill health who, though perhaps imperfect, was not a murderer.

Judge Durant entered the courtroom and took the bench. He was technically speaking to Dan, but his volume and demeanor suggested that he was speaking to the entire room. Not surprising, since today the gallery was full of reporters.

"On my docket this morning I find that the Donovan case has resurfaced, this time in the form of a motion to reconsider the court's ruling on the previous motion for new trial." He paused. "The only thing a court is less likely to spend time on than a motion for new trial would be a motion to reconsider the court's failure to grant a new trial." His eyes slowly scanned the horizon. "But this situation is different. Different from anything I've seen in thirty years on the bench."

No doubt true, but it didn't necessarily mean he'd changed his mind. They'd presented all the evidence in their brief, including Herwig's arrest, plus Zhang's recent murder attempt. But thus far, neither she nor Herwig had been charged with Claudia's murder.

"I've read the motion and brief submitted by the defendant, now the moving party, and I have also read the response brief filed by the State." He nodded toward ADA Chee. "And I can't help but notice how little the State disputes the newly acquired evidence. They argue about timelines and procedural matters, plead for the sanctity of the jury verdict, but can't deny the facts and for the most part don't try."

Dan was getting anxious. Enough with the prologue, judge. Let's get to the heart of the matter.

"Here's what we've got. The defense has produced new evidence indicating that a man named Herwig, currently under arrest for aggravated assault and attempted murder, is the actual murderer of Claudia Wells. But he hasn't confessed to the crime and so far hasn't been charged."

Dan cleared his throat. "They're negotiating, your honor. He wants a plea deal and so does Zhang. In exchange for information about who else might have been involved."

"Understood," the judge said, raising his hand in a way that Dan interpreted to mean, Don't interrupt me again.

"The court also recognizes that it would be awkward for the prosecution to charge someone with this crime when they already have a conviction on the books," the judge continued. "No one wants to admit that they convicted an innocent man. But that does not mean it never happens. The court notes that the Amati violin that belonged to Claudia Wells was found in Herwig's home, and when confronted, Herwig attempted to kill both defense attorneys."

Chee gave Dan a look suggesting that, if she got her wish, the attempt would've been successful.

The judge removed his glasses and wiped his forehead. "This is... unusual, to say the least." Durant looked out into the gallery. This time, he appeared to be speaking not from rote, but from the heart. "Judges have to defend the system, and that includes preserving the integrity of the jury system. Verdicts are supposed to bring finality, and we don't want to turn them into the first step in an endless chain of motions. When the appeal process started to get out of hand, we curtailed it. We don't want to recreate the same monster."

The judge appeared to be looking directly at David. "But the primary object of the justice system must be justice. When we use the phrase "beyond a reasonable doubt," that should mean exactly what it says. A virtual certainty. And in this case, every time we reconvene, it seems like there was less certainty than before."

Another deep long breath. Dan could almost feel the regret in Durant's words.

"And all this while, the defendant has remained behind bars. Months now, despite suffering from a potentially fatal illness and requiring dialysis three times a week. And it appears..." Durant stopped himself. "At the very least, it appears the jury did not have all the evidence. Significant evidence. Evidence that might have altered its verdict. On that basis, and that basis alone, this court will reconsider its ruling on the motion for new trial. Given the magnitude of the newly discovered evidence that appears to be potentially convincing—potentially damning—this court will grant the motion for new trial. You'll be notified of the trial date by my clerk, but I will direct her to set it down at the earliest possible opportunity."

David slowly raised his head. "Did I hear him say what I think I heard him say?"

Dan nodded.

He appeared almost dazed. "This really must be a dream."

Dan rose to his feet, but the judge waved him back down.

"I know where you're going, counsel. Bail. Which the court has already considered. Given the circumstances, and the court's belief that, at this time, the defendant is not a flight risk and presents little to no danger, plus considering his medical condition and the fact that the prosecution may well opt to drop the charges...bail is granted. Immediately."

David sat up, eyes wild.

"Mr. Pike, the defendant will be released on your recognizance. Make sure he shows up for the new trial. Though given what we now know, the DA might well reconsider this prosecution. Before more embarrassment ensues."

ADA Chee spoke. "I'll talk to opposing counsel about...working something out." She looked as if nothing could please her less. He didn't blame her. He'd be willing to bet the DA would drop all charges against David. Given the circumstances, David might have a civil claim against them.

Dan smiled. "Thank you, your honor."

The judge started to leave, then stopped. "No," he said, turning. "Thank you, Mr. Pike. Because, although I don't like to comment on the actions of jurors or law enforcement, I fear we came close to...to committing a grave injustice. You and your colleague prevented that from happening. I will always be in your debt."

---

DAN WAS FAMISHED. GARY HAD ARRANGED FOR A ROOM AT A LOCAL Italian restaurant called That's Amore. They took a private room in the back to celebrate the victory. In addition to the three lawyers and David, Christina and Maria also came.

Dan could barely control David, who was bouncing off the walls and giggling like a hyperactive child.

"I don't believe it," he said, over and over again, his hands pressed against the sides of his head. "I just do not believe it."

Dan laid a hand on his shoulder. "Believe it, kiddo. You're free."

"Pending retrial," Ben added.

"Sure." Dan winked. "But I'm betting that retrial never happens. And this should guarantee you get that kidney you need. There's no longer anything to disqualify you."

Christina had a bottle of white wine and made the rounds. She passed Dan a glass, then asked Maria. "Care for some adult pineapple juice?"

Maria shook her head. "Pass."

Christina nodded. "Thought so."

Ben raised his glass and toasted the beleaguered but now free defendant. "But we should be careful about overconfidence. I agree with everything Dan said. But I couldn't help but notice that, although he tiptoed around it, the judge never actually said David was innocent, or that the jury was in error, or that the police had failed to fully investigate."

"Because he doesn't want to fuel a lawsuit."

"That's going to happen anyway," Gary commented. "Good grief, David was in jail for months while the real killer ran free, playing his little violin every night in secret. I've already started writing the motion." He smiled. "I don't think I'll need you two boys for this one."

"Good," Ben said. "I miss my own bed."

Christina nodded. "It misses you, too." She turned. "Everything I've heard Ben say about you is right, Dan. You're a terrific courtroom attorney."

Dan pressed his hands against his chest. "Who? Me? Ben said that?"

Ben made a mock denial. "I must've been thinking of someone else."

Dan gave him a friendly slug on the shoulder. "Maybe you're not a grumpy old curmudgeon."

"No," Christina said, "you got that part right. Maria, let's get some food."

"At last. I'm starving. What does everyone want?"

"Two of every appetizer they make," Dan said.

Ben eyes widened. "For six people?"

"Well, you are the fabulously wealthy leader of the Last Chance Lawyers, right? Let's live it up."

"Ok," Ben said. "Two of every appetizer they make." And then in a much softer voice: "But I'm sending you the bill."

The women departed. Gary and David went to the digital jukebox to select something more jubilant. Gary favored Mariah Carey, but David picked Gloria Gaynor. Understandable, really. *Oh no not I...I will survive...*

Leaving Ben and Dan briefly alone.

"You know I was kidding, right?" Ben said. "You were great in court."

"Coming from you, that means a great deal." His eyes went into deep focus. "You know, I didn't realize how much I missed the courtroom."

"You can have it. I don't need that kind of stress in my life. Really wore me out."

"Did you forget to take your Geritol? Vitamin supplements?"

Ben ignored him. "You basically saved a man's life."

"Only because you figured out what was going on."

"We figured it out together. With a little help from our friends. Mike kept the cops off your back. Jones and Loving did critical research." He snapped his fingers. "That reminds me. Loving sent me something by email."

"He didn't send it by fax?"

"No, wiseass. We're not *that* old. Loving has been talking with the Unified Center for Organ Control. Said he found some interesting stuff. I haven't had a chance to review it."

He popped open his briefcase.

Dan laid a hand on his shoulder. "It can wait. Enjoy the celebration."

"But I'm curious. And an hour from now, I'll be too tired to read it."

Ben brought up the email on his new phone and scanned it. "Loving has done his usual thorough work. There are so many people who need replacement organs, not enough to go around, and major administrative problems. But I was hoping he could shed some light…"

Ben's voice trailed off.

"Yes?" When Ben didn't respond, he tried again. "You were saying?"

Ben stared at the piece of paper in his hands. "Oh my God."

"Are you doing that again? Stop teasing. What've you got?"

Ben fell into his chair. "The answer. At long last."

"I thought we already solved this case."

"We were wrong."

Dan pulled out a chair and sat opposite him. "You've got to be kidding. What have you uncovered?"

"The explanation for all the murders. And what has really been going on this whole time."

"I don't understand."

Ben shook his head from side to side. "And the sad thing is, the real answer has been in front of us the whole time. I was just too blind to see it."

# CHAPTER FIFTY-EIGHT

DAN NEVER EXPECTED TO BE HERE EVER AGAIN IN HIS LIFE. BUT THIS whole case had been a nonstop flurry of things he never expected. He never expected Maria's kidnapping, much less a road trip with his boss. He didn't expect to be trapped in a snowstorm or accosted by the FBI or—worst of all—subjected to Ben's taste in food and music.

But most of all, he never expected to be back in McAlester, Oklahoma, visiting the federal prison. It hadn't changed much since his visit a few days before. It was still dingy, poorly lit, and emanated an inescapable aura of despair. Sometimes he was amazed anyone survived prison, and marveled that through four thousand years of recorded history, no one had devised a better way of policing society.

They didn't have to wait long. Two guards escorted them into the visiting room. Then they brought in the man they came to see and, at the lawyers' request, cuffed him to a steel loop on the edge of the table.

Even when he wasn't wearing a cowboy hat, Jack Crenshaw always seemed to be wearing a cowboy hat. And boots. Even when he was handcuffed and in prison, he always seemed to be smirking as if he had the upper hand.

And maybe this time he did. Thus far.

"Thank you for seeing us," Dan said. "You didn't have to. And frankly, I didn't think you would."

Crenshaw smiled as if he were at peace with the universe. "How could I turn down the man who brought me a kaleidoscope? Best gift I've had in years. Gotta respect someone who makes a gesture like that, even if he is a polecat. How can I help you boys?"

Dan spread his hands. "You really can't. We've already figured it out."

Crenshaw arched an eyebrow. "Do tell." Crenshaw stared at him, as if debating internally how much he should say. "Then spill the beans, boys. Tell me what it's all about?"

Ben replied succinctly. "Caroline."

Crenshaw gazed back at him. "Dan, you should've partnered up with this old boy long ago. He's smarter than he looks."

Ben allowed a small smile. "It's the weak chin that fools people."

"I read that you boys solved the case. Got your client off the hook. Found the real varmint."

"We found that Professor Herwig stole the violin. Another woman, an FBI agent, played the Grim Reaper and orchestrated the rest, murdering people right and left and abducting Maria."

Crenshaw shrugged. "Well then. Case solved."

"Not exactly. At first I thought maybe Herwig hired Zhang, but that didn't make sense. He didn't have the means or the game. But someone put Zhang up to the job. And financed it."

"How can you possibly know that?"

"Agent Zhang doesn't need a kidney. She has no reason to eliminate potential donors or to interfere with David Donovan's defense."

"Maybe she just thought a rare organ should go to someone more deserving."

Dan shook his head. "She's not a social crusader."

"Then what is she?"

"Greedy. And—" He drew in his breath. "Easily manipulated."

"You think I'm the evil Svengali pulling her strings? May I remind you that I've been behind bars for years? Thanks to you."

"Yeah, that slowed me down for a while. You told us you were a changed man." He frowned. "Guess we just needed more details on exactly what had changed."

"I've never even met this agent."

"Quite possibly true. I've known gang lords who ran their business from prison. Some are allowed calls and some smuggle in cellphones. So I'm not surprised you could call someone. But I didn't think you had enough money to hire a killer."

"What changed your mind?"

He was clearly teasing them, trying to learn how much they knew. Dan decided to humor him. "Ben's investigator found your hidden bank account."

"What? A poor country boy like me?"

"Yeah. Under a false name. But he traced back the funds Agent Zhang was paid and found an account at Charles Schwab that you started, probably on a contraband cellphone. You used the name of an actual billionaire, which must've made Schwab eager to sign you up. When they requested an ID and utility bill, you sent digital photos you cribbed somewhere. In fact, you were so clever and they were so eager that after a few conversations, they allowed you to transfer four million bucks from the real billionaire's account to a precious-metals dealer so you could purchase over two thousand American Eagle gold coins. After that was deposited somewhere, you used it to hire a relentless killer who abducted my wife, tried to kill me and Ben, and did kill at least four others. Zhang even hired subcontractors, like the one at the gas station and the kid in Roswell. Who framed us. You knew we'd be going there because you're the one who sent us."

"Pardon me, boys, but that all sounds pretty complicated for a lowbrow owlhoot like me."

"Bull. You scammed ICE for years. You can scam banks just as easily. And the warden tells me that, despite their best efforts, guards confiscated over two-thousand contraband phones last year. So there must be a pipeline."

Crenshaw's smile faded. "Nice theory. But you can't prove anything."

"As we speak, guards are searching your cell. Are they going to find a phone?"

No response. Crenshaw just glared.

"Thought so. And the call record will likely confirm everything I just said."

Crenshaw's teeth scraped together.

"You can expect to be charged with conspiracy to commit bank fraud, aggravated identity theft, money laundering, conspiracy to commit money laundering, and of course, murder-for-hire."

"Meaning?"

"Before you had a life sentence, which would probably amount to around eighteen years. Now you're not going to see the outside of a prison for the rest of your life even if you live to be a hundred. Hope you're enjoying this prison life because it's all you're ever going to know." He paused, teeth clenched. "You know, I've always opposed the death penalty. But I think I might be willing to make an exception for you."

Crenshaw fell silent. He breathed heavily through his nose. Then all at once, the words tumbled out.

"I told you about my daughter. That she was sick. How important she is to me. I tried everything legal. Even reached out to Australia, where buying organs is legal."

"Which led to Maria getting calls from you and someone in Australia. Someone was doing a background check."

"And I knew I was unlikely to pass if she or you got involved. So I explored other possibilities."

"Like hiring the Grim Reaper?"

"I've known Zhang since my days with ICE. She's always been...useful."

"Having met the woman, I can state with certainty that she does not belong in government service."

"She's deeply religious. And holds strong political beliefs. Doesn't like what's happening in the world today."

"She's an assassin."

"Potato, potata. People have been killing each other in the name of religion for centuries."

"Most haven't run around dressed as Death."

"She needed a disguise. She's a good hand-to-hand fighter, but she doesn't look that imposing. Dress her up like something out of your nightmares, though, and people get scared."

"Which made it easier for your religious assassin to kill people."

"She believed in what she was doing and planned to use the money for a righteous cause. She went to confessional after every murder."

"The two of you were able to use your illicit government connections to get the list from the HSUS. You knew who was on the organ list. Granted, it's not a static list. Every time an organ arrives, a number of factors are reconsidered, like geography, age, need. But still. You knew who the top contenders were. So you set out to eliminate the competition."

Crenshaw shrugged.

"We like to believe prison serves some purpose. Reforms people. That's why I almost bought it when you talked about how you'd changed. But you haven't learned a damn thing."

"*She's all I have!*" At once, Crenshaw's eyes softened. "I lost my life. I lost my family, friends. Caroline is the only person who visits me. She's what keeps me alive. What gives me reason to get up in the morning. And then...then..."

"Then she tells you she has renal failure. Needs a kidney. And can't find one."

"She's not rich. She's not a kid. She doesn't have health insurance. And because of her condition, she needed a kidney from a live donor. She'd been waiting for more than a year and there comes a point when there's just too much waste for dialysis to clean effectively. She was rising up the list...but it looked like she would die before a kidney arrived. They said she had weeks. Maybe days."

"So you decided to eliminate the primary kidney candidates."

"Is that so wrong?" Tears actually appeared in Crenshaw's eyes. "To want your daughter to live?"

"No. But all those people on the list had fathers too. And families.

Who are now grieving the loss of a loved one. If you're waiting for my sympathy, it's going to be a long wait."

Crenshaw turned to Ben. "Don't you have daughters?"

Ben hesitated, but answered. "Yes. Two."

"What would you be willing to do to save them?"

Ben's voice dropped to a whisper. "Anything."

"Even a crime. Even murder."

Ben's voice was even softer. "Anything."

"Then you and I are exactly the same. Except I was trapped in prison. So I had to resort to desperate measures."

"We are not the same. Even if I were in prison, I'd find a different way. One that doesn't involve murder."

"Because you're rich. But most people aren't. Most people have to do as they're told or pay the price. We live our whole lives being pushed around by laws and cops and doctors and regulations. We're victims of the Combine. That's what America has become. An enormous monstrous Combine controlling everyone."

"Let's save the political theory for later," Dan said. "We just wanted you to know you might get a little time off from prison. Because you're going to have a lot of court dates very soon."

Crenshaw pursed his lips. "I never lied to you."

"Bull. You told us a cartel was involved."

"I knew you'd be interested if that cartel you buried raised its ugly head again. I made that up to get you to Roswell. I never intended any harm toward your companion. Zhang did that. Maria caught her rummaging around in your office."

"Zhang held her against her will for days. Do you have idea how scared she was? Do you have any idea what that does to a person?"

"Being locked up against your will. Yes, I definitely know what that does to a person."

"You didn't have the right."

Crenshaw's voice choked. "My daughter's illness gave me the right. To do anything."

Dan tried not to feel sorry for him—but it was challenging. "Did you really think you could get away with this?"

Crenshaw's eyes fell. "I don't know. I didn't care. I was desperate. I hoped no one would find out until after she got the kidney. What happens to me is unimportant." A look of terror spread across his face. "You're not going to screw this up, are you?"

"No," Ben replied. "David Donovan is already in line for a kidney, but I have some connections too, and I've been assured they've found a live kidney donor for your daughter. The surgery will happen as soon as they can get it to her. Sometime in the next forty-eight hours. There was concern about letting you...benefit from your crimes, but I convinced them that your daughter shouldn't be punished for your actions she knew nothing about. If all goes well, she should be much healthier soon. She'll be taking immunosuppressants for the rest of her life, she'll have to be cautious about infections...but she's not going to die from renal failure anytime soon."

"Thank you," Crenshaw whispered. "Thank you so much."

"There will be some medical expenses associated with Caroline's operation."

"And let me guess. You've seized my bank accounts."

"Of course. That money was stolen. But I will make sure your daughter's bills are paid."

Crenshaw gaped at him. "I—don't know what to say."

Ben pushed himself to his feet. "I didn't do it to be generous. I did it because...even if I don't approve of how you handled this...I understand the motivation. Daddies love their daughters." His eyebrows pushed together. "And love makes us do the crazy."

# CHAPTER FIFTY-NINE

DAN COULDN'T BELIEVE HIS BAD LUCK. AFTER ALL HE'D BEEN THROUGH these past few days—this had to be the worst. Ben and Maria and Christina left on an earlier flight while he stayed behind to clear up some of the details with law enforcement and file the necessary court documents to make sure David remained free. But now he was finally finished, boarding a full flight on a redeye back to Florida—

And he got the middle seat.

Life just sucks sometimes.

Worse, the man sitting beside him in the coveted window seat had a laptop and was banging away at the keys, which not only made noise but sent his elbow constantly flying into Dan's arm. He was a little guy, short and thin, bald with patches of gray on both sides.

Dan tolerated it as long as he could before he spoke. "Are you... going to be typing the whole time?"

The man did not look up. "Probably. Got to finish my chapter. If I don't do it now, I'll have to do it when I arrive. And I'd rather spend that time with my family."

"Chapter? You writing a book?"

"Yup. I make up stories. Have for a long time."

"Any lawyers in those stories?"

"Constantly."

"Are they all rule-breaking mavericks? Amoral narcissists? Alcoholics whose personal problems interfere with their cases?"

"No. I let other people write those stories. I like characters who do the right thing because they care about others."

"So this is fiction?"

The man just smiled.

"Let me tell you, I've just been through a case that would make a terrific book."

"I hear that a lot."

"Most of the time, I had no idea what was going on. My rep was ruined, my girl was gone—I wasn't in control of my own life."

The man kept typing. "Everyone feels that way at times. Like someone else is writing their story and they didn't even get to revise the rough draft."

Dan laughed. "I suppose." He tried to read the words on the laptop screen, but the typeface was too small. "Almost finished?"

"Writing the denouement."

"Heart-rending indictment of the American Way? Cold objectivity disdaining sentimentality? Huge bloodbath to prove how gritty and realistic your story is?"

The man shook his head. "Never."

"Don't want a Pulitzer?"

The man paused for a monent, then leaned back into the seat. "When I was younger, I had this cat. Percy. Short for Percival. God, I loved that cat. I don't think I'd ever felt love like that before."

"I notice you're using the past tense. What happened?"

The man's eyes became distant. "What always happens. Everything that lives eventually dies." He swallowed, then averted his eyes. "I was destroyed. I mean, destroyed. And I couldn't talk about it to anyone. I mean, he was just a cat, right? But to me—he was so much more. That was the worst pain I'd ever experienced. Couldn't shake it off. Still hits me, some days." He looked up and offered a wobbly smile. "I wouldn't inflict that kind of pain on anyone. Real or fictional."

"So…happy endings?"

"Always. No dead ends. Or no-win scenarios. The future always holds incredible promise."

"Not the worst rule."

"It works for me. At least for now. We all have to reconsider our decisions as we progress through life." He returned his attention to the laptop. "Who knows? Maybe it's time for you to do some reconsidering yourself."

---

By the time Dan arrived at the Snell Isle mansion in St. Petersburg—the LCL office—the party was in full force. Ben and Christina decided to spend a week with them in Florida. Maria was there with his former colleagues, Jimmy and Garrett. Dan's sister, Dinah, sported the honors cords from her recent law school graduation. The Kool-Aid flowed freely. The music was just loud enough. Everyone seemed to be in an excellent mood.

Good, Dan thought. Maybe we can write our own happy ending.

Maria gave him a smack on the cheek. She'd been dancing with Christina. Her hair was tousled and sticking to her face on one side.

"Can we talk later? We never got to finish our conversation."

"Of course." Because she had a surprise for him. "Whenever you're ready."

She kissed him again and grinned. "Tonight will be soon enough. When we're alone." She ran her fingers through his hair. "You've come a long way since you were repping drug dealers for Friedman & Collins, lover."

He nodded. "Because I finally fell in with the right crowd."

Dan danced, pranced, even sang a little. As it turned out, Christina knew how to throw a party. He beamed at his sister. "Thanks for holding down the fort, sis."

She was about his height, slim and muscular thanks to daily workouts. She had settled on pink for her current hair color. "Anything for my big bro. I had time. I'm still job hunting."

Despite graduating Order of the Coif. "Ben is also grateful. He instructed me to tell you that anytime you want a position with the LCL, all you have to do is ask."

"Wow. That's…massive."

"Take it from me. It's the best job you could possibly have. No worries about finding clients. No fretting about financing. All your cases are worthwhile and you'll have the resources to do right by them."

"And he's offering that to me? I haven't even tried a case yet."

"Ben has been known to go to extremes for friends."

"That is so extra. But very kind." She smiled. "I'll keep it in mind. But it's too soon. Let me try some baby cases and acquire some skills. Then we'll see."

He nodded. "What's most important is that you find work that makes you happy."

"What's most important is that I find a way to help others. That's what we're here for. And you know where I learned that? From my big brother."

Dan could only smile. If Dinah represented the future, then everything Zhang believed about America was dead wrong.

After an hour or so, Dan decided to sit for a moment. He was surprised when, barely a moment later, Ben lodged beside him.

"Great party, huh?"

"Love the music," Dan said. "Are we actually listening to vinyl records?"

"What can I say? Herwig is vile, but he was right about that. Christina bought you and Maria a turntable and a bunch of LPs."

"That was generous. And no occasion?"

Ben didn't look at him. "Not yet."

Dan paused. "Wait. Are we listening to…Harry Chapin?"

"One tune in ten. Christina allows me one song worth hearing for every nine pop songs that all sound exactly alike."

"Does Christina throw bashes like this in Oklahoma?"

"She would. But I hate parties. Torture chambers for the socially awkward."

Dan laughed. "You picked a good one when you hooked up with that lady."

"As well I know."

"There's something I've been wanting to talk to you about—"

"You want to get back into the courtroom. Start practicing law again."

Dan felt as if someone had stolen the words from his mouth. "How did you know?"

"Could see it in your eyes as soon as you tore into that first witness. Actually, I could see it as soon as we entered the courthouse."

Dan bit down on his lip. "I appreciate the faith you've put in me. Running the Last Chance Lawyers network has been an amazing experience. But I feel like...being in the courtroom is my highest and best use."

"And you're probably right. You should get back to your highest and best calling. Chart your own destiny."

"No hard feelings?"

"None. Actually, I think I know someone who might be qualified and willing to replace you."

"And that would be...?"

"Maria."

Dan laughed. "Good luck with that. She'll never give up legal work. She's a total workaholic."

Ben pursed his lips. "That might be...about to change."

"Well, whatever she wants to do is fine with me. She can chart her own destiny, too. Christina had a legal career, didn't she?"

"Till the girls came along." He looked at Dan as if hoping to see something. "Christina has been the best part of my life, the best thing that ever happened to me. And those two girls...well, you heard what I told Crenshaw. They are my life now. Those three women are the miracle I never deserved."

"Lucky man."

Ben took the plunge. "You will recall, Dan, that Maria mentioned that she had a surprise for you?"

"Yeah. Sports gear, I'm thinking. Maybe a new pair of collectible Air Jordans."

"Dan..." He took another breath, then looked at Dan sternly. "That's not what it is."

"How would you know?"

"I have a few more years under my belt than you do. And with age comes—"

"Bursitis?"

"No."

"Please don't say wisdom. That's so cliché."

"I was going to say, experience. Pattern recognition. Even you, the Great Observer, can be blind sometimes."

"I'm not getting the message."

"Did you hear Maria and Christina discussing their favorite baby names?"

"I must've been distracted."

"Did you observe that Maria is not drinking wine tonight?"

"Can't say that I did."

"Did you notice when she ran to the bathroom in a mad rush?"

"Was that before I arrived?"

Ben grabbed Dan by the shoulders. "You're about to be a father, you blithering idiot."

Dan's lips slowly parted. "I—what—how can you—"

"It's obvious. To everyone but you. I know you love that woman. It's time to make a commitment. Get a ring. Get a bigger house. Maria can handle most of the LCL administrative work from home. Which I think she will like once the baby arrives."

"I—I don't—I—I don't know if I'm—"

"Listen up, pal. That woman is the best part of your life. I didn't think I needed a family either. I was wrong. Your family will be the same unearned miracle for you that it was for me."

"But I—this is—"

"Sure, go back to practicing law, but make sure you spend as much time as possible at home. And get some sensible hobbies, for God's sake. You can't be risking your life out in the ocean every morning. Take up stamp collecting or something."

Dan gazed into the living room, where Maria and Christina were leading the bunny hop. "You sure about this?"

"Yup. And I'm sure about you, too."

"We all have to reconsider our decisions as we progress through life."

"Exactly."

Dan's eyes turned inward. "If I'd heard this a few weeks ago...I'm not sure how I would've reacted. When I grabbed you, I was feeling... mostly miserable. Maria was gone, the office was in shambles, someone was trying to kill me, and I...kinda blamed you. I was in a bad place. I was trapped in an ugly cage of my own making. But now...I don't know if I can even explain it. I feel like I've been set free. I'm ready to start a new adventure." He glanced over at Maria, who was still laughing and dancing. "Everything seems much brighter than it did before."

Ben nodded. "No matter hard dark the night becomes, the sun always rises. Eventually. Sometimes you have to wait for it. But you should always wait for it."

# ABOUT THE AUTHOR

**William Bernhardt** is the author of over sixty books, including *The Last Chance Lawyer (#1 National Bestseller)*, the historical novels *Challengers of the Dust* and *Nemesis*, three books of poetry, and the Red Sneaker books on writing. In addition, Bernhardt founded WriterCon Programs to mentor aspiring authors. He hosts an annual conference (WriterCon), an annual cruise, small-group writing retreats, a magazine for writers, and the WriterCon newsletter and podcast.

Bernhardt has received the Southern Writers Guild's Gold Medal Award, the Royden B. Davis Distinguished Author Award (University of Pennsylvania) and the H. Louise Cobb Distinguished Author Award (Oklahoma State), which is given "in recognition of an outstanding body of work that has profoundly influenced the way in which we understand ourselves and American society at large." In 2019, he received the Arrell Gibson Lifetime Achievement Award from the Oklahoma Center for the Book.

In addition Bernhardt has written plays, a musical (book and score), humor, children stories, biography, and puzzles. He has edited two anthologies (*Legal Briefs* and *Natural Suspect*) as fundraisers for The Nature Conservancy and the Children's Legal Defense Fund, and has also raised funds for Safe Haven animal shelters. In his spare time, he has enjoyed surfing, digging for dinosaurs, trekking through the Himalayas, paragliding, scuba diving, caving, zip-lining over the canopy of the Costa Rican rain forest, and jumping out of an airplane at 10,000 feet.

In 2017, when Bernhardt delivered the keynote address at the San

Francisco Writers Conference, chairman Michael Larsen noted that in addition to penning novels, Bernhardt can "write a sonnet, play a sonata, plant a garden, try a lawsuit, teach a class, cook a gourmet meal, beat you at Scrabble, and work the *New York Times* crossword in under five minutes."

# ALSO BY WILLIAM BERNHARDT

**The Daniel Pike Novels**

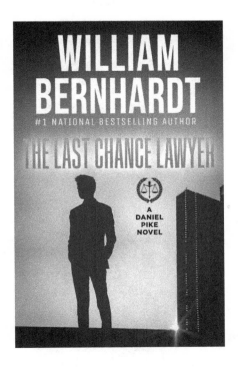

**Getting his client off death row could save his career... or make him the next victim.**

Daniel Pike would rather fight for justice than follow the rules. But when his courtroom career goes up in smoke, he fears his lifelong purpose is a lost cause. A mysterious job offer from a secretive boss gives him a second chance but lands him an impossible case with multiple lives at stake...

Dan uses every trick he knows in a high-stakes trial filled with unexpected revelations and breathtaking surprises.

The Last Chance Lawyer (Book 1)

Court of Killers (Book 2)

Trial by Blood (Book 3)

Twisted Justice (Book 4)

Judge and Jury (Book 5)

Final Verdict (Book 6)

**The Ben Kincaid Novels**

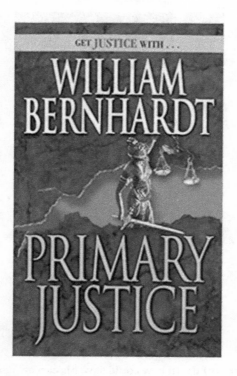

"[William] Bernhardt skillfully combines a cast of richly drawn characters, multiple plots, a damning portrait of a big law firm, and a climax that will take most readers by surprise."—*Chicago Tribune*

Ben Kincaid wants to be a lawyer because he wants to do the right thing. But once he leaves the D.A.'s office for a hotshot spot in Tulsa's most prestigious law firm, Ben discovers that doing the right thing and representing his clients' interests can be mutually exclusive.

Primary Justice (Book 1)

Blind Justice (Book 2)

Deadly Justice (Book 3)

Perfect Justice (Book 4)

Cruel Justice (Book 5)

Naked Justice (Book 6)

Extreme Justice (Book 7)

Dark Justice (Book 8)

Silent Justice (Book 9)

Murder One (Book 10)

Criminal Intent (Book 11)

Death Row (Book 12)

Hate Crime (Book 13)

Capitol Murder (Book 14)

Capitol Threat (Book 15)

Capitol Conspiracy (Book 16)

Capitol Offense (Book 17)

Capitol Betrayal (Book 18)

Justice Returns (Book 19)

**The Splitsville Legal Thrillers**

**A struggling lawyer. A bitter custody battle. A deadly fire. This case could cost Kenzi her career—and her life.**

When a desperate scientist begs for help getting her daughter back, Kenzi can't resist...even though this client is involved in Hexitel, a group she calls her religion but others call a cult. After her client is charged with murder, the ambitious attorney knows there is more at stake than a simple custody dispute.

Splitsville (Book 1)

Exposed (Book 2)

Shameless (Book 3)

**Other Novels**

The Florentine Poet

Plot/Counterplot

Challengers of the Dust

The Game Master

Nemesis: The Final Case of Eliot Ness

Dark Eye

Strip Search

Double Jeopardy

The Midnight Before Christmas

Final Round

The Code of Buddyhood

**The Red Sneaker Series on Writing**

Story Structure: The Key to Successful Fiction

Creating Character: Bringing Your Story to Life

Perfecting Plot: Charting the Hero's Journey

Dynamic Dialogue: Letting Your Story Speak

Sizzling Style: Every Word Matters

Powerful Premise: Writing the Irresistible

Excellent Editing: The Writing Process

Thinking Theme: The Heart of the Matter

What Writers Need to Know: Essential Topics

Dazzling Description: Painting the Perfect Picture

The Fundamentals of Fiction (video series)

**Poetry**

The White Bird

The Ocean's Edge

Traveling Salesman's Son

**For Young Readers**

Shine

Princess Alice and the Dreadful Dragon

Equal Justice: The Courage of Ada Sipuel

The Black Sentry

**Edited by William Bernhardt**

Legal Briefs: Short Stories by Today's Best Thriller Writers

Natural Suspect: A Collaborative Novel of Suspense

Printed in the USA
CPSIA information can be obtained
at www.ICGtesting.com
LVHW090715141023
761104LV00017B/61/J